Bad To The Bone

Second Edition

Bad To The Bone

Second Edition

Mike Faricy

Library of Congress Control Number: 2023918903
paperback ISBN: 978-1-962080-47-7
e-Book ISBN: 978-1-962080-48-4

MJF Publishing books may be purchased for education, Business, or promotional use. For information on bulk purchases, please contact the author directly at mikefaricyauthor@gmail.com

Published by

MJF Publishing
https://www.mikefaricybooks.com

Acknowledgments

I would like to thank the following people for their help and support:

Special thanks to my editors, Kitty, Donna and Rhonda for their hard work, cheerful patience and positive feedback.

I would like to thank Ann and Julie for their creative talent and not slitting their wrists or jumping off the high bridge when dealing with my Neanderthal computer capabilities.

Special thanks to Ann for her patience.

Last, I would like to thank family and friends for their encouragement and unqualified support. Special thanks to Maggie, Jed, Schatz, Pat, Av, Emily and Pat for not rolling their eyes, at least when I was there, and most of all, to my wife Teresa whose belief, support and inspiration has from day one, never waned.

Prologue

The server said, "Can I get you a glass of wine?"

"Actually, I think I'll order a bottle of…" It was my third date with Sandie, which meant this was the one where we finally got down to business. On the first date, we learned a little about one another. On the second date, she had to prove she wasn't a slut, so I got a lingering kiss on the cheek. Now tonight, our third date, with all that out of the way, well, let's just say tonight would be memorable.

Of course, she was stylishly late, but that had been the case on our previous two dates, so no big deal. The server returned with the bottle of wine and showed me the label. It didn't make any difference to me, so I just nodded. She poured a small amount into my glass, which I was supposed to sniff, sip, savor, and hopefully give approval. Instead, I just said, "Go ahead and fill my glass."

Sandie entered about five minutes later. She was an attractive blonde with a great figure. She glanced around the restaurant and caught sight of me just as I raised my wine glass toward her. As she headed over, I noticed two guys at different tables giving her the once-over. Ever the gentleman, I stood and pulled out the chair for her.

"Thanks," she said but didn't follow up with a peck on the cheek. "What a day. I gotta tell ya."

"Crazy?" I asked and took hold of the wine bottle to fill her glass.

"Oh, thanks, no wine for me tonight. Excuse me, ma'am?" she said to our server who was stepping away from another table. "If I could get something from the bar?"

"Certainly. What would you like?"

I was hoping she'd order a triple martini or a double manhattan.

"I think just a glass of sparkling water with a twist of lemon."

I felt a cloud suddenly descending on my hopes for the night. "You feeling okay?"

"Me, yeah, not a problem. Why? Are you upset just because I'm not drinking?"

"No, no, not upset. I wanted to make sure you were feeling okay, is all." I thought her tone came across as a little aggressive, but I let it go. Maybe this was her way of getting me to have a little too much to drink and lower my moral standards, not that I really had any.

"I feel fine."

"So, how was your day?" I asked and followed up with a smile.

"Could we just talk about something else?"

"Yeah, sure. Not a problem. I had an interesting thing happen today. My office mate is an attorney and—"

"Yeah, I know, you told me that the last time we met."

Things more or less went downhill from there. We ordered dinner, and it could not have been on the table for more than five minutes when Sandie signaled our server.

The woman plastered a smile on her face and hurried over to the table. "Is everything all right?"

"Actually, would you mind placing this in a takeout container? I'm going to have to leave."

"No, not a problem. Back in just a moment," the server said. She picked up the plates with Sandie's main course and her salad and hurried off to the kitchen.

"You're leaving? What's the problem? Something I said?"

"I shouldn't have to tell you, Dev."

"I thought we were just having a nice conversation. You were telling me about the lake place your folks have and—"

"Yes, and you said you'd like to see it sometime, basically inserting yourself into my personal life. Turns out you're just like every other guy I've dated. You want to line up my family against me, isolate me, and—"

"Sandie, what are you talking about? It sounded like a nice place. What lake did you say it was on?"

"See, there you go. Next thing I know, you'll be up there knocking on the door, introducing yourself, and I'll—"

"Here you are, ma'am," the server said, placing two boxes on the table in front of Sandie. She glanced at me for half a second.

"Thank you," Sandie said. Once the server left, she stood, picked up the boxes, and said, "Call me if you want to get together this weekend." With that, she turned and headed out the door. I poured myself another glass of wine and shoved a forkful of ravioli into my mouth. I paid the bill, ninety bucks, by the way, plus a tip, and headed home. Morton, my golden retriever, met me at the door. We watched a movie we'd seen before and then went up to bed.

One

I was up before my alarm went off. Morton wandered downstairs an hour later. I let him outside, filled his food and water dishes, and let him back in.

I was on my computer going through emails. I deleted just about all of them until I reached the email from Heidi Bauer, my on-again, off-again friend with benefits. I hadn't heard from her in over a year. There were actually two emails. One was sent last night, about the time I was listening to Sandie as she went off the deep end. I clicked on the first one.

Hi Dev. Long time no see. Interested in coming over for dinner tomorrow night?

Coming from Heidi, I knew or used to know, that was big. The second email was sent this morning, just after 5:00 am.

Please tell me you can make it tonight and you're not going to the meat raffle at The Spot bar or leering in some poor woman's bedroom window.

I dialed her number. She answered on the second ring. "Dev?"

"Hi, Heidi. Long time since I heard from you."

"I know, I know. Of course, that works both ways. I've missed you," she said, ignoring the fact that the last time we spoke, she told me not to call her and then followed up with telling me she never, ever wanted to see me again.

"Yeah, I've missed you too, Heidi," I said and meant it, not that I hadn't been enjoying myself, well, with the exception of last night and maybe a half-dozen other dates that had gone that way over the last year.

"Can you come over tonight?"

"You bet I can. You name a time and tell me what I can bring."

"Is 6:00 too early?"

"No, I think I can do that. Let me just cancel a meeting I've got and—"

"Oh, you don't have to do that, Dev."

"It's not a problem," I said since the meeting was a lie. "I didn't want to go anyway. It's a meeting with city staff. You know how boring they can be."

"Oh, good. I can't wait to see you, Dev."

"What can I bring?"

"Just yourself and make sure you're well rested."

"You sure? I could—"

"No, Dev. I *need* to see you." She emphasized the word *need,* suggesting all sorts of wonderful options.

I was whistling "Walk on By," an ancient hit by Dionne Warwick from back in the 1960s, when we arrived in the office. Morton waited patiently until I tossed him a biscuit then hurried over to his bed so he wouldn't have to share with me. I put the coffee on, and my officemate, Louie Laufen, wandered in about twenty minutes later. I heard the stairs creaking as he made his way up to our office and had a coffee mug waiting on his picnic table desk when he entered. True to form, he was red-faced and gasping for breath. He gave me a little wave and settled into his desk chair. It took a couple of minutes and a half-dozen slurps of coffee before he had recovered enough to talk.

"Sounds like your dinner date was a success," he eventually said.

I'd switched from whistling to humming and suddenly couldn't remember the song I'd been destroying. "Oh, actually, it was a complete and utter disaster. A ninety-dollar dinner bill, and she left five minutes into the meal."

"You're kidding. She left? What did you do to cause that?"

"Nothing I can think of." I went on to give him the details.

"Holy cow, Dev. It almost sounds like she set you up right from the get-go and had planned all along to run off with a meal. I'd say you dodged a bullet."

"Gee, I never thought of it like that, but maybe you're right. Anyway, what's the old adage, 'when a door closes, you can climb out a window'?"

"I think it's 'when one door closes a window opens.' Alexander Graham Bell. Actually, his original quote was—"

"Something I don't need to hear. Right now, I'm more in the mindset of having dodged a bullet. Good riddance to gorgeous, crazy, Sandie. Guess who sent me an email last night?"

"I give up. Who? The IRS?"

"Not even funny, Louie. No, Heidi sent an email last night and another one this morning."

"Heidi? When was the last time you heard from her? She's not asking to be repaid for the time she had to post bail for you, is she?"

"No, and I don't see any point in even going in that direction. If you must know, she invited me over for dinner tonight. Told me I should probably rest up."

"That sounds rather promising," Louie said and slurped some more coffee.

"You think? Perfect timing. I only wish I could let Sandie know I already have a hot date for tonight."

"Call her and tell her."

I shook my head. "No, at best, she was just scamming dinner. I'm thinking she was really going crazy, and I intend to stay away, as far away as possible."

"You can sure pick 'em, Dev," Louie said just as my phone rang.

"Haskell Investigations."

"Hi, Dev, a voice from the past, Augie Douglas." We'd played hockey together in high school. He was a lot better than me, and we thought he'd go pro. A broken leg from a car accident put an end to that dream.

"Hey Augie, great to hear from you. It's been what, ten years?"

"More like twenty, dude."

"What's up?" I asked, figuring he wasn't calling just to catch up.

"A problem in the family I'm hoping you might be able to help with."

"What kind of problem?"

"You read in the newspaper where they arrested this kid for murdering the girl on the front porch?"

"Was that a week or two ago? She was a teenager, a college kid if I remember correctly. Was she going to the U?"

"Yeah, that's it. The boy's mother is a cousin of Mary Beth's. He swears he's innocent. Doesn't know anything about it."

"He was dating this girl, wasn't he?"

"I think that's what led the cops to him. Apparently, she broke up with him a few weeks earlier."

"I'm vaguely aware of the situation. I don't know anything other than what I heard on a couple of news reports," I said.

"You think you could maybe check some things out? See if you think he's getting screwed on this deal. From what I know of the kid, he's a nice guy, smart, just treading water after high school while he figures out what he wants to do."

"Yeah, I suppose I could check it out. You remember Aaron LaZelle? He works in homicide now."

"LaZelle? He's a cop?"

"Yeah, and a good one."

"Humf, I had no idea. Obviously, this doesn't sound good. To my knowledge, the kid doesn't have a record. At least, I don't think he does. I know he had a job bussing dishes at Tracy's bar."

"That place down on Robert Street?"

"Yeah, that's it. He'd been working there for almost a year. Unfortunately, he didn't show up for work the night the girl was murdered."

"Where was he?"

"He maintains he was out running."

"Does he have an attorney?"

"I believe someone has been appointed. Kid lives with his mother in a small apartment. There's no money."

"What's his name?"

"Cornell Thomas, his mom is Christine. She's a single mom, works in the school system, food service at a grade school. She lives—"

"Before we get to that, let me check out a couple of things. If he's got a court-appointed attorney, I'd like to see who it is. Let me touch base with the cops and find out what they have, and I'll get back to you."

"What's this gonna cost me?"

"Well, for starters, I'm thinking at least a lunch or dinner. Let me see what I find out, and we can take it from there."

"You mean that?"

"Yeah, at least to begin with. Let me check things out and we'll see what we're dealing with."

"Oh, thanks, Dev. That's really kind of you."

"I'll check things out and get back to you, Augie. Great to hear from you. Sorry it's under these circumstances."

"Thanks, Dev. Let me know when you have something, and I'll buy lunch or dinner."

"I'll hold you to that, Augie," I said, and we disconnected.

"New business?" Louie asked.

"Maybe, a freebie unfortunately," I said, turning on my computer. "You going to be here for a while?"

"I'm here all morning," Louie said.

"You mind if I leave Morton in your trusted care? I should be back before noon. You got plans for lunch?"

Louie shook his head and said, "I was thinking a barbecue from Rooster's might be just the thing."

"Consider it done, Louie."

I googled the Pioneer Press, our local newspaper, and searched for any articles on the murder. There were two, one the day following the shooting mentioning the victim, Penny Larson. A picture was attached of a pretty blonde girl. It may have been a high school yearbook photo.

The second article was two days after the shooting and was two paragraphs long. Cornell Thomas had been arrested the day before. The article mentioned that he

had a prior relationship with Penny Larson. No specifics
were given as to the reason he was linked to the murder.

TWO

I drove down to the courthouse. I had to park a block away in front of the public library. I could probably get the information by making a phone call, but I wanted to be there in person just in case someone gave me access to the files. I walked over to the courthouse, went through the security check, and then took the elevator up to the fourth floor. I stepped into the clerk's office and walked up to the counter.

"Hi, how can I help you?" a young man asked and smiled. He looked to be in his late twenties. I wasn't sure, but I pegged him for a law student.

"Hi, I'd like information on a murder case that has yet to go to trial. The defendant is a young man by the name of Cornell Thomas. I'd like the name of the attorney for the defense."

He ran his fingers across the keyboard, looked up after a moment, and said, "The court-appointed defense attorney in that matter is Martin Meyer."

"Would you happen to have an office address?"

He stared at me for a few seconds and then gave me the address. The office was over on University Avenue. I wrote it down in my notebook.

"Anything else I can help you with?" he asked, suggesting no other information was forthcoming.

"No, appreciate the help. Thank you."

He flashed a one-second smile, and I headed out the door.

Martin Meyer's building was a two-story structure on University Avenue. His office was a small storefront with his name on the door. My first thought was that it looked more like the office for someone who was handling evictions and speeding tickets, not a murder defense. The unit to the right was vacant and had a dusty 'For Rent' sign leaning against the front window. The unit to the left was a Cambodian restaurant. I pulled on the door to open it, but it was locked. Given the neighborhood, I wasn't surprised. There was a woman inside seated at a desk, and I knocked on the door. A lock buzzed. I opened the door and stepped inside.

The floor was concrete. There were four folding metal chairs arranged against a wall that looked like they'd been stolen from a church basement. The ceiling was open. There weren't any ceiling tiles, just steel beams, dangling light bulbs, and concrete slabs that made up the second floor. The woman at the desk looked up from her computer screen. "May I help you?"

"I hope so. I'd like to see Mr. Meyer."

"Do you have an appointment?"

"No, I'm afraid I don't. I'm here on behalf of an individual he's representing, Cornell Thomas."

That seemed to get her attention. "And you are?"

"My name is Devlin Haskell. I'm a private investigator."

"Let me check with him. Wait just a minute," she said as she pushed her chair back and stood. She knocked on the door in the corner and stepped inside, closing the door behind her.

I looked around the office. Not so much as a picture frame hanging on the walls. Other than the four metal folding chairs and the desk, chair, and computer, the only other item was a black plastic wastebasket. There was a pleasant scent that must have come from the Cambodian restaurant next door because my stomach suddenly growled.

The office door opened. The woman stepped out and said, "He can see you for a minute." She held the door for me.

As I stepped into the office, she closed the door behind me. Martin Meyer was seated behind his desk. He smiled at me, extended his hand, and didn't stand. "Hi, Martin Meyer," he said.

"Dev Haskell," I replied as I stepped over and shook hands with him. He had an iron grip, and it felt like I was squeezing a brick. It was then that I noticed he was seated in a wheelchair.

"Take a seat. Mind if I call you Dev?"

"God, no. I'm called a lot worse by this time on any day."

"Please call me Martin. Edith said you're working for Cornell Thomas?"

"Not exactly." I went on to explain my phone call from Augie Douglas. "So I'm just taking a perfunctory look at things. I'll visit the police next. At this point, all I know about the case is what I heard on the news. I couldn't pick Cornell Thomas out of a crowd of two."

He nodded a couple of times as I spoke, then seemed to think for a moment. "Here's the deal. I was appointed to represent Cornell. I've met with him three times over the last seven days. Right from the start, I believed he was innocent. Let me be clear here. Because of my physical condition, I could just as easily back out of representing him. On the other hand, my physical condition has a tendency to make me rather stubborn at times, and this is one of those times. The boy is innocent. I have no doubt. It's my opinion that, in an effort to close this case quickly, he was arrested without any real evidence and locked up."

"Do you know who the arresting officer was?"

He nodded and said, "A detective by the name of Norris Manning." The expression on my face apparently gave me away. "You know him?"

"Oh yeah. I'm lucky he didn't arrest me. Any crime that occurs in this city, Manning has me at the top of his suspect list. We are not what you would call friends. That said, I would have to admit that he is otherwise very good at what he does."

"Arresting the innocent?"

I smiled. "Current case not included. My understanding is your client claims he was out running at the time."

Meyer nodded. "He runs five to ten miles every other day. On the evening in question, he ran the length of Summit Avenue from the Cathedral down to the River Boulevard and back."

"That's nearly ten miles," I said.

"You're familiar with it? Are you a runner?"

"No, I live about three blocks from the Cathedral. I'm familiar with the streets. Lots of runners up and down Summit. Is there any proof of his running? Did anyone see him?" I was replaying the length of Summit Avenue in my head, wondering if any businesses or homes may have had security footage.

"You seem to be thinking of something."

"Wondering about security cameras that may have caught Cornell running past. Unfortunately, that was over a week ago. We could check, but it's a pretty thin chance there'd be a digital file."

As he wrote something down on a yellow legal pad, he asked, "Are you planning to go to the police today?"

"Yes, but informally. I have a friend down there I can talk to, provided he's in the office."

"You're not going to talk with Detective Manning?"

"Not at this point. I'm just trying to get some general information. Over the years, I've found it seems to work out best for all involved if I can avoid Manning."

"Would it make sense for me to list you as an associate in this investigation?"

"Maybe hold off on that and let me see what I can pick up in a friendly conversation. Once things become official, everyone tends to act as if they're on thin ice. One thing that would help, Cornell lives with his mother?"

"Yes."

"Would you happen to have an address? I'd like to get a sense of the home life."

Meyer nodded and ran his fingers over his keyboard. "Yeah, here we go. Christine Thomas, age thirty-seven. Her address is 422 Ravoux Street"

"Is that Capitol Plaza?"

"It is. You're familiar with it?"

"Somewhat, it's been a couple of years since I've been in the place. My memory is the units were awfully small."

"Well, nothing's changed. Christine has a two-bedroom unit. I think it's just seven-hundred and fifty square feet. Pretty tough to get any privacy unless you want to lock yourself in a bedroom. Might be one of the reasons Cornell ran so much."

"Does he own a car?"

Meyer shook his head. "No. He's been saving his money to pay for classes this fall at a community college. Unfortunately, now that's been put on hold."

"Let me see what I can learn this afternoon, and I'll get back to you," I said and stood.

Meyer held out his hand, we shook, and he handed me a business card. I pulled one of my cards from my wallet and gave it to him.

"I look forward to hearing from you, Dev."

Three

I stopped at Rooster's on the way back to the office and purchased three barbecue pork shoulder sandwiches. I parked in front of my building and took two of the sandwiches up to the office. Louie and Morton were both asleep when I stepped inside. Louie blinked awake as I set a Styrofoam tray on his picnic table desk. Morton remained asleep.

"Mmm-mmm, perfect timing," Louie said and stretched.

"Busy morning?"

"I got a lot accomplished. But all of a sudden, I found myself nodding off while on the computer, and experience has taught me that, in that situation, whenever possible, close my eyes for twenty minutes and then get back to work. One of the benefits of being self-employed. How was your morning? Did you learn anything?"

"Yeah, I did. You know an attorney named Martin Meyer?"

Louie shook his head.

"He's the court-appointed attorney representing Cornell Thomas. The guy has an office over on University Ave. Not the best part of town. The place is pretty much bare bones." I went on to describe Meyer and his office. "Anyway, he believes the kid is innocent and decided he wanted to represent him. Oh, and then he just happened to mention that the arresting officer in the case was Detective Norris Manning."

"Oh, really. Your favorite person. Gee, small world."

"Yeah, I'll be down there after lunch. Hopefully, just chatting up Aaron. The less Manning knows about me looking into things, the better it will be for everyone involved, me especially."

"He'll find out sooner or later."

"Yeah, I know that. But the longer he doesn't know, the better it'll be for me, well, and this kid, Cornell Thomas."

"Sounds like you're already on board," Louie said and took a large bite of his sandwich. A chunk of barbecue pork bounced off the cuff of his formerly clean white shirt and landed on a document resting on his desk. He frowned and then picked up the piece of pork, crammed it into his mouth, and licked his fingertips.

"Yeah, from the little I know, it looks like they could use some help. The arrest, at least initially, appears to be based on some awfully thin ground, but you know how that works. You get the wrong prosecutor on the case, and you've suddenly got a real uphill battle on your hands," I said.

We talked as we worked our way through the sandwiches. Just as I was finishing up, Morton stretched and groaned but remained on his pillow. He looked at Louie and me for a couple of minutes. Eventually, he got to his feet, stretched once more, walked over, and stood at the door.

"Oh, I guess that's my sign to get up and take him for a walk." At the word, 'walk,' Morton's tail began to wag back and forth. I clipped the leash onto his collar, and we headed out the door. Morton visited his favorite fire hydrant and then sniffed every front gate and every other boulevard tree. We were back in the office twenty minutes later. I tossed him a biscuit which he inhaled in three quick bites.

"Hey, I was thinking about this kid you're going to be checking out," Louie said.

"Cornell Thomas."

"Yeah. Be interesting to find out how they landed on him. Did a friend of the victim friend him? The girl's parents?"

"Yeah, I'll keep that in the back of my mind. To tell you the truth, I'm not expecting much."

"Well, good luck. I'm here for another hour at least, and then I've got a 2:00 at the courthouse. Morton should be okay," Louie said.

"Thanks. I'll be back as soon as I can." I headed out the door. I climbed in my car, which now smelled like barbecue pork since the sandwich I was taking to Aaron had been resting on the passenger seat for the better part of the past half-hour.

Ten minutes later, I pulled into the gravel parking lot across the street from the police station. I managed to avoid the two large potholes and found an empty parking spot. I grabbed the barbecue sandwich and headed into the station.

Four

I recognized the desk sergeant and read his name tag. "Hi, Sergeant Cody, Dev Haskell to see Aaron LaZelle in Homicide."

"Is he expecting you?"

"No, I just wanted to drop this off for him," I said and lifted the Styrofoam container up toward him.

"Mmm-mmm, that wouldn't happen to be from Rooster's, would it?"

"As a matter of fact, it is."

"Lucky, LaZelle. Take a seat, and I'll see if he has time. You may just have to leave that meal with me," he said, then laughed at his joke.

I sat down on an orange plastic chair and waited for just a couple of minutes. A door suddenly opened, and a guy yelled, "Haskell?"

"Yeah, right here," I said as I hurried over. The guy was dressed in a blue shirt with the sleeves rolled up to his elbows. His pistol and badge were attached to his belt. As I approached, I looked at Cody behind the front desk and said, "Sorry, Sarge."

We took the elevator up a couple of floors. "Thanks for coming to get me," I said and got a nod in return. I followed the guy down the hall. He input his code into the keypad next to the Homicide door. The door buzzed, and he pulled it open. We stepped inside the squad room. Just like always, there was a bunch of activity. People talking on phones and typing away on computers.

"The LT is in his office," the guy said and headed over to a desk buried under stacks of files.

Aaron's office door was open, and I knocked on the doorframe. He was on the phone, and he waved me in and pointed to the two chairs positioned in front of his desk. "Yeah, I get it, but that still doesn't change the fact that he used a crowbar to make his point. The medical examiner is saying five blows to the head. I think at that stage, we're beyond this being an unfortunate mistake."

I set the Styrofoam container on his desk, and he raised his eyebrows, pulled it in front of him, and opened it up.

"Yeah, I guess that will be for the jury to decide. No, I can't comment on that at this time. Yes. Thank you," he said and hung up.

"That sounded lovely," I said.

"Someone's lawyer fishing for an excuse."

"And let me guess, he didn't find one."

"She actually," Aaron said and picked up the sandwich. "Mmm-mmm, perfect. I'm guessing from Rooster's?"

"Yeah, where else? Only the best for you, Aaron."

"So, to what do I owe the pleasure, a driving while intoxicated charge? Indecent exposure? Sex with a minor?"

"What? All of a sudden, I can't come down here and just be nice without getting accused. And besides, that girl said she was almost eighteen."

Aaron stared for a second.

"Okay, bad joke. No, actually, guess who I heard from this morning?"

Aaron had just taken a large bite and pointed to his bulging cheeks.

"I got a call from Augie Douglas. Haven't talked to him, let alone seen him, in twenty years."

Aaron chewed for a long moment then swallowed and said, "What's he up to? God, I thought he'd really go places. He was skating for the U and getting calls from all sorts of agents when he was in that car accident. Who was the girl that was driving that night?"

"Mary Beth Angelo. Guess what? He married her."

Aaron stopped in mid-bite. "Really?"

"Yeah."

"Mmm-mmm, I never would have guessed. What's he doing now?"

"We never really got into that."

"Why'd he call you?" Aaron asked and took another bite.

"Well, he wanted me to look into something. In fact, I'm hoping you might be able to help me."

Aaron set his sandwich back in the Styrofoam tray. "I knew this was too good to be true. You get nailed on something?"

"No, honest, Aaron, this isn't about me. It turns out Augie's wife, Mary Beth, has a cousin. She's the mother of a kid named Cornell Thomas, and he's been arrested for the murder of—"

"The Larson girl. Penny Larson. Did Augie happen to mention that Penny and Cornell had a fight, broke up, and a week later, he shot her?"

"No, he didn't say anything about that."

"That would suggest that he failed to mention the kid was in possession of the murder weapon."

"In possession of the murder weapon?" I asked.

"Yeah, a Glock 17. The serial numbers had been filed off the weapon. We've run a ballistics test, and at no surprise, it's a match to the round that killed the Larson girl. She was shot at about twenty-five feet. Murdered on the front porch of her home, one round to the head, just above her left eye."

"He had the weapon?"

"Yeah, of course, he denies having it. The only problem is, it was found in his bedroom. Right under his pillow as a matter of fact. He said he'd never seen it before."

"Fingerprints?"

Aaron shook his head. "Wiped clean, but DNA was—"

"That could have come from the bed. If someone had put it there to—"

"Really, Dev. The kid's room is searched, and the pistol is found. Now either he put it there, or his mother did. My money is on him."

"But under his pillow, why not at least stuff it beneath the mattress or tape it to the bottom of a chest of drawers?"

"Yeah, or better yet, drop it off a bridge and into the Mississippi. But he didn't do that, Dev. He was probably going to toss it in a dumpster the next day but was just too busy to do it that night. Or maybe, he just thought he'd never be caught, and now, after taking a life, he's a big bad gangster, and who wouldn't want to have him in their gang?"

"He's into gangs?"

"Not that we know of, yet. But we're checking it out."

"He's being represented by an attorney named Martin Meyer," I said.

Aaron took another bite of his sandwich and nodded. "Yeah, he's pro bono, and from what I know, this is his first time in the big leagues. Look, Dev, at this point, the case is out of our hands and is on the district attorney's desk. I basically told you everything we got. I'm not trying to be a wise-ass, but it has all the looks of an open and shut affair. As for his attorney, I'm sure Martin Meyer is a hard-working guy who just wants to see justice served. But if I found out he was one of those happy thoughts guys where everyone deserves a second chance, and they didn't mean to do something bad, well, tell that to the Larson family. Tell it to the girl's folks."

"The kid didn't have a record, did he?"

"No, he didn't, but he jumped right into the big time, and now he's about to get thirty years to think about the decision he made. It's an open and shut case, Dev. Mmm-mmm, thanks for the sandwich, by the way."

Five

I headed home from the office just after 5:00. I pulled on a fairly clean shirt, a nice pair of jeans, and my favorite pair of snakeskin cowboy boots. I'd stopped at the wine store up the block and picked up two bottles of a Pinot Noir that Heidi liked. Then, just to be safe, I bought a bouquet of flowers. I forgot to ask her if she was still living in the same house, but I figured she would have mentioned something if she'd moved in the last year. I was a stylish ten minutes late when I pulled in front of her place. I didn't want to appear too anxious.

Heidi must have been watching out the window because she answered the door just before I rang the doorbell. She was barefoot, wearing one of my Saint Paul Saints t-shirts and a smile. As I stepped inside, she took the flowers and the bag with the two wine bottles and said, "Oh, how nice. Thank you." She dropped them on the couch, attacked me with a passionate kiss, and then began to undo my belt.

It was close to 9:00 when we climbed out of bed. Heidi slipped into a red silk robe and said, "I'd better order that pizza before it's too late. Okay with you if I tell them no anchovies?"

"Yeah, yeah, I'm fine with that."

The pizza arrived twenty-five minutes later. I was dressed, answered the door, and paid thirty-five bucks, including the tip. Heidi was filling our wine glasses as I set the pizza box on the kitchen counter.

"You want me to get a couple of plates?" I asked.

She shook her head, pulled some paper towels from the dispenser beneath a cabinet, and handed a couple to me. Apparently, we'd both worked up an appetite because we finished the pizza in about twenty minutes. We chatted for the next hour and a half, mostly just gossip.

I mentioned checking out Cornell Thomas for my pal Augie, and Heidi asked, "Are you busy at work?"

"Not too busy. I'm always looking for the next client. You know how that goes."

She nodded and said, "Oh, believe me, I do. I might have something I'd like checked out, you know, if you can fit it into your schedule."

The only thing I had planned for the rest of the week was reading the Cornell Thomas file. Based on what Aaron LaZelle had told me, I figured that would take all of thirty minutes. "I might be able to fit it in. What do you have in mind?"

She smiled and said, "Just a second." She stepped into the rear entry off the kitchen, opened a drawer in the built-in cabinet, and pulled out a green cardboard file.

The thing was actually a hanging file about six inches thick. A number of manila folders were arranged inside.

"What's all that?"

"Information on an investment, a recycling company actually. It seemed to be going rather well, but all of a sudden, I'm not so sure. I'd like you to check these guys out. The business address is in the files, but I want you to check them out personally, too. I don't think I should say any more other than let me know what you think."

"Are you on any schedule with this?"

Heidi shook her head. "No, not really. Obviously, the sooner, the better, but be thorough."

We had another glass of wine and went back to bed. After six minutes of getting reacquainted, we were both asleep within a minute or two. The next thing I remembered was Heidi kissing me on the cheek and telling me she had an early meeting. She said the coffee was on and to let myself out. I never went back to sleep, and after ten minutes, I got dressed, filled a travel mug with coffee, and headed home. I was cooking French toast and humming a happy tune after my great night when Morton wandered down from the bedroom. I let him outside and filled his food and water dishes.

We headed down to the office once Morton finished eating. He settled into his bed in front of the file cabinet. I put the coffee on and started in on Heidi's six-inch file. Louie showed up a half-hour later.

I'd watched him pull his faded Ford Fiesta behind my car. The thing seemed to shudder for a moment before a black cloud of exhaust exploded from the rear, and Louie climbed out. I had a mug of steaming coffee waiting for him on his picnic table desk. I heard the stairs creaking as he climbed up to the second floor. Just like every other day, he was red-faced when he opened the office door. He didn't say anything. He just gave me his usual little wave as he tossed his briefcase on the picnic table and settled into his desk chair. Five minutes and a half-dozen slurps of coffee later, he said, "You're in early."

"Yeah, I'm plowing through all of this," I said and nodded at Heidi's file.

"New client?"

"New case, actually. It's for Heidi."

"Heidi? Didn't she tell you she never—"

"Water over the bridge," I said.

"I think you mean water under the bridge, but what brought that on?"

I nodded at the file in front of me. "She wants me to check out a business and the two guys running it."

"And she's paying you?"

"Well, we didn't actually get into that, and I—"

"Please, no details. Hopefully, you at least got dinner before she took you to bed."

"Actually, we had dinner afterward, umm, pizza delivery, and I paid for it."

Louie stared for a moment and then said, "Good luck."

"It was worth every penny," I said and smiled.

Louie shook his head.

Six

Heidi had always been an advocate of saving the environment and recycling. So it was no surprise that the file was on a company founded two years ago, RIP, Inc., short for Recycled Industrial Plastic, Incorporated. Apparently, they were or hoped to be, big in recycling plastics. There was just one problem, well actually, a number of problems that all boiled down to the bottom line. They had never been profitable, although their stock price had gone from $1.47 to a current price of $83.12 over the course of not quite twenty-four months. It seemed like a good deal to me, but then, what did I know?

From the articles I read in the first file, the company was looking for investors. RIP was run by two individuals, Franklin Lanzo and Russell Greeney. Their concept was to recycle plastic and, in the process, create a fire-resistant product. The articles listed a number of performance tests that rated the product as the 'latest and greatest.' Recycling plastic and turning it into a fire-resistant product sounded like a natural winner.

Two small files were next in the stack and consisted of a brief bio on Lanzo and Greeney. Both men were educated at Ivy League schools. Greeney apparently held a master's degree, but there was no mention of the specific field. They seemed to have held a variety of positions over the past twenty years. In a broad and ever-changing market like recycling, that didn't really strike me as strange. The offices were located downtown on the thirty-fourth floor of the Wells Fargo building, the tallest building in St. Paul. The actual recycling facility was located on River Road down in Inver Grove Heights, an area just fifteen minutes from downtown. It seemed to make more sense to check out the recycling facility before visiting the corporate offices.

"You in court today?" I asked Louie.

He shook his head, "No, busy writing an appeal that's going nowhere. But I have to submit it to keep my client happy, well, and charge him."

"Mind if I leave Morton here and take off for an hour, maybe two? I'll grab some barbecue pork shoulder sandwiches from Rooster's on the way back."

"Not a problem. By the way, I'm in the mood for some extra fries."

"Consider it done," I said. I wrote down a couple of items from the file and headed out the door. Morton was napping in his bed and didn't so much as open an eye when I left. I hopped on Highway 52 and took that down to 70th street in Inver Grove and headed toward the river.

The RIP plant was supposedly located on River Road. Only it wasn't.

The address I had looked like a one-time three-story warehouse or factory building that had been converted to offices. A sign out front announced, 'Office Space Available.' The parking lot looked like it could handle maybe fifty cars. As I pulled in, I counted three other vehicles in the lot. One was a black Prius; the other was a white Prius. The third vehicle was a banged-up pickup truck with an old box spring mattress in the back.

I parked almost next to the front door. Actually, there were two doors. But one of them had a sheet of plywood over it with red spray paint that said 'Use Othr Door.' An arrow pointed to the door next to it. I followed the misspelled directions.

I stepped into a lobby of sorts with a four-step staircase leading up to the main floor. The building was quiet, and my footsteps echoed as I walked down the hallway. The doors along the hall lacked any form of identification, no numbers or business names. The first four doors were unlocked, and I peeked inside. The offices were pretty much the same; empty and dusty, with worn carpet and outdated telephone jacks attached to the walls. One of the offices had what appeared to be a sleeping bag stretched out. I couldn't think of anything positive happening by checking it out and closed the door.

At the far end of the hall was an office with a two-inch-wide strip of masking tape. Handwritten on the masking tape was the name Bunker Real Estate. The door was locked, and no one answered when I knocked. I stuck one of my business cards into the end of the masking tape.

RIP was supposedly up on the second floor. The elevator had a handwritten 'Out of Order' sign attached to the door, so I took the stairs to the second floor. I heard voices as I stepped into the second-floor hall and headed in that direction. I passed two more unlocked doors with empty office space.

The third door was where the voices were coming from. The door was labeled RIP Production in raised white letters. I tried the doorknob. It was locked, and I knocked on the door. The conversation immediately stopped. I waited a bit and knocked again. A moment later, the door opened maybe an inch, and a guy peeked out. He was shorter than me. I could only see the one brown eye.

"Can I help you?"

"I hope so. I'm looking for Franklin Lanzo or Russell Greeney."

"What's this concerning?"

"An investment," I lied.

He opened the door and smiled. He stood about five feet five inches, needed a shave, and looked about fifty pounds overweight. He was dressed in jeans and a t-shirt with faded blue letters touting the band Nirvana. "Terry Nelson, pleased to meet you," he said as he flashed a grin and held out his hand. As we shook hands, he said, "Always a pleasure to meet an investor."

I could have sworn I heard a conversation going on just before I knocked on the door, but no one else was in sight. Maybe I'd just heard a radio or a video on a computer. Either way, Nelson appeared to be the only guy in the office.

"Haskell, Dev Haskell," I said as we shook hands. Nelson stepped back, crossed his arms, and studied me.

"Well, you've come to the right place. Looking to invest? Maybe retire early?" Nelson said.

"Yeah, I hope so. At least that's my plan. Is your facility out back or—"

"Actually, it's not too far from here. I'd be happy to give you a quick tour if you're interested."

"Yeah, I'd love to see it."

Nelson pulled out his cellphone and said, "Let me just send a quick message. I've got some folks coming over for a board of directors meeting. They can start without me. I'll give you a quick tour, shouldn't take more than twenty minutes or so. After you, Mr. Hassle," he said and nodded toward the hallway. I stepped out into the hall, and he followed, closing the door behind him. "I'm parked right out front. Tell me, what is it you do, sir?"

"Please, call me Dev. I just dabble in things that interest me. Been lucky enough to be able to keep it up. RIP struck me as an interesting concept."

"How'd you hear about us?"

"Oh, I was at a social hour sort of thing and overheard some folks talking about you. Apparently, you've had a nice steady increase in stock value over the last year or so. I'm always interested in getting in on the ground floor. Tell me, how long have you been located here, in this building?"

"Oh, bit of a temporary move. We've architects working on a new office building, but even if they started tomorrow, it would be at least a year before we could move in, so here we are." He gave a little chuckle as we headed out the front door and into the parking lot. He pulled out a set of keys as we walked past the black and white Priuses and headed for the pickup.

He looked back over his shoulder at my black car, and the smile suddenly left his face. "You some kind of cop?"

"Me? No, why would you—Oh yeah, of course. My car. That's a 2009 Ford Crown Victoria Police Interceptor. I actually bought it at a police auction. A guy I know works on cars for the department. They'd just finished servicing that vehicle and put it on the auction block. So I was fortunate enough to get it. Nice car, serves me well. I'm not doing any long hauls. Although, since I started driving that thing, I think someone asks me if I'm a cop every other day."

Nelson seemed to think about that for a moment and then nodded and smiled. "Hop in," he said as he hurried around to the driver's side of the pickup. I pushed a couple of McDonald's wrappers onto the floor, climbed in, and buckled up. A naked lady air freshener hung from the dash. We pulled out of the lot and headed down the road.

Seven

The RIP building sat on a raised foundation along the Mississippi River and appeared to be at least a hundred years old. It was a two-story brick structure with a double-door entrance centered on the first floor and then two loading docks on either side of the entrance. The windows on the second floor were partially bricked up and obviously not original to the structure.

What appeared more interesting to me was the cyclone fence with three lengths of barbed wire on top surrounding the building. The double gate at the entrance was padlocked. Three homemade cardboard signs were tied to the gates. 'Stop RIP', 'Polluters', and 'Plastic is not Fantastic'.

"Oh God, will you look at this shit? Hang on a minute," Nelson said as he shook his head. He climbed out from behind the wheel and unlocked the padlock that held the chain around the gates. He tore off the cardboard signs, tossed them onto the ground, and swung the gates open.

He climbed back into the pickup, still shaking his head. "I tell you, a bunch of wackos decided to protest us taking plastic out of the environment and finding a useful purpose for the stuff. You gotta wonder," he said, then put the pickup into gear, and we drove up to the building. Remnants of a red spray-painted 'Stop RIP' remained across the two loading dock doors on the right half of the building. Someone had attempted to cover it with some cheap white paint and hadn't done a very good job.

"You have any problems with protesters? You guys are taking plastic out of the environment, aren't you?"

"Yeah, exactly. We've developed a process to convert plastic waste into a fire-resistant material. It's a winner for everyone, well except for this bunch of college-age protesters with too much time on their hands and no idea about what's involved."

"What were they protesting?"

"Plastic. The fact that we're converting plastic refuse into a usable fire-resistant material apparently doesn't matter. I guess they'd like the world to go back to glass bottles, paper bags, and buttons made from metal or seashells. I tell you, you can't make it up."

I gave a quick glance to the empty parking lot. "Is anyone working?"

"Today? No, we decided to give the crew a break. They, umm, have really been going at things nonstop, and we figured we better rest up before we have an injury."

"How many people do you have working here?"

"Oh, it depends. I don't have an exact number, but I can tell you it's lots. Come on inside, and I'll show you around."

We climbed out of the pickup, and I followed Nelson up the three steps. He unlocked the double doors, and we stepped into one large open building. It was literally one big room, two stories tall. There were windows on the second story on all four walls, but there wasn't a second floor. Literally mountains of plastic bottles were piled up against the walls. A path maybe four feet wide wove through the mounds of plastic bottles.

"You're recycling all these?" I asked.

Nelson nodded and said, "We plan to. Come on, let me show you something."

I followed him along the path until we came to a small office room. He opened the door, and we stepped inside. A worn wooden desk with two red bricks holding up one corner was against a far wall. Three pieces of lumber, about a foot long rested on the desk, and a folding yellow lawn chair stood behind the desk.

"Check this out," Nelson said as he pulled open the bottom desk drawer. He took out what looked like a standard long reach butane lighter. It was the kind you light a grill with, black with a red trigger. He picked up one of the pieces of lumber, clicked on the butane lighter, and held the flame beneath the piece of lumber. Nothing happened. No smoke, no scent of burnt wood, the thing never caught fire.

"How come that lumber isn't burning? What kind of wood is that?"

Nelson grinned. "Because Hassle, this isn't lumber. It's our product, fire-resistant plastic made to resemble a piece of lumber. Functional from minus 100 degrees Fahrenheit to over 700 degrees Fahrenheit."

"That board is actually plastic?"

"You bet it is, one hundred percent fire-resistant plastic. These three pieces are our pine pattern. We're currently developing an oak, redwood, and birch wood grain pattern. Take a moment and think of the potential. Fire-resistant kitchen cabinets, trim, furniture, and no one would be able to tell the difference. We're right on the edge, and now is the moment for smart people, such as yourself, to jump in."

"That's absolutely amazing."

He turned off the butane lighter and said, "You're right, it is, and you are among the fortunate few to have the opportunity to get in on the ground floor. Here," he said, pointing the fire-resistant plastic board toward me. "Check it out. But be careful. It'll be hot."

I took hold of the board to look at it, but he gently pulled it away. I couldn't detect any damage from the flame. I touched the end where he had held the flame with my index finger and snapped my hand back. It was hot, very hot, but visually, it was undamaged.

"I don't know what to say. This is amazing. You're manufacturing this here?"

"Once we have our new building built, that will be the plan. As I mentioned earlier, we're in the beginning stages. We've had these prototypes produced in a lab. We've performed all sorts of tests. Everyone we've met with wants to be involved. This is bound to be the next best thing since Apple or Amazon, and you, sir, are looking at a ground floor entry. Just think of the opportunity, the potential. Invest fifty or a hundred thousand dollars, and in twenty-four months, you'll be looking at places to retire. Are you married, Hassle?"

"No, haven't found a woman patient enough to deal with me."

Nelson chuckled. "You invest in RIP, and in twenty-four months, women will be chasing you all over the world promising to do anything your little heart desires. Believe me."

"Sounds great."

"Oh, it will be. And the opportunity is yours for the taking. What do you think?"

"Like I said, I think it sounds great. I want to get in touch with my financial advisors and go over a few things so I can—"

"Well, let me give you a little inside information, a bit of a warning." He looked around as if there might be someone nearby listening to our conversation. Maybe someone was hiding beneath one of the two-story mountains of plastic bottles. "Here's the deal. We're about to close the door to new investors. The business is on the verge of really taking off, and rather than spread the results, we're looking to reward the folks who were with us from the start. So a word of advice, don't delay. Let me give you this," he said and reached for the middle drawer in the desk. He pulled a couple of times, flashed a smile at me, and then repositioned himself and pulled even harder. The drawer flew open, and Nelson took a step or two back. He reached in and pulled out what looked like a three-panel brochure. He refolded it and handed it to me.

"Here's all the information you'll need. Once you invest, you can start to google the vacation spots that appeal to you because that's what the future holds for our investors."

"Thanks, Mr. Nelson, much appreciated."

He nodded and said, "Come on, I'd better get back to that damn board meeting. Glad you took the time, Hassle, and let me just say, welcome aboard." With that, we followed the winding path around the mountains of empty plastic bottles toward the front door. Along the way, Nelson kicked two or three bottles off the path. We pulled outside of the fenced area. He reconnected the chain around the entrance gates, ignored the cardboard signs he'd tossed on the ground, and we headed back to the mostly empty office building.

We shook hands, I promised to be in touch, and as he entered the building, I climbed into my car. If there was a board meeting, the members must have walked because the only other vehicle in the lot was Nelson's pickup with the box spring mattress in the back. The black and white Priuses were gone, and I thought back to hearing multiple voices just before I knocked on the office door. On the way back to the office, I tossed around a number of thoughts in my thick skull, none of them very positive.

I have to say I was impressed with the flame against the fire-resistant plastic. That was good. Among my many questions I wondered if that was an actual sample of the product they planned to produce? Or was it some other company's product and everything he told me was a big lie? Why was it so heavy? And what about the protesters? Someone somewhere had enough information on the company that they were willing to give up personal time to protest the organization, not that anyone would be aware of the protests. The place was in the middle of nowhere. No traffic, no cars in the parking lot, just a building full of empty plastic bottles. I didn't buy the line about giving workers time off. The whole thing seemed more than a little sketchy.

I headed back to the office and parked behind Louie's Ford Fiesta. I left a good deal of space between the cars just in case the Fiesta exploded when Louie turned it on. He was typing away when I entered the office. Morton rose from his bed and looked longingly at his leash hanging from the nail in the wall. I clicked the leash onto his collar and said, "See you in fifteen minutes, Louie."

He nodded and said, "Don't forget the barbecue pork sandwiches."

Morton and I headed out the door.

Eight

We walked for close to twenty minutes, Morton sniffing the gate on every fence and getting up close and personal with two fire hydrants. I didn't think much of it at first, but the third time a black Prius drove past, I started to pay attention. We walked into Rooster's, and I ordered two sandwiches, one with extra fries.

Taffy was the girl working the counter, and she rang up my order and then looked down at Morton. "Hey, Dev, would it be okay if I gave Morton a treat?"

"A treat? You mean like a candy bar or one of your blueberry muffins?"

"No, silly. We've got a bunch of bones in the back. I'll get one for him, just a minute," she said and stepped through the swinging door. She was back a moment later with my order and a large bone for Morton. "Here you go, boy," she said. As Morton grabbed the bone she gave him a good scratch behind his ears.

"God, Taffy, you've got a friend for life. Thanks, that's really nice of you."

"Oh, I love him, and when you think of all he has to worry about," she said and nodded at me.

"Yeah, I see your point. Hey, thanks, catch you later."

"You two behave. Be patient, Morton, you've got a lot to deal with," she said as we headed out the door.

When we stepped outside, I happened to glance up the street. A black Prius was parked across the street and up maybe three doors. A guy was sitting behind the wheel. It looked like he had on a suit coat with a white shirt and a tie, but with the tinted windows, I couldn't make out a face. I was tempted to walk in that direction but decided against it, and we walked the two blocks back to the office. Just as I opened the door to the building, the Prius drove past. I only got the first three letters on the license plate, MEW.

"Perfect timing," Louie said as I set the white Styrofoam tray on his desk. He tapped a half-dozen keys on his laptop, pushed it off to the side, and pulled the tray in front of him. I unclipped Morton's leash. He hurried over to his bed and settled in with his bone so he wouldn't have to share. "Oh, lucky Morton," Louie said.

"Yeah, Taffy, she's his big fan."

"Mmm, perfect, extra fries. Everything go okay for you this morning?" Louie asked and proceeded to take a large bite from his sandwich. Experience had taught him to lean forward over the tray, so when the sauce and bits of meat fell, they landed in the tray rather than on the desk or him.

"Yeah, I suppose. You know how it goes. You start looking at things, and it seems to bring up more questions than answers."

"Anything I can do to help?"

"Thanks for offering, but at this stage, no, not really. You're here all day?"

"Mmm, yeah. You want to go check something out, be my guest. I'm here, and it looks like Morton will be involved with that bone for the better part of the afternoon."

We chatted a bit, then Louie went back to typing, and I headed out to the Ramsey County Adult Detention Center, formerly known as the jail. I went through three levels of security before I was ushered into a room with sectioned-off areas and white Formica counters. It was a long fifteen-minute wait before Cornell Thomas was ushered into the area. He was clean-shaven with closed cropped hair on the sides and a little longer on the top but nothing wild or crazy. I figured him to be around my height and average weight. If it weren't for the orange jumpsuit, the ankle cuffs, and the handcuffs attached to a chain around his waist, he'd look like a nice guy. He got a questioning look on his face as he shuffled to his chair and sat down. I reached for the receiver and placed it against my ear. He stared through the thick glass for a long moment before he reached up with his cuffed hands and took hold of the receiver.

"Hi, Cornell. My name is Dev Haskell. I'm a private investigator. I got a call from your uncle, Augie Douglas. We played hockey together a thousand years ago."

He seemed to think about that for a moment and asked, "Are you the guy that dates a bunch of different women?"

"Yeah, and I'm the guy all those women tell they never, ever want to see again." He smiled at that and nodded. "Your uncle told me a little bit about what happened. I spoke with your attorney, Martin Meyer. He's convinced you're innocent. What can you tell me?"

"I am innocent! I'll tell you anything and everything you want to know. I shouldn't be here. I didn't do it. I didn't shoot Penny. Honest, I didn't. I hadn't seen her since the night she dumped me. That was almost two weeks before," he said, and his eyes began to water. He sniffled a bit and ran a hand beneath his nose.

"We're going to start to get this thing on the right track, namely getting you out of here. First thing we have to do is set things straight. What can you tell me? I'm gonna take some notes, so don't let that worry you, okay?"

"Yeah, okay. I just want to get out of here. The sooner, the better."

"Let's get started then. What can you tell me about the night Penny Larson was shot?"

"What can I—The night Penny was shot, I was out for my run. I'm running every other day. I do six or nine miles, depending on what I feel like. I did my run, went home, watched a couple of episodes of NCIS on TV, and went to bed. The first thing I heard about Penny being shot was the police knocking on the door of our apartment."

"What time was that?"

"When the cops came? It was maybe 10:30 in the morning. My mom had left for work, and at first, I thought maybe she forgot something. I opened the door, and these guys slammed me up against the wall, and they're shouting that I'm under arrest and shit. I tried to tell them I didn't do anything, but they just kept shouting at me. One of them was waving a gun at me."

"How many officers were there?"

"I can't really be sure. Three or four in uniforms and I think maybe four more in civilian clothes, two of them in suits, the other two were in jeans and shirts, I think. It all happened so fast I have a tough time remembering what they looked like."

"They say anything to you?"

"They were yelling about being under arrest for murder. I don't think they mentioned Penny's name, at least not until they were locking me up. I kept telling them I didn't kill anyone, but they didn't listen."

"Where were you running that night?"

"Same place I always go, Summit Avenue. We live in Capitol Plaza South. I always walk down to John Ireland Boulevard and then right where it turns into Summit Avenue, you know in front of the Cathedral, that's where I start running. I ran down to the River Boulevard that night. You familiar with Summit Avenue?" I nodded. "I run in the bike lane up to Lexington, and then once I cross Lexington, I run the rest of the way in that center boulevard."

"What time did you start?"

He seemed to think about that for a moment. "It was probably around 7:30, maybe a little later. I was looking at schools online. I've been thinking of going to college, but now…"

"Don't worry about that. You said you ran down to the River Boulevard?"

"Yeah."

"If you're running down there and back, that's gotta be nine miles."

"Nine and a half, actually. That's why it's the perfect run for me to start at the Cathedral because that's my start and finish point. It's about a four-block walk to our apartment, and it's the perfect way to cool down after my run. Once I walk back to the apartment, I hit the shower."

"How long does it take you to run that far?"

"Down to the Boulevard and back? I run at an average pace. Maybe a nine-minute mile, so call it a little more than an hour and a half."

"So you would have been home around 9:00, maybe 9:15?"

"Yeah, that's about right."

"Was your mom home?"

He shook his head and said, "No, she was out grocery shopping."

"You didn't go out after your run?"

He shook his head. "No, I'm trying to save money so I can go to college. I figure I can do the first two years at a community college and save some dough not paying all that tuition they charge you at the U. The last thing I want to do right now is go out and spend money."

"Sounds like a good plan. Can you think of anyone who might have seen you on your run that night?"

He shook his head slowly. "No, when I run at night, there aren't many other people running. In fact, the only thing I remember was a wedding reception at that place next to the Governor's mansion. They have wedding receptions there all the time."

"Oh, you mean the College Club. It's a gray limestone building."

He nodded. "Yeah, that's it. The bride, and I guess the guys in the wedding—"

"The groomsmen."

"Yeah. They were wearing different colored suits, red, yellow, blue, white, and even pink. They were taking a picture with the bride when I was running past."

"And you weren't at work that day. Where were—"

"Not at work? I worked that day. I switched hours with another guy there, Joey Castelana. I worked his shift, 11:00 to 4:00. He had a job interview somewhere that afternoon. So I covered for him, and he was supposed to cover my shift from 4:00 till 10:00." I nodded and made another note.

The guard suddenly appeared behind Cornell and said, "Time has expired."

I held both hands up, suggesting ten more minutes. He looked at me, nodded, and left.

"Tell me about your breakup with Penny Larson."

"Not much to tell. I'd had the sense something was gonna happen for a couple of weeks. I mean, there was no yelling or screaming if that's what you're thinking. She just said she wanted to move on. I don't think there was another guy or anything, least as far as I know."

"Where'd this happen?"

"The breakup? We were at a birthday party for a girlfriend, Casey Jenson. She's one of Penny's roommates. Like I said, I kinda had a feeling something was up. In fact, I was ready for it. Casey and Penny lived with three other girls in a house down on Marshall Avenue. I was getting weird looks from a couple of the girls that night, and then when Penny wanted the two of us to go out onto the porch, I just had a feeling it was gonna happen."

"What time was this?" I asked.

"Maybe 10:30. We sat out there, and she was just talking about dumb stuff. I finally asked her, what's going on? That's when she told me she wanted to breakup. She said there wasn't anyone else, and we talked for a while, and I left. She even offered to give me a ride home, but I told her no thanks, and I caught a bus. It wasn't a screaming or yelling thing if that's what you're thinking. To tell you the truth, with her getting so involved with all her protests and stuff, she just made the decision before I did. We—"

The guard suddenly appeared, "Sorry, time is up."

I nodded at him and said, "You got an address on that house?"

"I can't remember it exactly, but it's sky blue with a white front porch. It's on Marshall about two doors west of North Moore Street."

"Okay, Cornell. You hang in there, and we'll talk some more. I'm going to see if next time we can't be in one of the interview rooms with no time constraints. Okay?"

"Time's up," the guard said a little more forcefully.

Cornell nodded and said, "Thank you. The sooner you can get me out of here, the better." Then he hung up the receiver, stood, and the guard led him away.

Nine

I debated going to see Aaron LaZelle at the police station and quickly decided against it. I drove back to the office. Louie was still typing away, and Morton was still focused on his bone. As I stepped into the office, Morton looked up, licked his lips, and returned to the task at hand, namely gnawing on his bone.

"How'd it go?" Louie asked.

"Good. Cornell seems like a nice kid. I have a number of things to check on, not the least of which is a house with a bunch of college girls."

"You think he did it?" Louie asked.

I shook my head. "Unless he's a very good actor, I would say the cops made a quick arrest, cleared the books, and moved on. He seems like a nice kid caught in an unfortunate circumstance through no fault of his own."

"He has an alibi?"

"Yeah, he was out running that evening and got home from his run about 9:15. The problem is there's no one to attest to it. He goes home, showers, settles in front of the TV, and then goes to bed. Next thing he knows, the police are pounding on the door. I need to talk with his mother, check with Tracy's bar, and talk with these girlfriends of Penny Larson's."

"You're suddenly a very busy person. You think you might have time for a moment of relaxation at The Spot?"

"I think that might be just what the doctor ordered. Let me take the gnawing champion on a walk, and we'll meet you at The Spot in about fifteen minutes."

"Sounds like a plan," Louie said and began the process of shutting down his computer.

I pulled Morton's leash from the nail in the wall. That was usually the move that had him jumping to his feet. This afternoon he gave me a quick glance and started to gnaw even more aggressively.

"Come on, Morton. We're going for a walk."

He shot me a look that suggested 'really?'

I clipped the leash to his collar and pulled. He slowly climbed off his pillow. He gave a little stretch and quickly snatched up the bone and headed toward the door.

"All right, fine, you can bring your bone," I said, and we headed out the door and down the stairs. We walked for fifteen minutes. Even while reestablishing his relationship with the two fire hydrants, he never let go of the bone. At one point, a dog tied to the front porch of a house barked at Morton, and he just wiggled his head back and forth and showed off the bone.

We eventually made it to The Spot. I kept an eye peeled, but I never saw a black Prius or a white one, for that matter.

The Spot was maybe half-full when we entered. Mike, the bartender, nodded at us as we walked in and asked, "The usual?"

"Yeah, and better give Louie a refill, too," I said as we headed along the bar to where Louie sat on his semi-permanent stool. As we approached, Louie reached over and pulled a bag of pork rinds from the rack and opened the bag.

There was no way Morton could have seen what Louie did, but somehow he knew and sped up, pulling at his leash. Louie had the bag open as we came around the corner, and he poured half the bag into his hand. Now Morton was faced with a decision. Did he drop the bone and go for the pork rinds, or did he hang onto the bone?

He glanced around the bar just to make sure there wasn't anyone who looked like the type to grab his bone. Then he dropped the bone on the floor and, using his right paw, shoved it halfway beneath him, making it almost impossible for anyone to grab.

Louie started laughing and nearly fell off his stool, scattering pork rinds across the floor, which Morton just as quickly snatched up.

"Oh, God, you two are quite the pair," I said, and we both laughed. Louie poured the remainder of the bag into his hand and leaned down toward Morton, who inhaled everything in about five seconds.

Mike arrived with my beer and Louie's Jameson. Louie handed him the empty pork rind bag and said, "Put this on Dev's tab."

"Be glad to," Mike said and headed back down the bar to fill another order.

After a toast to one another and a couple of sips, Louie said, "I made a few calls on Martin Meyer, the attorney representing this kid you're looking into."

"Cornell Thomas."

"Yeah," Louie said and nodded.

"What'd you find out?" I asked and took a sip.

"Very solid reputation. From what I could determine, this is his first criminal defense case. That said, something interesting came up. I don't know if you're aware of this."

"Maybe I am. What is it?"

"Meyer is in a wheelchair," Louie said.

"Yeah, and from the looks of it, I would say permanently."

"He's the victim of a shooting. You remember maybe six or seven years ago, there was a shooting at the courthouse?"

"Some idiot was trying to sneak a pistol into a trial, if I recall," I said.

"Yeah, he's stopped just inside by security. Pulls the gun and starts shooting," Louie said.

"I think they killed the guy, didn't they?"

"Yeah, they did, but he wounded three people before he was killed, two security guards and a gentleman in the process of leaving the courthouse."

"Let me guess, the guy leaving the courthouse was Martin Meyer?"

"Correct," Louie said and took a sip from his drink.

"Hmm, interesting he would take this case at all, let alone pro bono."

"Maybe. Or perhaps, he has a true sense of what it means to be in the wrong place at the wrong time. And that seems to be the situation with this Cornell Thomas."

I nodded. "Well, let's just say it's beginning to look like he was a convenient candidate for the title of guilty party. If I can get a couple of things to click, I think we can get him off. I'd like to keep my involvement as low-key as possible. If Manning finds out I'm involved, he's going to figure Cornell is definitely the shooter, and I put him up to it."

"Your close personal friend Detective Manning."

"Yeah, there hasn't been a crime committed in this city that he doesn't think I was somehow involved."

Louie ordered another round. Morton remained focused on his bone, and we chatted about everything and nothing. We headed home, and I took the three pieces of pizza in the refrigerator and ate them cold in front of the TV. We both dozed off halfway through whatever movie we were watching and woke up to a tv screen that read,

'Are you still watching?' I let Morton out into the back-yard. I got the coffee ready for the morning, and then we headed upstairs to bed.

Ten

I hit the alarm the following morning just before it went off. I climbed out of bed and headed for the shower. Morton didn't so much as open an eye. He remained curled up on the far side of the bed with his bone tucked between his front paws.

I was down in the kitchen on my second cup of coffee when Morton wandered in carrying his bone. I gave him a head scratch and let him outside, then went back on the computer. I googled the street corner Cornell had mentioned, North Moore Street and Marshall Avenue. Once the image appeared, I moved it three houses to the west, and suddenly, there it was, a sky blue three-story house with white trim and a front porch. It was a nice enough looking place with a large boulevard tree that shaded the front yard. I envisioned Cornell maybe sitting on the porch railing on the night Penny Larson told him she wanted to breakup, never a fun time for either individual.

I let Morton back in, and once he finished breakfast, we climbed in the car. I decided to drive past the house on Marshall Ave. Morton was busy working on his bone as we headed down the street. When I got to the corner of North Moore Street, I slowed down. There were two girls sitting on the front porch of the sky blue house. It looked like they were drinking coffee and chatting.

I pulled to the curb and climbed out of the car. When I stepped onto the sidewalk leading to the front porch, they abruptly stopped their conversation and stared as I approached.

"Good morning," I said and smiled in an attempt to appear nice. They didn't move or respond. "I'm hoping you might be able to help me out. I'm a private investigator. I've been hired to look into Penny Larson's murder. Would you mind if I asked you a couple of questions?"

One of the girls immediately stood and hurried into the house. The other girl studied me for a long moment as she took a sip from her mug. "So, who are you working for?"

"I'm just trying to find out the details. From what I've heard, Penny broke up with her boyfriend a couple of weeks before."

"Yeah," she said and took another sip.

"Were they having problems?"

"Problems?" she asked and shook her head. "Not that we were aware. We thought he was a nice guy. At least he seemed to be until he killed her."

"Did you see him do that?"

"See him? No, I was working that night. Came home to cop cars all over the place and learned that he had killed Penny."

"Did anyone see him?"

She seemed to think about that and finally shook her head. "No, I guess not. She was out here alone. We all work nights, waitressing and bartending. She had a bunch of her protest pals over for a get-together. The cops arrested him the next day. So there you go. Besides, who else would have done it? She quit her job the month before, so it's not like she had any work problems."

"Why'd she quit her job?"

She shook her head. "She was all about ecological restoration, stopping global warming, encouraging sustainability. She turned into a fanatic, protests, demonstrations, signs all over. Our landlord warned her a number of times to take her signs down. God, she didn't want us to turn on the heat or the air conditioner."

"Sounds like she really practiced what she preached."

The girl nodded, "Oh yeah, definitely. We'd all be the first to agree. But there has to be some middle ground. I like to take a hot shower. It's Minnesota. We need the heat on in the winter. Don't get me wrong. I loved her, and we all really miss her, but she was starting to turn into Miss Crazy. She was studying to be an English teacher and then switched majors last spring to ecology and systematics biology."

"I don't think I could spell that, let alone study it," I said.

Fortunately, she smiled. "I think her breaking up with Cornell was just another step in the process. She was involved with protests around town. You know, fossil fuels and stuff."

"So was there ever a big battle between her and Cornell? Did he have a temper?"

She shook her head. "No, like I said, we all thought he was a really nice guy. But you know, sometimes things just don't work out. We were all shocked when we found out he was the guy the cops arrested. Maybe Penny had a sense something wasn't right there. I don't know. She never mentioned anything. Now it's too late."

"Okay, well, thanks for filling me in. You mind if I leave my card with you? If anything comes to mind or one of the other girls thinks of something, please give me a call," I said and handed her a card.

She took my card and studied it for a second or two. "Yeah, we'll be sure to call," she said in a way that suggested I'd never hear from any of them.

"Thanks for your time. Oh, I didn't catch your name. I'm Dev Haskell."

"Yeah, I saw it on your card. Diane Haggerty, good luck."

"Thanks, Diane. Appreciate your time," I said and walked back to my car. I watched her reflection on the car window, expecting her to give me the finger or toss my card, but she just took another sip from her coffee mug. I climbed in the car, and we headed down to the office. Louie was there, and the coffee was on. Morton made a beeline for his pillow and continued to gnaw.

I poured myself a mug of coffee and topped up Louie's.

"How was your night?" Louie asked.

"I started to watch a movie and fell asleep halfway through the thing. How about you?"

"I left The Spot about thirty minutes after you two took off. Court appearance later this morning, so I was in early."

"I've got to make a phone call and then work my way through that file Heidi gave me. Not looking forward to it."

"Good luck," Louie said and went back to the file he was working on.

I settled in at my desk, glanced out the window to see if there was any activity in the apartment across the street. Unfortunately, the shades were pulled. I took out my cell and called Cornell's attorney, Martin Meyer.

"Martin Meyer Legal Office," a female voice answered.

"Is this Edith I'm speaking with?"

"It is. Who's calling, please?" she asked in a no-nonsense tone.

"Hi Edith, this is Dev Haskell. I was in the other day to talk with Martin. Would he happen to be in?"

"Just a moment, and I'll see if he's available," she said. The phone clicked, and she put me on hold before

I could give her a clever response. After a long moment, she was back on. "I'll transfer your call now," she said then did just that before I could reply.

The phone rang three times before Meyer picked up. "Martin Meyer," was how he answered.

"Hi Martin, this is Dev Haskell."

"Haskell, good morning. How can I help you?"

"I was able to visit with Cornell Thomas yesterday for a few minutes."

"How did that go?"

"It went well, considering." I went on to explain the surroundings, the glass partition, speaking on a phone receiver, and, most important, the time constraint. "I would like you to list me as a member of the defense team, so I can discuss things with Cornell in private and for longer than a few minutes."

"I can do that. Have you discussed compensation with Cornell?"

"No, I have not, and I don't intend to. I'll follow your lead and do this pro bono. I'm pretty certain he's been railroaded. Maybe it's the police being a little too aggressive in attempting to close the case quickly. Maybe they were fed some bad information. At this stage, I don't know, but I intend to find out. If you could add me to your list and submit that to the powers that be, I'll get started."

"I'll have the update delivered this morning. Anything else?"

"Have you spoken with the roommates?"

"The roommates? Are you referring to the women sharing that house over on Marshall Avenue?" Meyer asked.

"Yes, I am. I swung past there this morning."

"And?"

"And their friend was murdered on the front porch. To tell you the truth, I'm more than a little surprised any of them are still there. The cops arrested Cornell, and their attitude is, 'He seemed like a nice guy. Too bad we didn't know.' The girl I spoke with suggested that the victim, Penny Larson, may have gone a bit off the deep end. Apparently, she was all involved in ecology and protesting against fossil fuels and that stuff."

"So making the world a better place."

"To a point. She said Penny Larson wasn't too happy when they wanted the heat on in the winter, and she wasn't too thrilled with using air conditioning in the summer. She changed her major in college from studying to be a teacher to recycling or something. Are you aware of anything along those lines that would have set Cornell off?"

"No, I'm not aware of anything that would have upset him. The breakup didn't seem to be that big a deal to him," Meyer said.

"I had the same impression. He mentioned that he'd felt the relationship slowly drifting apart for a number of weeks. I got the distinct impression, while it's never fun to be told that, he wasn't really surprised. The police suggest anything to you besides the breakup as a reason he would do this?" I asked.

"No, nothing. They were set on the breakup as the reason."

"Which suggests maybe there's someone out there who had a reason to want her dead," I said.

"I'll get you listed as an associate on the defense team. You should be good to go by the end of the day."

"Thank you, Martin. I'll plan to meet with Cornell tomorrow morning. Do you want to be there?"

"Would you mind?"

"Not at all. I'll call you tomorrow with a time. I'm going to aim for 10:00. Would that work for you?"

"I'll make it work," he said. We chatted for another minute or two, and I hung up.

Louie was in the process of stuffing files into his briefcase when I hung up. "With any luck, I should be back by mid-afternoon," he said as he closed his briefcase.

"Good luck," I called as he headed out the door.

I'd done everything I could and now stared at Heidi's six-inch thick RIP file on my desk. I took a deep breath, opened it, and started reading. Over the course of the next three hours, I drank all the coffee, scribbled a half-dozen pages of notes on a yellow legal pad, and in the end, didn't feel any further ahead.

I kept thinking about the little demonstration Terry Nelson had shown me, holding the flame beneath the fake board and it never catching fire. He was right. If they could produce that stuff at an economical level, it really did have the potential to change the world. And yet, Heidi was worried enough that she wanted me to check out the two principles, Franklin Lanzo and Russell Greeney. That was very unusual for her. In fact, she'd never come to me with a concern like that before.

Eleven

The RIP, Inc. website had a photo of Franklin Lanzo and Russell Greeney along with a paragraph of general information on each of them. Greeney appeared to be the older of the two, with thinning gray hair and blue or gray eyes. He was originally from Santa Barbara, California, and graduated with a master's degree in environmental ecology from Princeton University. Franklin Lanzo graduated from Columbia. He appeared to be a little younger and heavier with dark eyes and hair. Both men lived in the suburb of Dellwood, an area just north of the city.

I looked up the zip code and then did a search. I came up with three addresses and wrote them down. I grabbed the leash and took Morton on a walk before we got in the car. His work on the pork bone must have been more or less completed because he was happy to leave it on his pillow after I clipped the leash to his collar.

We headed out the door for a three-block spin. We came across a truck blocking the sidewalk and unloading furniture. I counted five guys carrying chairs and a mattress into a house with a sold sign out front. It was a nice-looking two-story brick place. A blonde woman in shorts and a white top was standing on the front porch talking on her cellphone. I wondered if she was the owner or maybe one-half of the couple that had purchased the place.

Morton did his duty, and I dropped the plastic bag in the trash bin a half-block away. I let him in the backseat, and we drove up to the 35E entrance and headed north to Highway 61. We drove through White Bear and into Dellwood. It's more of a rural area. Homes were all a bit off the road and usually behind trees and large plots of land. We passed a number of small bodies of water, some downright swampy areas, and then every so often one hell of a large, fancy home. The first address I checked was listed to a Roberta Greeney, and I wondered if she was maybe a sister or daughter of Russell Greeney. At the moment, there was no way to find out, and the house looked like a pretty standard three-bed-room suburban home. The second address, maybe three miles away on the same road, had a three-car garage, trimmed hedges, and a gorgeous brick home with a red tile roof. What appeared to be a greenhouse was attached to one side of the house. It looked like a swimming pool area was behind the structure, but I couldn't see an actual pool from the road. The address on the mailbox matched the one I'd found for Franklin Lanzo. I took four photos with my cellphone.

I drove past the Dellwood Country Club toward the north side of White Bear Lake. The homes along the shore were hidden from the road by bushes and trees. I pulled to the side of the road and stopped next to the mailbox that corresponded to the address I had for Russell Greeney. With all of the shrubbery, the only thing I could see was the roof of the house. Suffice it to say, the place was huge and on the shore of White Bear Lake. I counted five dormers with rounded roofs along the roofline, suggesting a three-story structure. The entrance from the road featured a curved brick driveway that disappeared behind the shrubbery.

Morton was asleep in the backseat, no doubt exhausted from gnawing on the pork bone for the past day and a half. On the twenty-minute drive back to the office, I came to the conclusion that it looked like money did not appear to be a problem for either Lanzo or Greeney. That made the building filled with empty plastic bottles seem even more strange. You'd think two successful businessmen would know how to get things moving in a start-up company.

As I parked in front of the office, my cellphone rang. I pulled it out and checked the screen, caller unknown. I debated answering, thinking it was probably another recording about the warranty on my car, and I'd add the number to the dozen or so I'd already blocked. I answered anyway.

"Hello."

"Devlin Haskell, please."

"You got him."

"Toby Bunker, Mr. Haskell. How are you today?"

"What can I do for you, Toby?"

"I think it's more, what I can do for you. You're looking to buy or sell a house?"

"Buy or sell a house? No neither. I think you've got the wrong number and—"

"I'm sorry, I found your card attached to my office door this morning. You didn't put it there?"

"No, someone must have… Wait a minute. Is your office at the end of the hall on the first floor?"

"It is."

"And I think the only other office in the building belongs to a company named RIP, is that right?"

"Yeah, they're a little different."

"Toby, have you had lunch today?"

"No," he said, drawing out the word as if to ask, 'What's this about?'

"I'd love to buy you lunch if you've got the time. You tell me where, and I'll meet you there."

He seemed to think about that for a moment and then asked, "You know where Jersey's Bar and Grill is?"

"Yeah, I think so. It's on Concord Boulevard, right?"

"That's the place. Can you meet me there in, oh say a half-hour?"

"I can. Thanks for making the time. I'm wearing a Saint Paul Saints t-shirt."

"Perfect, I've got my Coldplay t-shirt on today, well and yesterday too, now that I think about it. First one there grabs a table. I look forward to meeting you, Dev."

"Likewise, Toby, I'll see you in a half-hour."

I took Morton up to the office. Louie wasn't due back for at least another hour. I tossed Morton a biscuit, and he settled onto his pillow. He devoured the biscuit in three bites, then started in again on the pork bone and seemed content. I left Louie a note, hurried back to the car, and took off for Jersey's Bar and Grill.

Twelve

The route was a quick drive through a corner of downtown. I took the Robert Street Bridge over the Mississippi and then turned onto Cesar Chavez Street, which turned into Concord Boulevard after a mile. I pulled up almost in front of Jersey's and hurried inside.

The building had a rough stone facade on the first floor and aluminum siding made to look like cedar shakes on the second floor. It had been a couple of years since I'd been in the place. I couldn't remember the name of the woman I was with at the time. Nothing seemed to have changed, a nice-looking U-shaped bar that seated maybe forty with a wavy yellow neon light along the ceiling above the bar. Tables and booths were on either side of the bar. Just now, the place was close to half-full of people finishing up lunch. I didn't see anyone wearing a Coldplay t-shirt, so I grabbed an empty table.

A waitress appeared about thirty seconds later and handed me a menu. "Anyone joining you today?"

"Yeah, another guy should be here soon."

"Can I get you something from the bar?" she asked as she set another menu on the table.

"Maybe just a coffee when you have time, no rush."

She smiled and headed toward the bar. She was back a moment later with a mug of coffee. No more than a minute after that, a guy about my age entered wearing a faded gray t-shirt with the word COLDPLAY in different faded colors across the front of it. I waved to catch his attention, and he headed for the table. The t-shirt was stretched tight across his chest but not from being a poster child for 'in shape.' I guessed his weight at north of three hundred pounds as he bounced and jiggled toward the table. "Toby Bunker," he said upon arrival and extended his hand to shake.

"Dev Haskell, thanks for making the time, Toby."

He pulled out a chair and sat down just as the waitress showed up wearing a smile. "Hi, Angelina, just the usual for me. Can I get you anything from the bar, Dev?" he asked and glanced at my coffee mug.

"Thanks, but I'm fine for right now," I said.

Angelina hurried back to the bar.

"So you said you wanted to talk about RIP. Is there a problem? And before you say anything, I've spoken with Terry Nelson a little bit, most times nothing more than a 'hello,' but I don't know that much about the company. To my knowledge, no one but Terry is in that office. A couple other guys are in and out once or twice a week, but they don't office there."

"Those 'couple other' guys you just mentioned, do they drive a black or a white Prius?"

"Yeah, as a matter of fact, they do. Sounds like you might know more than me. Who are they? Clients?" Bunker asked.

I shook my head. "No, they're the principles of RIP. They actually office downtown in the Wells Fargo building. I think they're up on the thirty-fourth floor."

"Jesus, you do know more than me. Oh, thanks, Angelina," he said as the waitress placed a beer on the table.

"Are you ready to order?" she asked.

"I know what I'm getting, my usual, the cheeseburger special."

The waitress nodded, smiled, and looked at me.

"Same thing for me, Angelina."

"Your coffee okay?" she asked.

"Yeah, just fine."

She picked up our menus and hurried off. "Nice girl," Bunker said, watching her head back to the bar. "I think the guy she dates is trouble. So RIP, like I said, you seem to know more than me."

I shook my head. "Not really. I've never met the two principles. I've only met Terry Nelson the one time, and that was the other day. I was interested in maybe investing. The company stock seems to have done well, and Nelson gave me a demonstration of their fire-resistant plastic product." I went on to describe Nelson holding the flame beneath the foot-long board.

"And this was in that two-story brick building down along the river?"

"Yeah, it's got a cyclone fence around it. There were a couple of cardboard protest signs hanging on the fence when we pulled up. Nelson unlocked the gate and pulled the signs off the fence. The building was actually just one big room filled with mountains of plastic bottles going all the way up to the second-story windows."

"Yeah, I'm familiar with the building. It's been for sale for years. It was originally built to manufacture buggy whips or something; it's been that long ago. Problem is, being that close to the river, it floods every four or five years. I've actually had a couple of folks interested in buying the place. But once they get a look and see the flood history, they move on."

"So RIP doesn't own the place?"

"I'm sure they don't. They're probably renting that space for next to nothing. Because of the light snow and the slow thaw, we didn't really have much of a flood this year. But if they brought in any equipment, you'd want to be out of there from March to early June just to be safe."

"Is there much activity in the office above you?"

He shook his head. "Not that I'm aware. Terry's pickup is parked out there just about every day. The funny thing is he's usually there at the end of the day. A couple times, I've had to do some work, you know, present an offer or something, and I'm in the office at night, maybe 8:00, once in a while 9:00 or later, and his pickup is always parked there. It's almost like he's living up in the office, but I've never actually asked him if that was the case."

Angelina suddenly appeared with two platters. Each featured a three-story cheeseburger, a large stack of onion rings that looked like doughnuts, and a pile of lettuce, tomato, pickles, and onions.

"Can I get you anything else?" she asked.

I just stared at the platter and shook my head.

"Yeah, I better have another beer," Bunker said. He piled the tomato slice, some lettuce, and three onion rings on top of the three-story cheeseburger. He placed the top of the bun on the stack and pressed it down, causing juice from the three burgers to squirt onto the platter and his side of the table. He picked the thing up and took a gigantic bite. "Mmm, I just love these things," he said, spitting bits onto his plate. He chewed, swallowed, and took another bite.

I couldn't bring myself to do it, and I cut into the stack with a knife and fork. Bunker set down his triple cheeseburger and attacked the pile of onion rings just as Angelica set Toby's fresh beer on the table. "Everything okay with you guys?"

"Just fine," I said.

"Mmm," Bunker nodded. He washed down the onion ring with two or three gulps of beer, burped, and said, "Yeah, everything is just fine."

We chatted for the next fifteen minutes, but truth be told, I did most of the talking while Bunker cleaned his plate. I finished half of my triple cheeseburger and was stuffed. Once I set my fork down, Bunker asked, "You going to finish that?"

"No, you want it?"

"You mind?" he asked, handing his empty plate to me and picking up mine with the onion rings and half the triple burger.

"Help yourself, man," I said, and he did just that.

It took him about three minutes to clean my plate, and then he ordered a piece of chocolate cheesecake for dessert. I got a fresh cup of coffee and the bill. Once I paid, we chatted for another five minutes and walked out together. "Let me know if anything strange ever happens up in the RIP office. I think I'm going to hold off for a bit before I decide to invest."

"Yeah, can't say as I blame you. I got the card you left at my door. Anything happens, I'll get in touch. You know, the strange thing is they never changed the locks on their door. I changed mine before I moved anything in. The building locks are a joke. You can go into any office in the building, just walk right in."

"I peeked in a number of empty offices just to see what they were like, but the doors were unlocked. In fact, a couple of them were wide open."

"Yeah, like I said, the locks are so bad a kid could open them with a bobby pin. I'm not kidding, literally with a bobby pin. If the doors do happen to be locked and you left your bobby pin at home, you can just give them a hip check, and the door would fly open."

Yeah, maybe I thought, but then, how many people were walking around with hips the size of Toby Bunker's? We said goodbye, shook hands, and I watched as Bunker waddled around the corner and into the parking lot. I slid behind the wheel and waited to see what he was driving. He pulled out of the parking lot a couple of minutes later. He was driving a faded black Buick Regal with a long white scratch along the left side of the car. He gave a quick glance in my general direction, but I'm pretty sure he never saw me. He pulled into the street and drove away.

I noticed the rear panel on the left side of the car was dented, and the left taillight was broken. It looked like he had taped some red plastic film over the taillight. The rear window had an Uber decal in the righthand corner, and I wondered if he was driving for Uber when he wasn't working at his real estate business. As he sped off, the car definitely leaned to the left from his weight.

I pulled a U-turn in the middle of the street and headed back to the office. When I arrived, Morton was asleep on his pillow, and Louie was nowhere to be seen. Morton slowly opened one eye and looked at me. He closed his eye a moment later, snuggled a little deeper into his pillow, and took a deep breath. I made some notes on the yellow legal pad, tore off the sheet of paper, and slipped it into Heidi's file.

When I opened the file, I noticed the brochure Terry Nelson had pulled out of the desk and handed to me. The brochure looked worn and had a number of photos of the plastic lumber similar to the three pieces I had seen yesterday. In fact, they could have been the same three pieces for all I knew. There was a phone number scribbled along the side of the brochure.

I was thinking of calling the number just to see who would answer when I heard the stairs begin to creak. A moment later, the door opened, and a red-faced Louie walked in. He gave me a little wave, tossed his briefcase on his picnic table desk, and settled into his desk chair. Morton opened his one eye, then snuggled down into his pillow and went back to sleep.

I busied myself paging through Heidi's file for a couple of minutes before I glanced over at Louie and asked, "So, how did things go in court?"

"Reasonably well. My client won't have to spend any time in the workhouse provided she attends the AA meetings. Fortunately for her, it was her first offense."

"You think she'll act accordingly?"

"Oh yeah. She was absolutely mortified she'd been arrested. She'll be driving to and from work, and I'm pretty sure, if she's driving, she won't be having anything to drink. In all honesty, it was an unfortunate bit of bad luck, but I doubt she'll ever get behind the wheel again after drinking."

Thirteen

Louie was on the phone when Morton woke up. I figured it might be a good time to take him for a walk. As I pulled his leash off the nail, he rose from his pillow, stretched, and turned his head left and right, apparently getting all the kinks out before he met me at the door. I attached his leash, gave a wave to Louie, and we headed out the door.

We took our usual route through the neighborhood. Morton marked his appearance at both fire hydrants. We walked down the street, and just as we came to the house where the guys had been moving in furniture, the blonde woman I'd seen on the phone was walking down the front steps with an almost white lab on a leash. Morton stopped and stared, and I had to pull on the leash to get him moving.

"Sorry about that. He's always into making friends," I said.

"Oh, that's sweet. I'm Becky Desjardins, by the way, and this is Princess. She's a fair-haired yellow lab. We just moved in."

"Dev Haskell. Nice to meet you, Becky, and you too, Princess. This is Morton, my Golden Retriever. We saw the guys here unloading the truck yesterday."

"Yeah, I've got things stacked everywhere inside the house. It'll be a year before I can get through it all. Do you live nearby?"

"No, I mean not really. I live up the hill, and then if you know where the cathedral is, I just live a couple of blocks from there."

"Oh wow, I'm impressed. That's a pretty long walk."

"Yeah, it is, and we didn't make it. My office is just kitty-corner from The Spot bar. So it's only a couple of blocks from here, but it's nice to get out and do our constitutional duty."

"Yeah, I saw that place, The Spot. Is it nice?"

"I like it. It's a neighborhood place. Local folks in there. Nice bartenders. It's not crazy, and if you're wondering if you'd be okay going in there alone, the answer is yes."

"I'll have to check it out."

Morton was now in the process of sniffing Princess's rear end. She responded in kind. "We were just getting started on our walk. You want to join us for a quick tour of the neighborhood?"

"Would you mind?"

"No, not at all. In fact, I'd enjoy the company."

She smiled at that, and we headed off down the street. Morton and Princess seemed to strike up an immediate friendship. We walked along a couple of streets, and I occasionally mentioned the history of a house or a corner. I told Becky more about The Spot and Rooster's barbecue. I mentioned a couple of grocery stores and a gas station nearby. I told her about the restaurants on Selby near me and the ones on Grand Avenue. We'd been talking and walking for the better part of an hour, but suddenly we were back at her corner.

"Oh, Dev, this has really been nice. Thanks for making the time. I'm sure there are other things you'd rather be doing. At least now I know where to get gas and groceries."

"My pleasure, Becky. Nice to meet you and Princess. Now don't be a stranger, oh, and here, let me give you a card," I said and pulled a business card out of my wallet. I checked both sides to make sure I hadn't written down a phone number. "Yeah, here," I said and handed her the card. "If you have a question or you're lost on the streets, feel free to give me a call."

"Oh, thanks, Dev. I just might do that. Well, umm, thank you for the tour, and I hope we see more of you two."

"Yeah, me too. Thanks for letting me bore you."

"Oh, it was anything but. I really appreciate it," she said, and they headed down the street to her house. Princess looked over her shoulder three times as they walked away.

Morton didn't bark, but his tail was wagging a mile a minute.

"Well, finally. I was starting to get worried," Louie said when we stepped into the office. I tossed Morton a biscuit, and he settled onto his pillow. He finished the biscuit before I sat down.

"Morton introduced himself to a lovely white lab, and then we took her and her owner on a little neighborhood walk. She just moved into a place about two blocks away."

"What's her name?"

"Princess."

"Not the dog, Dev, the woman. What's her name?"

"Oh, yeah, sure. Umm Becky. Becky Desjardins. Just moved in yesterday. In fact, there was a moving van outside the place, and we saw the guys hauling all sorts of furniture in. Nice lady."

Louie looked at me for a moment and then shook his head.

"What? I was just being nice. I told her where the grocery stores were and gas stations. Told her The Spot was a good place."

"Yeah, no doubt all in the interest of just being a good neighbor. You're the original gentleman, Dev."

"What do you mean?"

"I don't suppose you happened to mention your phone number. Did you invite her over to your place for a nightcap? You know, classy guy that you are."

"There you go, Louie. I'm a nice guy, helping a stranger, and now I'm being criticized. That's okay. I know I did the right thing."

"I'm thinking of going over to The Spot in about an hour. You interested in joining me? Be a good opportunity to spread some more of that charm of yours around."

"Let me think about it. You know what they say. You're known by the company you keep."

We headed over to The Spot an hour later. I took Morton on a short walk before we were settled in at the bar. We took a different route rather than walk past Becky's house again. I didn't want to appear too anxious.

Once we entered The Spot, Morton pulled me along the length of the bar to Louie's semi-permanent stool. Louie already had a handful of pork rinds ready. We hung around for two beers and then headed home. It would have been nice if Becky had shown up, but I really didn't expect her to.

I found a chicken drumstick in the refrigerator along with a piece of lasagna that didn't taste too bad once I warmed it up. We watched a movie I'd already seen once or twice and then headed up to bed. I slept through the night and was up just before my alarm.

Fourteen

I was on the computer when Morton wandered down. He did his usual stretch when he entered the kitchen and then wandered over for his head scratch before I let him out into the backyard. I filled his food and water dishes, let him back in, and continued my exploratory work on the computer. At the moment, I was looking up Becky Desjardins. I found the name, actually a couple hundred women with the same name, but not the specific person I was looking for. I went through Google, Instagram, Facebook, Twitter, and LinkedIn. Lots of women with the same name, just not the one I'd met yesterday.

Eventually, I gave up, and we headed down to the office. Louie wasn't in, so I dumped the remnants of coffee down the sink and made a fresh pot. I pulled the RIP brochure that Terry Nelson had given me from Heidi's file and did a search on the phone number written inside. Nothing came up. I debated for a second or two and called the number. The phone rang three times, suggesting the number was at least in service, and then a recording said, 'Leave a message.' I ended the call.

I phoned Martin Meyer, and amazingly, Edith, his secretary, was pleasant and put my call through.

"You've reached Martin Meyer," was how he answered.

"Hi, Martin, Dev Haskell calling. Just checking in. Were you able to add my name as an associate on the Cornell Thomas case?"

"You're official, Dev. You'll be able to meet with Cornell and discuss things privately. Just a word of advice. Give them some leeway on scheduling a meeting. They've got a lot of people in there and a very limited number of rooms. Schedule a time as much in advance as possible for your own sanity."

"Thanks, Martin. I'm planning on going over a little later. You still interested in being there?" He seemed to think about that for a long moment. "Martin?"

"Oh, sorry, Dev, just going over my schedule. I'm really pressed for time today, especially during the afternoon. Would you mind swinging by after you meet with Cornell to give me an update?"

"Not a problem. I can do that. Let me schedule that interview, and I'll call whenever I finish up with Cornell. If you're available, I'll swing by. If not, you can call me when you have a moment. Will that work for you?"

"Yeah, that works fine."

"Okay, Martin, I'll call them now and try to schedule that interview."

"Thanks, Dev. Hope to see you later this afternoon," Meyer said and disconnected.

I phoned the Ramsey County Adult Detention Center. It took three different phone transfers, but I finally ended up with the person who was able to schedule my interview with Cornell Thomas. She came across as a no-nonsense individual, and I figured rather than say a couple of stupid one-liners I would just thank her for the help and get out of her hair. I had a 1:00 appointment.

Louie eventually showed up around 11:00, and I had a mug of coffee waiting for him on his picnic table desk. After a couple of sips, he said, "You look all bright and cheery. Did you phone your new friend last night and—"

"Becky Desjardins? No, I thought it best not to interject myself until she's emptied most of the boxes she said were stacked around the house. Actually, Martin Meyer put me on the associates' list for the Cornell Thomas case, and I was able to schedule an appointment to interview him this afternoon."

"Oh, hey, congratulations. That's good news."

"Well, we'll see. As a matter of fact, I want to go down to Tracy's and check out Cornell's schedule. He mentioned covering for someone, and the guy was supposed to return the favor and cover for him the night of the Penny Larson murder, but apparently, he never showed up."

"Good luck with that."

"Yeah, hopefully, they'll confirm Cornell's version. In fact, I'd better get going. Are you going to be around for a bit?"

"I'm here for the rest of the day, Dev. No worries, take as long as you want. If we're not here, it just means Morton wanted to go over to The Spot, and that's where you'll find us."

"Thanks, Louie. I took him on a walk a while ago, so he should be okay."

"Good luck," Louie called as I headed out the door and down the stairs. I looked up and down the street for the black Prius and decided I must have been mistaken. Maybe it was just a guy trying to find an address, and he'd pulled over a number of times to talk on the phone. Yeah, maybe, but then again…

Fifteen

At one time, maybe forty or fifty years ago, Tracy's was one of the top three 'after work' bars downtown. It was a block and a half from the city courthouse, and the place would be jammed for two martini business lunches and the two or three drinks everyone stopped for after a tough day at the office. Of course, that was in the day when everyone worked downtown. Times change.

Nowadays, the lunches at Tracy's are more of the fast-food variety. Martini lunches had been out of style for decades. Anyone who's working is drinking coffee or a Coke. In the evening, what's left of the dinner crowd is sixty-five or older, and you'll still see the occasional tie on an older gentleman. Still, it was where Cornell Thomas worked, and I wanted to check out what happened with the guy he'd traded working shifts with, Joey Castelana.

Tracy's was located on St. Peter Street. It had been in the same place since its inception back in 1923. The two-story red-brick building had been around since 1858, ancient history for Minnesota.

I parked across the street, which spoke volumes that I could even get a parking space in the middle of a workday. I stepped inside and looked around. I was sure my grandparents wouldn't have noticed any change. The bar on the left ran almost the entire length of the dining area. Currently, there were two tables occupied. The four or five people in the place looked to be well past retirement age. Two guys were wearing ties and sport coats.

"What can I get you?" the bartender asked.

I hadn't seen him in years, but it clicked as soon as I read his name tag. Dick Tracy. Fourth or fifth-generation owner. The commercial lot the building was on had to be worth millions, but he was happy just tending bar and running the business, such as it was.

"Hi Dick, Dev Haskell, long time no see," I said and held out my hand.

"Haskell?" he said and then smiled. "Yeah, didn't I throw you out years back for being underage?"

"You did, and I deserved it. I still remember you let me finish my beer then told me to get lost."

"Yeah, and you left me a dollar tip, didn't you?"

"Not exactly, it was monopoly money."

"Yeah, that's it right there," he said and pointed to a small black frame hanging behind the bar with a white one-dollar monopoly bill.

"You actually kept the thing. That's the one I gave you?"

"Believe me when I say you're the only guy who has ever done that. Now, what can I get you?"

"Sorry to say just a coffee and maybe a minute or two of your time."

"Well, you can see we're really busy," he said and shook his head. He poured me a coffee and then filled a shot glass with Baileys Irish Cream and slid it next to the coffee.

"Thanks, Dick, that's mighty kind of you."

"It's good to see you, Dev. Usually, we ask customers for their AARP cards, but since you're at least thirty years away from qualifying, I'll make an exception. So what are you doing? I think the last I heard, you'd gone in the army."

I nodded and said, "Yeah, I have the honor of knowing I served, and the army is happy with the knowledge that I'm out."

He laughed at that, "So what are you up to?"

"I'm a private investigator. Have been for a number of years, now."

"No kidding. That's great. You must have a ton of stories."

"A few. Probably just like you, the craziness becomes more of an everyday event." He nodded. "Actually, that's why I stopped by. I'm looking into a case. A young girl was murdered a few weeks back, and I—"

"You mean the Larson girl? On a front porch? Cornell Thomas was involved. God, I still can't believe it. He was a good employee. Wish I had more like him, to tell you the truth. Kid worked his rear end off. I don't think he ever missed a day."

"You sure about that? See, the cops are telling me he missed work the night of the murder."

Tracey thought about that for half a second and said, "That's not exactly what I told them. I said he was supposed to work that night. It was his usual shift, and I ended up bussing the dishes. Cornell had covered the shift for our afternoon guy, Joey Castelana. He had a job interview that afternoon. I guess some idiot ran a red light and broadsided his car on the way to the interview. Put the kid in the hospital with a broken hip. That's why I ended up bussing tables. I had to call my son-in-law in to help out. Castelana is still out, probably will be for another month or two," he said and shook his head. "It don't look like it now, but I could use both of them back. They were good workers."

"Would you be willing to swear to that? If I had Cornell's attorney contact you, would you be willing to go on record?"

"You mean swear to the fact that the kid covered for his pal that afternoon? Sure thing. I don't know Dev, is that going to make a difference? That girl was shot at night, wasn't she? All my statement is going to do is convince the powers that be that Cornell wasn't working that night and had the time to commit the crime."

"Yeah, I get that, but it's the first step in building his case. You wouldn't happen to have contact information for Joey Castelana, would you?"

He seemed to think about that for a moment before he said, "Hang on just a minute. I've got it in the office."

He stepped out from behind the bar and headed for the swinging door that led to the kitchen.

I took a couple of sips of coffee and then poured the shot of Baileys into the mug. Tracy was back a couple minutes later. He handed me his business card and said, "I wrote Castelana's phone number on the back. He's a good kid, and as far as I know, he's pretty much confined to home. He'd probably love a visit from someone. Even if it was someone like you," he said and laughed.

We chatted for a few more minutes. I finished most of the coffee and left a ten-dollar bill on the bar despite his objections. I got in my car, drove around the block, and parked. I phoned the number Tracy had written on the back of the card. The phone barely rang once before it was answered.

"Hello," a male voice said.

"Hi, I'm calling for Joey Castelana."

"That's me."

I went on to explain who I was and why I was calling. "Would you have time to talk to me today?"

"You kidding, the only things I got scheduled this week are breakfast, lunch, and dinner. Yeah, please come over and talk to me."

He gave me his address, and I told him I'd be right over. I pulled in front of the house ten minutes later.

Sixteen

The Castelana family home was in West St. Paul, a municipality actually south of St. Paul but on the west side of the Mississippi River, hence the name. Just one more thing to confuse visitors.

I guessed the house might be thirty years old. It was located in a nice suburban area of similar structures. The area consisted of three and four-bedroom homes with attached garages and nicely paved streets. The house had wooden shakes painted a light gray with white trim on the windows and doors. The front door was painted black and had a large brass door knocker centered on the door.

Joey Castelana had instructed me to walk around to the back of the house and knock on the sliding glass door in the walkout basement. I followed his directions and walked down a set of steps to a well-manicured backyard. A wooden deck came off the main floor of the house. Below the deck was a brick patio with two wicker couches, chairs, and a gas grill that looked like it could cook steaks for thirty. The sliding glass door was behind the chairs.

As I approached the sliding door, a guy in a wheel-chair knocked on the glass and signaled me to pull the door open. "Dev Haskell?" he asked as I slid the door open.

"Yeah, and you're Joey?"

He nodded, and we shook hands. "Nice to meet you. Come on in and grab a seat," he said, then rolled backward, clicked the remote resting on his lap, and turned off what looked like an eighty-five-inch flatscreen hanging on the wall. I happened to know Castelana was twenty years old, although sitting in the wheelchair, he looked like some high-school kid. He had neatly trimmed dark hair slicked back. His eyes were dark brown, in fact almost black. It was tough to determine his height, but I guessed he was maybe about 5'10".

I settled into a wingback chair, and Castelana positioned himself more or less across from me. There was a coffee table off to the side with a half-dozen prescription bottles arranged in a straight line.

"So, you just came from Tracy's?" he asked.

"Yeah, Dick was tending bar, and after I told him what I was doing, he thought it might be best to talk to you."

Castelana nodded and smiled. "Well, what can I do to help Cornell?"

I went on to explain the record the police had established and finished up with, "So, a sworn statement from you wouldn't change anything. You still didn't show up for work. But what it does establish is the fact that there is a reason you didn't show up. Namely, you were hospitalized and unable to work."

"Yeah, hospitalized for four days. Two of which I was unconscious."

"Not to joke about your situation, but that's exactly the kind of credibility we need to build and convince people that there is no way Cornell was involved in the murder of Penny Larson."

"I'll be happy to give a statement."

"Do the docs have you doing any therapy?"

"You kidding? I go through torture six times a day. I get out of the chair, turn from side to side. Walk a few feet between a pair of railings. It's really fun," he said, meaning anything but.

"How are you holding up?"

"Pretty good. They gave me a bunch of painkillers," he said and nodded at the line of plastic bottles on the coffee table. "Fortunately, I'm pretty much off those except just before I go to bed, and even then, I'm just taking one. I want to get off that shit as soon as possible."

"So, Tracy said you were on the way to a job interview, and someone ran a light?"

"Yeah, the guy's been charged with a DUI. I think they got him in the workhouse."

"Did you get his name?"

"Yeah, Spenser Buchner. He tried to flee the scene, but two guys who saw the accident blocked his car and called the cops. Turns out his car wouldn't have been able to go anywhere. I don't think it was his first DUI, but I'm not sure about that."

"You suing him?"

"Yeah, my dad has an attorney friend, and he's going after the guy."

I handed him my card and said, "You need any help nailing this guy, Joey, give me a call or have that attorney call me. I'll help you in any way I can."

"Thanks, I'll pass this on, Dev."

"Good. Now, if it's okay with you, I'm going to have Cornell's attorney get in touch. I'm guessing he'll want a sworn statement. Just tell the truth. We're establishing the fact that Cornell had nothing to do with this unfortunate incident, and it's a case of the cops getting the wrong guy."

"I'll be happy to do that. It was nice to meet you. I've never met a private investigator."

"Well, there you go, cross that item off your list and set your sights higher."

We both laughed, shook hands, and I thanked him again and then headed out the sliding door. I drove back to the office. Louie was typing away on his keyboard, and Morton was lying on his pillow. As I entered, Morton raised his head. He stared for a moment before he got up and walked over for a head scratch. Once that was finished, he stood by the door and looked over his shoulder at me.

"Oh, apparently, I'm supposed to take him for a walk. We'll be back in a bit, Louie," I said, and we headed out the door. We did a quick walk through the neighborhood. Once again, we took a slightly different route and didn't pass Becky Desjardins' place. We stopped at Rooster's on the way back to the office. I almost had to run to keep up with Morton pulling on his leash once he saw the place. I ordered two barbecue sandwiches from Taffy. She placed the Styrofoam trays in a bag and then placed another bone wrapped in cellophane on top of the trays.

"Oh, gee, thanks, Taffy. Would it be possible to get a second bone from you? We've got a new neighbor with a white Lab, and she—"

"Is her dog named Princess? Attractive blonde woman?"

"Yeah, has she already been in here?"

Taffy nodded. "They were in last night, said you told them about us. Thanks for spreading the word, Dev. Much appreciated," she said as she tossed a second bone into our bag.

I paid the bill and added a nice tip for Taffy. On our way back to the office, Morton kept banging his head against the paper bag. When we stepped into the office, I reached into the bag and pulled a bone out for Morton. I removed the cellophane wrap and handed the bone to him. He snatched it from me and hurried over to his pillow.

"That's bound to keep him busy for the rest of the afternoon," Louie said.

"Little something for you, too, Louie. Figured you'd need the energy." I set a Styrofoam box down on his picnic table. He pulled it in front of him. "Oh, thanks." He opened the top and inhaled, causing his stomach to growl. "Apparently, just in time. Mmm, thank you. I take back some of the things people have been saying about you, Dev."

I settled in at my desk and proceeded to wolf down half of the barbecue sandwich. When I'd finished, I closed the lid on the Styrofoam container and placed it in the bottom drawer of my desk along with the bag holding the second bone.

"You're already full?" Louie asked.

"No, I'll grab the rest later. I've got a 1:00 appointment at the Adult Detention Center with Cornell, and I don't want to be late."

I tossed a yellow legal tablet into my computer bag, shoved in my laptop and a small recorder, and zipped the thing closed. "No idea how long this is going to take," I said.

"Don't worry. If we're not here, we'll be over at The Spot."

"Okay, thanks. See you later, Morton."

He gave me a quick glance and then returned to the new pork bone. I headed out the door and drove over to the Adult Detention Center. It's located more or less behind the police station.

Seventeen

I was fifteen minutes early for my appointment, but I figured it would take a couple of minutes to get checked in and set up in a private interview room. It took closer to a half-hour. The first thing I did was hand my pistol over to the officer at the front desk. I showed him my license to carry, and he locked my pistol in a metal box, one of about twenty in a rack behind the desk and gave me a receipt. I went through three security stations, not that I blamed anyone. Better safe than sorry. Eventually, I was led into a small windowless room with a round Formica top table and four chairs. At least the chairs weren't bolted to the floor. The floor was gray concrete, and the concrete block walls were painted a lighter gray.

I pulled out my laptop, the recorder, and the legal pad and arranged them on the table. Once that was done, I sat in the room for another twenty minutes before Cornell was ushered in. He was dressed in an orange jumpsuit with 'Ramsey County Correctional Services' stenciled on the back. One of the guards stepped in before him and held the door. As soon as Cornell entered, the guard stepped out of the room. He closed and locked the door behind him.

Cornell stared at the door for a moment, then approached me with a smile on his face. "Great to see you, Dev, and finally get to shake hands with you. Pardon our surroundings, but it was the best I could do under the circumstances," he said and chuckled.

"How's it going, Cornell?"

"Okay, I guess. I just wish I was out of this hellhole."

"Problems?" I asked.

He shook his head. "No, other than I wish I was anywhere but in here."

We sat down at the table. I pressed the button on the recorder, gave the date, time, and location, and said, "Cornell Thomas, I'm about to tape our conversation. Do I have your permission to do that?"

"Yes, you have my permission."

"So, tell me what you're doing."

Cornell looked at the recorder for a moment, nodded, and said, "I eat breakfast, lunch, and dinner at seven, noon, and five. I do five miles on the treadmill every afternoon. I'm reading about a book a day. Busy, busy, busy."

"Anything affecting you, like depression?" I asked.

He shook his head. "No, don't get me wrong. I don't want to be in this God-forsaken place, but I'm on my best behavior. The last thing I need is someone testifying in court that I'm an asshole."

I nodded. "I met with Dick Tracy and Joey Caste-lana earlier today."

"How's Joey? I guess he had a car accident."

"Yeah, broadsided, broke a hip, but he's on the road to recovery. Exercising and doing physical therapy. I spoke with him at his folk's house. Has he been living there all along?"

Cornell nodded and said, "Yeah. He's been saving up to get an apartment. He has to pay a month in advance for a security deposit. He was planning to move in with another guy, but after his car accident, I don't know if that's still the plan."

"Well, your attorney, Martin Meyer, will be getting in touch with them and getting sworn statements from both of them."

"What good is that going to do? I wasn't at work that night, and Joey was in the hospital."

"We're going to present a number of things that es-tablish the fact you're a hard-working, decent guy who wasn't involved in Penny Larson's murder. Tell me again about your run that night," I said.

Cornell told me the same story as the other day. Where he ran, the distance, the time it took. He described everything from the run to his walk home after the run.

"The police report says they discovered a pistol in your bedroom. I think under your pillow."

"Yeah, except I didn't put a gun under my pillow. I've never had a gun to put under my pillow. I've never ever had a gun. And before you ask, no, I don't know how it got there. I've never shot a gun in my life. Never even held one."

"Let me ask a question, and don't get upset. When we go to court, the prosecution will ask this or something like it."

"Yeah, okay."

"Do you think your mother put it there?"

"My mom? No, absolutely not. She was as surprised as I was. Have you talked to her yet?"

"No, I wanted to speak with you first. I'll give her a call later today."

"Well, I'm absolutely positive she didn't put it there. The only other person who was in there was Javis."

"Who is Javis?"

"A guy who lives down the hall, Trenton Javis. I sort of know him, but we don't hang out together. He just stopped in to say hi. He brought some flowers for my mom, as a matter of fact. I was thinking he probably stole them from someone's garden, but he told me he just got a job at a flower shop."

"And he was in your bedroom?"

"Not that I know of. We talked at the door. I ran down to the first floor to grab the mail. He was talking to my mom. I was back in the apartment in a couple of minutes. He said he heard about Penny breaking up with me and was sorry about that. We talked for maybe all of five minutes, not much longer, and he had to take off. No big deal."

"Was he anywhere near your bed?"

"I don't think so. He just talked to my mom. When I came back to the apartment, he was in the same place as when I left, right by the door. He was sitting on the arm of a chair. They were talking about roses. Those were the flowers he brought."

"What time was this?"

"That Javis brought the flowers? Oh, maybe 8:30 or so."

"That's in the morning?"

Cornell nodded and said, "Yeah."

"And the cops were there two hours later, at around 10:30."

"Yeah. My mom had left for work by then. They pounded on the door."

"You got a phone number for him?"

"No, he just shows up once in a while. I guess you could say we travel in different circles, plus, well, I'm working, and he isn't, or wasn't. So we have different schedules. He's nice enough, and he's always bringing something. He brought flowers that day, but my mom was getting ready for work, so I put them in a vase on the kitchen table. He showed up with candy canes last Christmas, dropped off a chocolate Easter bunny. He carved a little pumpkin and had a battery-operated light in it so my mom could put it in the window at Halloween. She really thought that was cool. Like I said, he's a nice guy."

"Back up for a second. You said you put the flowers in a vase?"

"Yeah, and then I put the vase on the table."

"So your mom didn't do that?"

"No. Like I told you, she was getting ready for work. Javis was going on about how he liked roses, and that's why he chose those for her. As far as I know, it's the only job he's ever had, but he seems to like it, never stopped talking about it, as a matter of fact."

"So you went down to get the mail, and your mom is where? In her kitchen?"

"No, in her bedroom, and Javis was sitting on the arm of the chair. That's where he was when I left, and he was still there when I got back."

I made a note and said, "Tell me about the girls that lived with Penny Larson."

"Mmm, I didn't really know them except to say hi. They're going to college, and I mean, they're nice and all, but since I'm not in college, I got the impression they thought I was maybe second class."

"Even though you were going out with Penny?"

"Well, yeah, I guess. I mean, they were doing the same thing I was, you know, working in bars or restaurants. They never ever said anything mean if that's what you're thinking. But they all have cars, and I don't. They're in their own place, and I'm living with my mom. They're going to college, and I'm not. Sometimes, I thought Penny was going out with me just to piss them off, not that I was complaining. But, you know, right from the start, our relationship was kind of doomed. It started out fun, and then, well, like I said, I was getting the feeling Penny wasn't having as much fun as she did at first."

"Any reason why?" I asked.

"She was getting all involved with her protests and stuff, and that's not my gig. I even went to a few protests with her, two actually, and I figured, instead of doing that, I could maybe work some more hours and make a little extra cash. It just wasn't my deal, and that maybe turned her off, you know?"

I nodded and asked, "Did you talk to her after your breakup?"

He shook his head and said, "She called once. I think three or four days after she dumped me, but I didn't take the call. That was the last time she tried to contact me."

"You ever meet anyone from her family?"

"No, never. In fact, a couple of times, I called her, and she couldn't talk because her folks were coming over to visit or something. I don't mean to suggest that was a problem. I get it. But I never met anyone in her family. I never felt the urge to meet them, and I never thought about having her meet my mom. In fact, I think it would have been a little stressful, you know, hoping her folks would like me and all."

"Yeah, believe me, I get that. Let's go back to this Trenton Javis. You said he lives down the hall from you and your mother?"

"Yeah, three doors down. I'm not sure about his family. I know he's got a little brother and sister, maybe eight and ten. I think Javis is seventeen or eighteen. I don't believe he's in school. Not sure if he ever finished high school. I've seen his mom a few times but never said hi or anything. I've never seen a guy living there with them."

"And you said Javis just got this job?"

"Yeah, like I told you, he was all excited about it. I gotta say it was pretty cool, him giving my mom a dozen roses. As far as I know, that was the first time someone gave her roses, maybe even the first time someone gave her flowers."

"Does he have any other friends?"

"I suppose he does. I don't know any of them. Anytime we were together, it was usually due to him knocking on the door of our apartment. He'd always have something for my mom, and then we'd talk about, mmm, nothing important, I guess, and he'd leave. Never there for more than a few minutes. I've never seen him hanging around the building. I only knocked on his apartment door once. His mom answered and wasn't happy I interrupted whatever she was doing. I never knocked on their door again."

"Hmm, interesting. Well, that's about all I've got at the moment, Cornell. You have any questions for me?"

He seemed to think for a moment and shook his head. "No, I'm cool. Just want to say thank you for all you're doing, Dev. I really mean it. You, umm, you know I can't pay you, don't you?"

"I do, and that's not an issue, so don't even go there. I believe you're innocent. I believe you didn't have a thing to do with this situation, and we're going to get you out of here just as soon as we can. Your job is to hang in there because it's going to take some time."

"I can do that, but like I said, the sooner, the better."

"Then I'd better get going. This concludes our interview," I said and turned off the recorder. We walked to the door and then pressed a button on the wall. That turned on a blinking light out in the hallway above the door.

Two or three minutes later, there was a knock on the door, and it opened. Two guards were there, and one of them said, "All finished?"

"At least for the moment," I said.

One of them escorted Cornell back to his cell. The other one took me in the opposite direction. I went through the three security stations again and then was out in the main lobby. I handed my receipt to the officer at the front desk, retrieved my pistol, and placed it in my computer bag. I thought about going over to the police station to see if Aaron was in. It took about two seconds to decide that was not the best idea. Instead, I walked out to my car and phoned Martin Meyer. His secretary, Edith, answered just after the fourth ring. "Meyer Legal Office."

"Hi Edith, this is Dev Haskell. Is Martin available?"

"Let me put you through," she said.

"Martin Meyer," he said a moment later.

"Hi, Martin, Dev. Say, I just finished chatting with Cornell, and I wondered if you had some time."

"How did everything go?"

"Pretty well. He seems to be doing all right, under the circumstances. Mentioned more than once that he's anxious to get out of there, but then who can blame him? He said a couple of things that are interesting, and I met with Dick Tracy, Cornell's boss and the owner of Tracy's, as well as Joey Castelana. He's the guy who was supposed to cover for Cornell the night of the shooting."

"Why don't you head over if it works for you? Let's talk and compare notes."

"Good, I should be there in about fifteen minutes. I'll see you then."

"Looking forward to it," Meyer said and disconnected.

I pulled my pistol out of the computer bag, shoved it back in my belt, and started the car.

Eighteen

I drove over to the office on University Ave and pulled behind a classic Plymouth Barracuda. The thing was painted white with red and yellow flames on the hood and about a dozen coats of wax. The windows were tinted so dark I couldn't make out the interior. I grabbed my computer bag and headed into Meyer's office.

As I stepped inside the office, I was going over my conversation with Cornell and thinking it was strange the front door wasn't locked. I heard a voice shouting and looked up. Edith was standing behind her desk, wide-eyed and ghostly white.

Martin was in his wheelchair next to her desk. "I told you before, no. Now I'm going to ask you to leave, or we're going to have to call the police."

"You ain't going to do shit," a very large man shouted at Martin and then kicked the arm of his wheelchair, pushing it backward and into Edith's desk.

"Hey," I yelled without thinking.

The guy half-jumped, turned, and said, "You best get your dumb ass out of here."

"You should probably leave now. Call the cops, you guys. That will—" He suddenly growled and charged me. I wasn't thinking. Basic training from the army immediately kicked in. I dropped my computer case just as he slammed into me. I somersaulted backward, kicking the guy up and over me and hanging on for dear life. My drill sergeant would have been proud when I landed on the guy's chest.

He let off a large "Uff," and I think I knocked the wind out of him. I was running on autopilot, and I pulled the pistol from my belt, jammed the barrel into his mouth, and was ready to pull the trigger.

"Don't, Dev, don't shoot him. Don't shoot him," Meyer yelled and wheeled over to us.

"You had better hope I never, ever see you again," I said and grabbed the guy by his t-shirt as I climbed off him. I raised him to a sitting position. He coughed and spit blood onto the concrete floor. Blood was running out of his mouth and onto his t-shirt. "Get your ass out of here before I change my mind," I growled.

He crawled four or five feet, then rose to his feet and hurried out the door. He scrambled behind the wheel of the Barracuda, fired it up, and pulled into traffic without looking. A car screeched to a stop, missing him in the Barracuda by just an inch or two. The driver leaned on the horn as the Barracuda sped down the street.

"Sorry about that. I didn't mean to lose my temper, but that guy was about to hurt you."

Meyer was looking at the blood on the concrete floor and said, "I think those are teeth." Two pieces of what looked like teeth, maybe a quarter of an inch long, lay in the middle of a little puddle of blood.

"Are you guys okay?"

"We're just glad to see you. Let me get the mop," Edith said and opened a door in the opposite corner from Meyer's office, revealing a closet with a small washtub.

"Join me in my office," Meyer said. He rolled behind Edith's desk, pushed a button that locked the front door, then rolled into his office.

I picked up my computer bag and followed.

"So you met with Cornell," he said, changing the subject as he rolled behind his desk.

"Martin, that guy was going to beat the shit out of you and Edith. What was that all about?"

"A client unhappy with the decision the judge made. What can I say? Everyone is entitled to representation, but that doesn't entitle them to get away with a crime." He reached into the bag hanging from the side of his wheelchair and pulled out a pistol.

"You had a gun? You were armed?"

"Yeah. A Colt 45, 1911. I was all set to calm him down when you arrived and escalated everything."

"Escalated?"

"Relax, Dev, I'm joking. Thanks, nice work. I was afraid I would have to shoot him, the stupid bastard."

"You get that sort of thing a lot down here?"

"Whacko clients? No, not as often as you might think. It happens occasionally, and then, just like today, the word will go out this isn't a place to mess with. There's always another idiot somewhere who thinks that doesn't apply to him, and they're going to make a point. Anyway, take a seat. You said you met with Cornell."

"Yes, I did. Let me bring you up to date on a couple of things. I also met with Dick Tracy and Joey Castelana." I went on to describe those two conversations and finished up with, "So I told them you would be in touch with them, and you'll want to get sworn statements. I'm thinking this is going to be the long game, presenting Cornell as an upstanding person."

"Which I'm convinced he is," Meyer said.

"Thus far, I am too. He did tell me a couple of things. Did he ever mention a guy named Trenton Javis to you?"

Meyer seemed to think for a moment and then shook his head. "I don't recall that name."

"He's seventeen or eighteen and apparently lives down the hall from Cornell and his mother. The guy shows up occasionally with a little something for Cornell's mother, candy, flowers, that sort of deal. Then he and Cornell chat for a few minutes, nothing in particular, just a guy being a nice neighbor. The morning Cornell was arrested, the cops arrived about 10:30. Javis brought over flowers, a dozen roses in fact, for Cornell's mother around 8:30 that morning. Cornell went down to the first floor to get the mail, and then they talked for a couple of minutes. Cornell's mother was in her bedroom getting ready for work. Cornell is down on the first floor getting the mail. That's maybe a minute or two when Javis is more or less alone. Plenty of time to hide the murder weapon in Cornell's bed. The other thing is the police report I read indicated that the pistol was found under Cornell's pillow. Cornell told me he doesn't have a gun. He said he's never fired a gun and has never even held one."

"That lines up with what he told me, although this Javis person is news and makes the pistol under the pillow more credible. Actually, if you were a kid hiding a gun, that makes more sense."

"Yeah, or some guy from down the hall planting a gun to be found."

"You going to check him out?"

"Javis? Yeah, if I can find him. We also discussed the breakup. Cornell said he'd actually been expecting it. The excitement Penny first displayed had waned, and when the breakup actually happened, he wasn't all that surprised."

"It sounds like he has better luck than I usually do," Meyer said and laughed.

"He said she called him a few days after the breakup, he didn't answer the call, and that was the last time he heard from her."

"Thanks for your help, Dev. It would be great if you could find this person delivering the flowers."

"Javis."

"Yes."

"I'm also going to try to talk to Penny's roommates. There's something there, I think. The one girl I spoke with, Diane Haggerty, alluded to Penny becoming more and more involved in protesting some ecological stuff. Cornell mentioned it, too. I want to see what the others say. Maybe I can track down some of the protesters. I want to talk with Cornell's mom, too. Can you give me her phone number?"

Meyer nodded and clicked his keyboard a couple of times. "Yeah, here it is." As he began writing, he said, "We can't thank you enough, Dev. Oh, and thanks again for your timely arrival this afternoon."

"I'd guess that guy has some bigger problems than his court decision."

"You think? Just imagine the mess if I'd shot him. It would take all day to clean things up," Meyer said and chuckled.

"I'll keep looking into things. Call me with anything you think of," I said. We shook hands, and I headed out the door.

The concrete floor in front of Edith's desk was now spotless. "Thank you again for your acrobatic prowess," Edith said.

"Yeah, I'll need to go home and take a hot soak for an hour or two."

"We'll see you. You're always welcome here."

Thanks," I said and headed toward the door. Just as I approached, it buzzed and unlocked. Once I stepped outside, the moment the door closed, it buzzed once more as it locked. I gazed up and down University Avenue looking for a black Prius or a white Barracuda with flames on the hood. Thankfully, I didn't see either one.

Nineteen

I drove back to the office, checked the street for the Prius or Barracuda once again, and hurried up the stairs. "Well, perfect timing, we were just about to head over to The Spot," Louie said as he packed up his laptop.

"Hey, we'll catch up with you. Let me take Morton for a walk. I've got a spare pork bone for Becky Desjardins dog, Princess." At the mention of Princess, Morton stopped gnawing his bone and looked up.

"Well, you've certainly got Morton's attention. I'll be over holding court across the street. I'll see you two in a bit," Louie said. He picked up his briefcase and headed out the door.

I pulled the bone and the other half of my barbecue sandwich from the desk drawer. I clipped the leash onto Morton's collar and coaxed him out the door by repeating, "Princess," a number of times. I directed us past both fire hydrants, so Morton was in good shape in the event we chatted for a few minutes with Becky and Princess. Morton was parading through the neighborhood carrying his pork bone. As we approached Becky's house, I could see Princess in the front yard, apparently not on a chain or a leash.

Morton raised his head just a little higher and moved it from side to side, showing off his pork bone. Princess barked and jumped back and forth but never made an effort to leave the front yard. That's when I noticed the little white flags along the edge of the yard. A logo was on each flag, 'PETSAFE *Safe Pets Happy Owners.*' There must have been fifteen or twenty flags across the front lawn announcing the electric fence, which was why Princess hadn't made a move to join us.

Becky suddenly appeared on the porch, wiping her hands on a dishtowel. "Oh, hey guys, perfect timing. I was just about to sit down to some dinner. Can you join us?"

"Oh, we don't want to interrupt your dinner," I said, thinking it sounded a lot better than the half of the barbecue sandwich I was planning to eat.

"Are you kidding? You'd be saving me from myself. Otherwise, I'm going to be eating the rest of it tomorrow, and I really don't need to be doing that. Please stay. Besides, Princess needs someone to play with. She must be bored out of her mind listening to me complain all day about moving boxes."

"Are you sure?"

"Oh, yes, please. I really mean it, Dev. You would be just what the doctor ordered."

"Yeah, we'd love to if you're serious. When did you get the electric fence?"

"Oh, they installed that the other day, part of our purchase agreement. We had one in our old place, and it worked very well. Princess is used to it. Come on in. Can I talk you into a glass of wine? I've got a nice, chilled Sauvignon Blanc I was just about to open."

"Yeah, sure. That sounds wonderful. Just to even things out, we brought a bone for Princess. Is it all right if I give it to her?"

"Oh, my God. You'll have a friend for life. She would love it. Thank you. I see Morton is happy with his."

"Are you kidding? Don't even think of trying to get him to part with that thing."

"Let me pour the wine, and we can sit out on the porch," she said.

We were on our second glass of wine, chatting while watching Princess and Morton lying in the grass, gnawing contentedly on their pork bones.

"So, what kinds of thing do you investigate?" Becky asked.

"It's not as exciting as you might think. If you're thinking of detective movies or Sherlock Holmes stories, don't go there. Most of the time, I'm doing something like checking work histories on job applications or trying to find a former husband who suddenly decides to stop paying alimony."

"But you do investigate crime."

"Well, not paying alimony or lying on a job application is sort of criminal."

"But you do go after robbers and bad guys, don't you?"

"Yeah, sometimes, but not the real criminals, you know like politicians."

"Well, they're above the law," she said and set her wine glass down on the porch floor. "Give me just a minute. I'm going to bring out that pizza." I watched her as she headed into the house and went upstairs. I heard her come down the steps maybe five minutes later and go to the rear of the house. She was back out on the porch with a large pizza delivery box and another bottle of chilled white wine.

"Oh wow, that's one big pizza," I said and then immediately wished I hadn't said that.

She laughed and said, "That's what happens if I order food or go grocery shopping when I'm hungry. I always end up getting way too much. Your job tonight is to help get me out of this predicament, so eat up. It's got everything on it except anchovies," she said and opened the lid on the extra-large pizza box.

'Everything but anchovies.' For a second or two, I thought of Heidi but fortunately kept my big mouth shut. We ate about two-thirds of the pizza. I remember moving a number of boxes upstairs to different rooms. I moved two couches to opposite sides of her fireplace. I carried boxes of books into a study off the dining room. I know we opened at least one more bottle of wine.

"Dev? Dev?" Becky whispered in my ear. "Are you awake?"

I blinked my eyes open and stared up at our reflection in the mirror on the ceiling. The giant headboard was in the shape of a heart and upholstered with some kind of pink fiber surrounded by an elaborately carved gold frame. As I turned halfway toward her, it dawned on me that the sheets were white silk.

"I was going to make some coffee. Would you like some?"

"Coffee? Umm, yeah, yeah sure, that would be great."

"I'll put it on down in the kitchen. Come on down when you're ready. Okay?"

"Yeah, I'll be down in just a second."

"Mmm, no wonder you're tired. Moving all those boxes and then, well, who knew you had that much energy left. Talk about working up an appetite. Take your time," she said and gave me a kiss on the cheek.

She strolled out of the bedroom naked and into the bathroom across the hall. As she walked, I noticed a large red bite mark on the right side of her perfectly formed rear. God, I had no memory. How much wine did we drink last night?

She stepped out of the bathroom a few minutes later and called, "It's all yours," as she strolled naked down the stairs. I looked around for my clothes but couldn't see them anywhere. I climbed out of bed and looked underneath, no clothes. I headed toward the bathroom, turned at the door to look at the bed. Yeah, the pink headboard was indeed in the shape of a giant heart. I was in the bathroom for a couple of minutes. Fortunately, I didn't find any bite marks on me. God, what was I thinking?

I found my boxers halfway down the staircase. My jeans were on the floor in the entryway, just next to the front door, along with my shoes and one sock. My shirt was alongside the staircase. It was all crumpled up and apparently had been tossed toward an antique wooden wastebasket that held four umbrellas.

I heard the radio playing at the end of the hall. I pulled on my clothes and headed in that direction. I passed the living room and saw Princess asleep on the couch and Morton asleep on the floor. A pork bone rested about two inches from their respective heads. The empty pizza box rested beneath an end table near Morton.

As I stepped into the kitchen, Becky was just taking a pan out of a drawer beneath the stove. She was wearing a thong and a smile. The bruised bite mark on her rear was quite obvious.

"How does French toast for breakfast sound?"

"Oh, that sounds great, Becky, but you've absolutely been the most perfect hostess. We should get out of your way so—"

"Are you kidding? The least I can do is make you breakfast. Grab a stool at the counter and let me pour you some coffee.

"Oh, I don't want to impose on you and—"

"Dev, put your ass on a stool and let me do something to thank you for everything you did last night. And I mean everything."

"Yeah, about that. I'm sorry about the, umm, little bruise on your backside. I don't usually—"

"You mean the bite mark? Oh, God, yeah, thanks, but that's not from you. It's a tattoo I got with three other girls back in college. We were out on spring break. You thought you did it? Oh God, I'll have to call and tell them. That's really funny," she laughed.

My mood lightened up over coffee and breakfast. I counted four empty wine bottles on the back counter, which explained a lot. She told me she worked in IT for a large firm and had been transferred in from California. We had a great chat and kissed as we left. Morton and I walked back to the office. Princess remained on the couch when we left, and I never did find my missing sock.

We drove home. I filled Morton's food and water dishes and headed upstairs to shave and shower. I pulled on clean jeans and a sport shirt advertising Summit Beer. We headed back to the office, and I parked behind Louie's car.

Amazingly, he had a fresh pot of coffee on that I smelled the moment I opened the office door.

"Oh, you two are still alive. You had me worried last night when you didn't show."

"Yeah, sorry about that. We went for our walk, and I got roped into helping Becky move some boxes. By the time I was finished, I just felt like lying on the couch and watching TV.”

“What’d you watch?” Louie asked.

“Oh, man. You know, I fell asleep, and I can’t even remember.”

“Interesting,” Louie said in a way that suggested he didn’t believe me.

“No, really, I’m not kidding.”

“Don’t kid a kidder, Dev.”

Twenty

I read the phone number Martin Meyer wrote down for Cornell's mother and called her. I ended up leaving a message. I drove over to their apartment building, called the apartment on the security phone, but never got an answer. I waited around for twenty minutes hoping someone might come out of the building and I could step in, but it never happened. I called the number listed for the building manager and ended up leaving a message.

I went back to the office and was going to take Morton for a walk, but he was sound asleep. Louie was gone. I looked up the office address for Franklin Lanzo and Russell Greeney, the two principles at RIP, Inc. I'd completely forgotten that they were in the Wells Fargo building. I wrote down the office number, left Morton asleep, and headed downtown.

The Wells Fargo building is at the corner of 7th Street and Cedar Avenue. At thirty-seven stories, it's the tallest building in St. Paul and takes up an entire city block. It has a granite exterior and reflective windows. There's a parking ramp attached to the side, but I parked two blocks away and crossed my fingers I'd be back to my car before I was issued a parking ticket for not paying the parking meter.

I climbed the stairs at the entrance and walked into the three-story atrium of the Wells Fargo building. There were white marble floors and a fountain in the middle of the atrium. There was retail space surrounding the atrium, and I counted three 'Space Available' signs. A bank of six elevators was off to one side, and the doors on one of the elevators just happened to open as I approached. I pressed the button for the thirty-fourth floor and got a look from two guys in suits who were traveling up to nineteen.

They took turns giving me the evil eye until we stopped on the nineteenth floor. As they stepped off the elevator, I said, "Enjoy your day, gentlemen."

One of them turned and was about to say something but the door closed. I gave him the finger as the elevator rose. The doors opened onto the thirty-fourth floor maybe a half minute later. I stepped off and followed the directions for RIP, Inc. I passed two offices that were obviously vacant, and then there was the RIP, Inc. office.

The door was the same as the others in the hall, a dark wood, maybe a mahogany veneer. I tried the doorknob. Surprisingly, the door opened, and I stepped inside. I entered a moderate-sized room with a curved receptionist counter directly in front of me and a large desk area behind the counter. The area behind the counter was spotless. Not so much as a computer, a phone, or a file anywhere, not to mention an employee. There were open doors to what appeared to be two offices, one to the left and another to the right of the reception counter.

I popped my head in the office on the right. There was a desk with two chairs in front of it. A black leather couch and a coffee table were positioned against the far wall. At least there was a computer screen and a keyboard on the otherwise empty desk.

I peeked in the other office. It was empty with a mirror image of the same layout. The only difference was the coffee table had been pushed against the wall, and there was a putting cup with a putter and a half-dozen golf balls on the floor. A crumpled-up McDonald's bag was in the middle of the desk. I considered leaving my card but decided that might not be a good idea, so I left.

I walked down the hall to the bank of elevators and pressed the down button. A minute later, it dinged, and a green light appeared above one of the elevator doors. As I walked over, two guys stepped off the elevator. They looked about fifty, both wearing suits and ties. As if on command, they both frowned at me. Apparently, I was in the way and didn't realize how important they were. It suddenly dawned on me it was the RIP guys, Franklin Lanzo and Russell Greeney. They didn't see any point in halting their conversation.

"No, Russell, in just three weeks, we'll be ninety days past due. They're liable to call the loan, and that'll knock the entire house of cards—"

"Hold up," Russell Greeney said and turned to look at me just as the doors closed.

I wondered how many guys named Russell would be on the thirty-fourth floor of the Wells Fargo building. I pressed the button for the skyway level, which was the second floor, just in case they were going to hop on an elevator and try to catch me. I got off on the skyway level, eventually wandered out of the building, through the skyway one story above street level, and into another building. I walked out of that building at the Cedar Avenue exit and headed back to my car. Once behind the wheel, I wrote down what I remembered of their conversation.

'No, Russell. Just three weeks, and we'll be ninety days past due. They're liable to call the loan, and that'll knock the entire house of cards...'

I sat behind the wheel and thought for a couple of minutes and then climbed out of my car and walked back to the Wells Fargo Building. This time, I entered the parking ramp and headed toward the contract spaces. It turned out to be eight different levels. I found what I was looking for on the fifth level, a black Prius with the license number MWE 746 and, parked next to that, a White Prius with the license number 376 PCE, both Minnesota plates.

As much as I would have liked to, I didn't slit their tires. I wrote down the numbers and walked back to my car. I gave myself a fist bump for my good luck in not getting a parking ticket and drove back to the office.

Louie wasn't in, but Morton quickly took up a spot next to the door and looked at me. I clipped on his leash and took him for a quick walk. We skipped Becky's street just because and made our way back to the office. Louie was just settling into his chair when we arrived.

"Everything all right on your end?" I asked.

Louie gave a nod and said, "Just filing papers down at the courthouse. How about you?"

"I'm hoping to chat with Cornell's mother later today. I left a message for her. I'm looking into that RIP, Inc company for Heidi. The more I learn, the more it doesn't look like a very good investment. As a matter of fact, I should give her a call. She's probably wondering why she hasn't heard from me," I said, reminding myself not to mention Becky Desjardins to Louie and especially not Heidi.

I pulled out my phone, signaling I had some things to do. Louie turned on his computer and slid the keyboard in front of him. I hit the speed dial number for Heidi. She answered just before I was dumped into her voicemail.

"Hi, Dev, nice to hear from you. I was beginning to worry."

"Yeah, sorry it took this long, but I wanted to check a number of things before I got back to you."

"And?"

"Well, this is developing into a very complex issue." I went on to tell her about meeting with Terry Nelson and the ten-minute tour he gave me of the RIP facility along the river with the mountains of empty plastic bottles.

"But isn't that exactly what you would expect? If they're recycling plastic and they have all sorts of empty plastic bottles, that sounds positive. You know, like something's happening."

"Yeah, except nothing was happening. The gate into the place was padlocked. There were protest signs hanging from the gate. The building was locked. There weren't any employees around. This Terry Nelson guy gave me a used brochure that had a phone number written on it. I called it and got a recording. Some guy just said, 'Leave a message,' and that was it."

"Maybe it was a personal number, Dev. You know, not a business kind of thingy."

"Yeah, maybe. But the other thing is we were in this building, one giant room filled with mountains of empty plastic bottles and—"

"And like I said, Dev, that's what they do. They recycle plastic. There's such a need for effective plastic recycling that this appears to be a sure win for investors."

"Okay, but then how are they actually going to recycle the plastic? I didn't see any equipment, Heidi. I just saw a bunch of plastic bottles, oh and some samples of fire-resistant plastic that Nelson held over a lighter, and it never caught fire. That was pretty cool, but he said they made it in a lab."

"Yes, I've seen it. Very impressive."

"But making something like that in a lab and mass-producing a product are two different things."

"Which is exactly why investing this early is likely to pay huge dividends, Dev. You might want to think about it."

"But all he talked about was when they were going to build a building. I didn't see anything that suggested they were actually capable of creating the product. Then I went down to the Wells Fargo building."

"Yes, their office is on the top floor."

"Actually, no, it's not, Heidi. It's on the thirty-fourth floor, close to the top, but it's not on the top floor."

"Oh, well, please forgive me. Sorry I made a mistake," she said.

I ignored her comment and said, "I went into the office, and the place was empty. The reception counter was unoccupied. I don't mean like someone ran to the restroom. I mean, there was no receptionist. There were two offices. One had golf balls on the rug, a putter, and a crumpled McDonald's bag on the desk. The other had a computer and a keyboard but no sign of any activity."

"So what are you saying, Dev? The two successful principles are neat freaks?"

"No, I'm saying be careful. I'm getting a bad feeling about this company. The idea sounds almost too good to be true. Oh, and this is the best part. I leave their empty office, and I'm waiting for the elevator. The thing shows up, and two guys step off. One of them says, 'No, Russell, in just three weeks, we'll be ninety days past due.

They're liable to call the loan, and that'll knock the entire house of cards—' I didn't hear anything else because the elevator doors closed."

"And you're sure that was Lanzo and Greeney?"

"Yeah, I mean, I think so. One of them was named Russell. They looked like the pictures of the two guys in the brochure."

"You're sure?"

"Yeah, I think so. They were wearing suits and looked to be maybe fiftyish. I only saw them for a second or two before the doors closed on the elevator."

"So it could have been anyone."

"Heidi, how many people do you think are named Russell on the thirty-fourth floor of the Wells Fargo building?"

"There could be a couple."

"Really? Look, I'll keep checking, but just my initial investigation is beginning to suggest that this investment may, in fact, be too good to be true." I waited a long moment before I said, "Heidi, you still there?"

"Yes, just thinking. Oh, God, I want this to work. Okay, keep me posted, and thanks, Dev. I didn't mean to be so negative. I just want this to work on a number of different levels, not the least of which is beginning to deal with the plastic problem."

"I'll keep looking, Heidi," I said, and we disconnected.

I thought about calling her back and mentioning that Toby Bunker suggested Terry Nelson might actually be living in his office on the second floor, but then thought I'd given her enough to think about. I decided to check it out later that night before I mentioned anything to Heidi.

Twenty-one

I puttered around the office for a couple of hours. I pulled the binoculars out of the drawer and checked the apartment building across the street. Unfortunately, it appeared no one was home in the unit where the two women lived. Louie turned off his computer, closed his briefcase, and said, "You thinking of joining me over at The Spot?"

"That sounds like a pretty good—" My cellphone ringing cut me off. I pulled it out of my pocket and checked the screen. The number looked vaguely familiar, but it was labeled 'Caller Unknown.' "Haskell Investigations," was how I answered.

There was a pause, and then a woman's voice said, "I'm returning a call I received from a Devlin Haskell."

"Speaking, is this Christine Thomas?"

"Yes, it is."

"Miss Thomas, thank you for returning my call. I'm a private investigator working in conjunction with Martin Meyer, the attorney representing your son, Cornell. I've met with Cornell twice now, and just like Martin Meyer, I'm convinced of Cornell's innocence. I would like to meet with you and get some general information on a couple of things that will, no doubt, lead to a few more questions. Would you have time to meet with me this evening?"

"I'll meet with you anytime, anyplace if it will help Cornell's case. He's innocent, Mr. Haskell. He did not kill that young woman."

"That's exactly why I want to meet with you. I want to convince the powers that be of Cornell's innocence, and in order to do that, I need to talk with you. If I stopped over, oh, say around seven, would you be able to sit down and talk?"

"Of course. I'll be waiting for you. Our apartment number is two-one-six. Dial that on the phone in the lobby, and I'll buzz you in. I look forward to seeing you," she said and hung up.

"Sounds like you're going to be working late," Louie said as he pushed in his desk chair and picked up his briefcase.

"Yeah, afraid so. I should probably get Morton home and have some dinner. Depending on how well this goes, I might make it down later but don't count on it."

"I'll plan on seeing you in the morning," Louie said and headed out the door. I heard the stairs creak as he made his way down to the first floor. I watched out the window while Louie waited for a bus to pass and then waddled across the street and into The Spot. I glanced up and down the street but didn't see a black Prius or a white Barracuda with flames on the hood. Morton and I headed out to our car and drove home. I let him out into the back-yard, then rummaged around in the refrigerator, looking for dinner. I settled on a dish of sea salt caramel ice cream and two chocolate chip cookies.

The Thomas apartment building was five minutes from my place. Parking was allowed on only one side of the street, and with four apartment buildings next to one another, parking spaces were at a premium. Luckily, I found one about a block away.

The four apartment buildings looked exactly the same, two-story brick structures probably built in the 1950s. The Cornell's apartment was in the third building, the address was 422. I pulled the door open and stepped into the small lobby. Built-in mailboxes were on one wall, and a phone with a digital keypad was on the wall next to the security door.

I dialed two-one-six, and Christine Thomas answered on the second ring. "Hello."

"Hi Christine, Dev Haskell. I'm down in the entry if you can buzz me in."

"Our apartment is the same as what you just dialed, 216," she said, and then the security door buzzed as it unlocked. I hung up the phone, pulled the door open, and stepped into the hallway.

The air was stuffy. Two white plastic trash bags leaned against the wall next to apartment 102. The doors and the trim around the doors appeared to be oak with a blonde stain. The apartment numbers were black metal positioned on the center of the doors. Worn beige carpet covered the floor. Halfway down the hall, a staircase led up to the second floor. The carpet on the stairs was even more worn than the hallway. It appeared to be original to the building and was threadbare in spots. I went up to the second floor and took a right turn. Apartment 216 was at the end of the hall on the righthand side. I knocked on the door.

Christine Thomas answered a half minute later. She had dark-brown shoulder-length hair and brown eyes. She was a heavyset woman with an infectious smile. "Mr. Haskell?"

"Please, call me Dev."

"I will if you call me Christine. It's very nice to meet you. Please, come in."

I stepped into a small apartment. A gray couch was against the wall to the left. Next to the couch was a matching upholstered gray chair with a rectangle of white lace attached to the back of the chair. Beyond the chair was a small kitchen area. I thought the chair had to be the one that Cornell told me Javis sat in when he delivered the roses. A small table with two chairs sat at the end of the kitchen against the wall.

"I just put the kettle on. Would you like a tea?" Christine asked.

I nodded and said, "I'd love one."

"Please make yourself comfortable," she said as she walked into the kitchen. She opened a cabinet door and took out two mugs. "I hope you don't mind, but I phoned Cornell's lawyer, Mr. Meyer, and asked about you."

"Actually, I'd be worried if you hadn't done that."

"He spoke very highly of you."

"Well, I think he's very good. Tell me, how long have you been here?"

"Here? You mean in this apartment?"

"Yes."

"Oh, well, almost since Cornell was born."

"And he mentioned you work in food service for the school system."

"Yes, I've been doing that for almost twenty years. I've been at Randolph Heights Elementary for the past eight years. I head up the staff there."

"Sounds like a lot of work."

She nodded and smiled. "Not without its rewards. For a number of children, it's really the only meals they get. We serve breakfast and lunch, and then I've set up a program to send certain children home at the end of the day with a sandwich and maybe some fruit."

"That's wonderful. It's a different world from when I was in school. I know a woman who teaches, and she told me once that there are plenty of things to complain about with the school system. But, if you're going to complain, you first have to go to the school and see what's coming in the front door. It's not like twenty or even ten years ago."

Christine nodded and said, "Still, a lot of very wonderful children."

The water came to a boil, and she made the tea and sat down in the chair opposite me. I asked her about Cornell, and she gave me a brief history. No father, raised by his single mother. He was a decent student in school and ended up in about the same amount of trouble as the average kid, nothing really bad, just the normal dumb things that kids do.

I asked about Penny Larson, and she shrugged. She knew Penny's name and that she was in college, but Cornell had referred to her as a friend as opposed to a girlfriend. She wasn't exactly aware of the breakup but did notice that he hadn't mentioned her for a good week before his arrest.

She confirmed that Cornell had gone for a run that evening and mentioned that he usually ran in the morning before his work shift. She added that he'd covered for Joey Castelana that afternoon, and that was why he'd run in the evening.

I asked her about Trenton Javis.

"Oh, poor Javis, a bit of a lost soul. There doesn't seem to be much direction coming from his mother. I know she's gone through a laundry list of men. Three children, to my knowledge, she's no idea who the fathers are. That said, Javis is a kind boy. He's clearly looking for a direction, but he dropped out of school, I think, two years ago. I've encouraged him to get his GED, but to my knowledge, he hasn't made any effort. I've told him the loading dock jobs are disappearing, and they're not going to come back. He needs that high school diploma at a minimum, or he's not going to go anywhere. But there's only so much you can say, and then ultimately the decision is up to him," she said and took a sip of tea. "One step at a time, he's finally got a job, so that's something positive."

"Cornell mentioned that the morning of his arrest, Javis had dropped off some roses for you."

She smiled and said, "Oh yes, we see him every so often. He'll show up with some flowers, candy at Christmas. One time, he brought a Halloween pumpkin." She smiled at the memory. "He only stays for a few minutes. I'm not aware of him calling on anyone else in the building. Not sure why he chose us, but it's nice of him to do so. The bouquet of roses was beautiful. He works at a flower shop or the grocery store. I don't recall that he told us where," she said and gave a look. "I figured the best thing I could do was get them in some water. They were lovely, and he looked so proud."

"Cornell said he ran downstairs to get the mail when Javis was here."

"Oh yes, one of his responsibilities. It's delivered sometime just after 8:00 every morning. Unfortunately, we've had people breaking into mailboxes on occasion, so it's been Cornell's job to get the mail first thing every morning. Of course, that also serves as a wake-up call, no sleeping in until noon, if you know what I mean," she said.

"Yeah, I get it. So when he was down getting the mail, you were talking with Javis?"

"Well, yes, in a manner of speaking. I was actually getting dressed in my bedroom, and Javis was sitting on the arm of this chair. When Cornell came back with the mail, he got the vase out and placed the roses in the vase."

"Does Javis know which room is Cornell's?"

"Oh sure, he's been in there a few times. Not that there's a lot of room for two people. Why do you ask?"

"Cornell said the gun was a complete surprise. Shock might be a better word. He said he's never fired a gun, and he's never held a gun."

Christine stared at the floor for a long moment. Without looking at me, she said, "Cornell's father was killed in Iraq. We were going to be married when he returned. I… I never told him I was pregnant, and then one day, it was too late. But I have been very strict." She looked up at me with tears in her eyes. "I would never allow Cornell to be anywhere near a gun. He knows that, and he honors my wish. I think the police brought that gun with them and said they found it under his pillow."

"Have you ever considered the possibility that Javis might have placed it there?"

"Javis?"

Twenty-two

I went on to explain my suspicions to Cornell's mother twice.

"But he's such a nice young man. I mean, he brought me a dozen roses, for God's sake."

"But you said you were talking with him while you were in your bedroom getting ready for work. So I'm guessing that means the door was closed and—"

"And Cornell was back in just a minute, two at the most."

"How long would it take to run into Cornell's room, slip the pistol under the pillow, and sit back in that chair? Fifteen seconds? He could have done that five or six times while Cornell was getting the mail."

"He's such a nice boy. So kind, so generous, and he…"

"What is it, Christine?"

"He mentioned he lost his wallet and wondered if I'd found it."

"And did you?"

"No, I didn't know anything about it. But I suppose he could have gone in Cornell's room for just a second or two and—No, he wouldn't have done that. Would he?"

"You mentioned he just got this job?"

"Yes, that's what he said. But what has that got to do—"

"Christine, I'm just suggesting we have to consider every possible aspect in order to get Cornell out of this predicament. You told me you think the police planted that gun in Cornell's bedroom." She nodded. "Okay, I'm going to be checking that out. But Javis represents another possibility that I want to explore as well. We have to, just to be sure. The last thing we want is to have Cornell found guilty of the murder of this girl. So we have to look at everything, from all angles."

She nodded but didn't say anything.

"The roses were a lovely gift. A very nice gesture. A dozen roses, were they long-stemmed?"

She nodded.

"A dozen long stem roses run around thirty bucks. Even if he has a job, thirty bucks? It's one thing to bring a pumpkin or some candy canes but a dozen roses? That's a lot of money. Could you show me Cornell's room?"

She nodded and got out of the chair. I followed her down a short hall. "This is my room," she said, pointing at the closed door we passed. "Here is Cornell's room," she said and opened the door.

The room looked about the way Cornell had described it. There was a single bed, no head or footboard, just a pillow, a sheet, and a blanket. Opposite the bed was a small, three-drawer chest for clothes with a small flatscreen resting on top. Next to the chest of drawers was a rack with a pole maybe four feet long. A half-dozen shirts, two pairs of trousers, and three pairs of jeans were on hangers hanging from the pole. Three pairs of shoes, black, brown, and a pair of high-top tennis shoes, were arranged on the floor.

The room was small, about eight feet wide, and the only place to sit was on the bed. I stepped over and lifted the mattress. There was no box spring, just a metal frame. The pillow was sweat-stained and thin. Hiding a pistol under that particular pillow made even less sense.

"Is this where the police said the gun was?" I asked.

She nodded and said, "Yes, they said the gun was hidden beneath his pillow. How could anyone sleep with a gun beneath that pillow?"

I picked up the pillow. She was right. I would have found it next to impossible to sleep on such a thin pillow. A gun beneath it would be like having a brick under the thing. I placed the pillow back on the bed, pulled my phone out, and took a picture."Let's step out of here, and I'll take a couple of pictures from the doorway."

Christine stepped back into the hall, and I followed her, then turned and shot two pictures of the tiny room. The door directly across the hall from Cornell's bedroom was open, revealing a small compact bathroom. The bathroom appeared to be the same size as Cornell's bed-room, which really brought home just how small the room was.

"Anything else you can think of, Christine?"

She shook her head and said, "No, I mean, this whole awful event just came out of nowhere. I'm sorry this girl was shot, really I am. But Cornell didn't do it. He would never do it. Nothing against her. I mean, I never met the poor thing. But I never picked up so much as one hint of depression or anger from Cornell regarding their supposed breakup. You'd think that if he was so upset with the breakup that he planned to kill her, you'd think I would have seen or heard something, tears, anger, shouting, or swearing. But there was nothing. There's been nothing, and Cornell was just as shocked as I was that the girl was murdered."

"That's pretty much what he told me. I believe him, and now we just have to convince the authorities. Unless you have some questions, I'm going to leave and let you get back to your evening. Can I just say that Cornell is a wonderful young man, a genuinely nice guy, and we're going to get him out of this predicament."

"It was nice to meet you, Mr….I mean, Dev," she said, and we shook hands.

She walked me to the door, and as I stepped into the hallway, I said, "Say, you wouldn't happen to know which unit Javis lives in, would you?"

"Oh yes, across the hall and down three more doors. The fourth door is their apartment."

"Okay, thanks again for your time, Christine. It was a pleasure meeting you. Sorry it was under these circumstances."

She smiled and closed the door. I heard the lock snap a moment later. I walked down the hall to Javis's apartment, number 209, and knocked on the door. I could hear what sounded like a TV playing in the apartment.

The door appeared to be the same as all the other doors in the building, only in a little worse condition. The metal numeral '9' was gone and replaced with a length of silver duct tape with the number '9' written in black marker. Next to the doorknob, there was a hole in the hollow core door that looked like it had come from a kick or maybe even a knee.

I listened to the noise from the TV for a moment then knocked on the door again. After maybe a half minute, I knocked again, this time much harder. I still didn't get an answer, so now I pounded on the door. If someone was in there, they were either asleep or dead. Either way, they weren't going to open the door, so I took the stairs down to the first floor and stepped out of the building.

Three kids, maybe twelve or thirteen, were standing outside the building. "How's it going?" I asked. They eyed me suspiciously and nodded. "Hey, you guys know where I can find Javis? I owe him a couple of bucks and wanted to pay him back."

All three shook their heads. Clearly, even if they did know, they weren't about to tell me.

"Okay, great chatting with you," I said and headed for my car.

"You want to leave the money with us, we'll see that he gets it," one of them called out, and they all laughed.

I waved without looking back and kept walking.

Twenty-three

It was a little after eight, and my first thought was I could probably head down to The Spot and catch a couple of beers with Louie. I turned my car on, and my second thought was to have just one beer and then drive over and check to see if Terry Nelson was actually living in that building like Toby Bunker suspected.

I parked alongside The Spot and went in the side door. Louie was seated on his usual stool with his back to me, reading the paper.

"Looking for your name in the obituaries?" I asked.

Louie jumped and said, "Don't sneak up on me like that. God! You want a beer?"

"Yeah, but one is my limit tonight."

"Where's Morton?" Louie asked and looked around.

"I left him at home. I just finished talking with Cornell's mother and checking out their apartment."

"How'd that go?" Louie said then pointed at me and raised his index finger at Mike standing at the far end of the bar.

Mike gave a nod and grabbed a beer glass.

"How'd it go? Oh, she seems like a very nice person. Works for the school system. Raised Cornell as a single mom and understandably is worried sick about him right now."

Louie shook his head and said, "Anything look like you may get a break in the case?"

"Mmm, maybe, but it's a little too soon to tell. I've got a couple of things to check on."

Mike set my beer on the bar and asked, "How'd you find your way over here without Morton?"

"I got lost a couple of times, but I finally made it," I said.

Mike chuckled and said, "Well, that just proves he's done a good job training you. Louie, how about you? You ready for another?"

"I suppose one more wouldn't hurt," Louie said and drained his glass.

"Coming right up," Mike said as he grabbed the empty glass and hurried down the bar.

Louie and I chatted for a while. I finished my beer, debated having another, and decided against it. I said my goodbyes, headed out the door, and drove over to Inver Grove. I hopped on Highway 52, took that down to 70th street, then headed toward the river. The old three-story building looked awfully dark. At no surprise, the parking lot was completely empty, with the exception of Terry Nelson's pickup truck still hauling around that old box spring mattress.

I glanced at the clock on my dash, 8:53 p.m. I figured the odds of Terry having two vehicles were slim to none. So if he was still here, he was either working awfully damn late, or Toby Bunker had been right, and the guy was living in the building. I climbed out of my car, gave a quick look around for a black or white Prius, saw neither, and headed towards the front door. Someone had spray-painted 'Stop RIP' across two office windows, this time in green spray paint.

I opened the door and stepped inside the building. It was dark and got darker as I made my way up the stairs to the second floor. I remembered the RIP office was just three doors down the hall. I slowly walked in that direction, running my right hand along the wall so I could hopefully find the place. I stopped as my hand ran across the doorframe and then the door for the first office. A dozen steps later, I felt the doorframe for the second office. As I approached the third door, hopefully RIP, I began to hear noise. It sounded like a TV playing and grew louder as I approached.

Once I was at the door, I placed my hand on the door and ran it up until I felt the raised white letters that read RIP Production. I knocked on the door and waited. Nothing happened. Part of me wondered what the hell was with people who don't answer when someone knocks.

I tried the doorknob. Surprisingly, it turned, and the door opened. The lights were off in what would normally be the reception area. I could barely make out the wooden desk I'd seen the one time I was previously in here. There was light coming from a room down the hall to the right, and I wandered in that direction.

"Terry? Hey, Terry, it's Dev Haskell. Are you in here? Terry?" I called as I approached. I never did get an answer, and the noise grew louder with each step.

I stood in the open doorway, and there was Terry stretched out on a mattress on the floor, lying on top of a sleeping bag. At first, I thought he might be dead, but then he snored, and I saw the nearly empty vodka bottle and the empty glass lying on its side. What looked like a half-eaten taco was on the carpet next to the vodka bottle. So much for RIP Production.

I pulled out my cellphone and took a photo. Three paper grocery bags were lined up against the far wall. One looked like it held boxer shorts, another held socks, and the third held a pile of t-shirts. As long as Terry didn't appear to be in the conversational mood, I decided to look around. I stepped into the room across the hall and searched for the light switch. The light, such as it was, came on. If there were four fluorescent lights, only one was working, and that one was fluttering. Still, it was enough to see a small refrigerator, maybe three feet high, standing in the corner. A Formica topped table with folding legs was next to the refrigerator. The table had an electric burner resting on it. Off to the side was a pan and what looked like the cardboard lid to a shoebox with a knife, fork, spoon, and napkins resting in it. Next to that was a stack of white paper plates.

Home sweet home, I thought. There were two other rooms, presumably offices at one time. Both appeared to be empty, but since the lights didn't work in either room, I couldn't be sure. There was nothing else to look at, no files, no desks in either of the rooms. I walked out to the reception area and turned on the light. Thankfully, the light fluttered for a moment and then came on. I opened the drawers on the wooden desk. They were all empty except for a bottom drawer that held a stack of the Recycled Industrial Products pamphlets like the one Terry had given me in the building with the plastic bottles.

My conclusion was they were a bogus operation, and the sooner I let Heidi know, the better. I turned off the light and stepped into the hall, closing the door behind me. I slowly made my way down the stairs and out the front door. I caught some movement off to the left as I walked toward my car. I glanced over and saw some kid spray- painting graffiti across another set of windows.

I hurried toward him. Fortunately, he was so involved in his spray-painting that he didn't hear me until I grabbed him from behind.

"Ahh," came the scream and then the shot of spray-paint. I pushed him and knocked him to the ground. He was down for just a second or two then up on all fours, crawling as fast as he could.

"Not so fast, dip shit," I said and grabbed his belt to pull him back. It kind of worked; he couldn't go anywhere. Only it wasn't a him. It was a her. I'd pulled her jeans down, exposing a red and blue striped thong, a flowery tattoo across her lower back, and a pretty nice rear.

"Get away from me, you pervert. I'm going to call the cops."

"Go ahead. They'll arrest you for spray-painting graffiti on private property."

"They deserve it. Do you have any idea what they're doing?"

"You mean, RIP? Actually, that's what I'm trying to find out. Tell me what you know."

"You work for them, don't you?"

"You're talking about RIP, right, Recycled Industrial Plastic?"

"You don't work for them?"

"No, actually, I'm investigating them."

"Investigating?"

"Yeah, it's a long story. Here," I said, and reached into my pocket. I pulled out my wallet, and handed her a business card.

"You're a cop?"

"A private detective. I'm looking into that company. Some things just don't seem right."

"Don't seem right? I'll say," she said. She hopped to her feet and pulled up her jeans. They had designer rips on the thighs that I never really understood. She was actually attractive, probably about twenty, with dark hair and eyes. "Instead of reducing plastic waste, they're going to create even more, and you know what their plan is? They're going to grind it up into the consistency of dust particles and then dump it in the river. That's their plan for recycling."

"How do you know this? Oh, by the way, my name is Dev Haskell, and you are?" I asked, holding my hand out to shake.

She studied me for a moment and then took hold of my hand and said, "Beatrice Hilger. Everyone calls me Bea. Umm, sorry about the paint. I was afraid you were one of the creeps from RIP."

"No, like I said, I'm checking them out, and I just keep coming up with more questions."

She nodded and said, "I guess I had better get out of here. I'm just going to finish up if that's okay." She nodded at the words spray-painted across the window. 'RIP Resist Industrial Pol'

"You're misspelling plastic," I said.

"It's going to be Polluters," she said as she picked up her spray paint can.

"You got another can of spray-paint?"

"What for?" she asked, drawing out her question.

"If we both did it, you could be done in half the time."

She seemed to think about that for a moment and then walked over to a bag leaning against the building and pulled out another can of spray paint. "Shake it up before you use it," she said and handed me the can.

Twenty-four

We were finished in less than ten minutes. It would have been sooner, but I had to ask her how to spell 'polluters' twice. Once we were finished, I handed the can I'd been using back to her and said, "If you've got some time, Bea, I'd like to talk with you. Any information you have would be helpful."

She eyed me suspiciously and said, "Talk? Like where?"

"I don't know. You pick a place where you'll feel comfortable."

"There's a Taco John's not too far from here."

"That sounds good. We can meet over there, or I'd be happy to give you a ride over."

"I rode my bike, so I—"

"We can just toss it in my trunk."

"No offense, but I'd feel better if I rode my bike."

"Not a problem. Tell me where this place is, and I'll meet you there. I'll grab a table."

She gave me directions, and I drove over. It took less than five minutes to drive, and that included waiting for a traffic light to change. There were four cars in the parking lot when I pulled in and parked. As I walked in, I held the door for a guy just leaving. He gave me a weird stare as he walked past. It made me wonder what his problem was.

"Can I help—Umm, can I help you, sir?" the woman behind the counter asked. Her eyes seemed to widen as she looked at me.

I glanced up at the sign above the counter, and since I was close to starving, I ordered two burritos and a Dr. Pepper. As she placed my order in a bag, I noticed the two guys working the cooking area seemed to be laughing. I ignored them, paid for my order, shoved the change in my pocket, and settled into a booth next to the window in the back of the place. I got more strange looks from the two girls seated at a table across from me. I was beginning to wonder if it was something in the water.

Halfway through my first burrito, there was a knock on the window. I looked over and Bea gave me a wave, locked her bike in the bike rack, and headed inside. I was still staring at my reflection in the window. The left side of my face and my chin were spray-painted green. It must have happened when I grabbed Bea.

"Oh, wow, you must be hungry," Bea said as she slid into the booth across from me.

"Just looking at my reflection in the window and examining your artwork. I couldn't figure out why everyone was giving me these weird looks. You painted half my face green."

"Yeah, well, that was a mistake, and if you want to trade stories you pulled my jeans down."

"Do you want to get something to eat?" I asked, changing the subject.

"Oh, I'm not that hungry," she said, eyeing my untouched burrito.

"I'm buying," I said and reached into my pocket and pulled out a ten-dollar bill.

"Oh, you don't have to do that."

"Yeah, I know, but I'm hoping you can fill me in on what you know about RIP. At least get yourself a drink. I'm starting to feel guilty eating in front of you."

"You sure?"

"I insist, honest."

She grabbed the ten-dollar bill and hurried out of the booth. She was back in a couple of minutes with two tacos, a Pepsi, and a dish of tortilla crisps. "I thought we could share these crisps for dessert," she said.

If she was like most of the women I knew, that meant I could have one, and she'd eat the rest. "So, I take it you're not a fan of RIP," I said.

She shook her head then chewed for a moment and swallowed. "No, anything but. We've been protesting them for the past three, almost four months."

"How did you learn about them? I actually got a tour from one of their employees. He gave me a demonstration of their product. It's this fire-resistant material they've designed to look like wood. The guy held it over a torch, and it never caught fire, didn't produce any smoke, wasn't scorched. I have to say I was pretty impressed."

She nodded, finished chewing her taco, and said, "Yeah, I've seen a video of that demonstration. The wooden-looking thing is about this long, right?" she said and held up her hands about a foot apart.

"Yeah, so you know what I'm talking about."

"Yeah, I know exactly what you're talking about, and here's the problem. That isn't their product. It's not made from recycled plastic. They purchased those samples from a laboratory in New Mexico. Did he let you touch one of the so-called boards?"

"Touch it? Yeah, I mean, after he ran the torch on it, I touched it for a quick second. It was hot."

"Yeah, of course, but you didn't pick it up. You weren't able to bang it on the floor or on the edge of a table. Know why?"

I shook my head. "No, why?"

"Because it would have broken into a million pieces. He wouldn't let you pick it up because you would be able to determine it's fake. He probably did hand you a special piece to hold. It's actually metal painted to look like the other samples. It feels like wood, has the weight. But he'll never run the flame on that piece because the paint will blister off."

She'd just described the routine Terry Nelson went through with me in the building full of plastic bottles. "Are you aware of a guy named Terry Nelson?"

"You mean that drunk that lives in that empty building?"

I nodded and said, "There is one other office in there, a real estate guy."

"Yeah, Bunker. He's the only reason we haven't blown up the building. He seems like a nice enough guy, just caught in the wrong place at the wrong time. I know he's planning to move in the early fall, right after Labor Day."

"So you've spoken to him?"

"No, I haven't, but someone else in our group has."

"Was it your group that placed the signs on the gates leading into the facility along the river?"

"You've been in there?"

"Yes, just a few days ago. As a matter of fact, Terry Nelson took me down there. I pretended to be interested in investing in the company, and he took me inside the building. That's where he gave me the demonstration with the torch on the fire-resistant material. He said they were going to be producing furniture, homes, just about anything you can think of, basically replacing lumber."

"What's in that building now?" she asked and started in on the tortilla crisps.

I chuckled for a moment. "There's an old wooden desk in a small office room, and the rest of the place is one large two-story room filled with mountains of empty plastic bottles."

She nodded, grabbed another tortilla crisp, and said, "We've kept an eye on the place. You didn't see anything resembling industrial equipment, did you?"

"No, nothing like that. I asked and he sort of dodged the question. More or less implied they have a crew of people working there, but they'd been working so much they gave everyone the day off."

"Yeah, that's what they tell everyone who's been in there. They just happen to be there on the day the workforce is resting. We've watched it for weeks, months, actually. The only person who goes there in daylight is Terry Nelson. At night, two guys have been spotted there. They both drive a Prius and—"

"A black and a white one?"

"Yeah, how did you know that?"

"You know who they are?"

She shook her head. "No, we've been trying to find out, but it's not every night. It's not even every week. In fact, we've only seen them in there twice, I think. Late hours, like after midnight. Way after midnight. Our protests have been more successful in attracting public attention. We were on the news last month for a full minute and a half. Did you happen to see it?"

"I guess I must have missed that one. Tell me about your group. Do you protest anything else?"

She looked at me for a long moment before she said, "We're focused on protesting against RIP. Hoping to stop them in their tracks."

"How large is your group?"

"We're constantly growing. The more we get the word out, the more people want to join. Say, I should probably take off. Umm, thanks for paying for dinner. It was nice talking with you. You can finish up these tortilla crisps. They're really good."

"You want a ride. We can put your bike in the trunk of my car, and I could drive you to wherever you—"

"Thanks but no thanks. Maybe I'll see you around," she said and hurried out of the booth. She appeared a few seconds later on the other side of the window. I was going to give her a wave, but she never looked at me. She just unlocked her bike and took off.

Obviously, my questions about the group are what brought our conversation to a close. I wanted to ask her if maybe she knew Penny Larson. I pulled out my pocket notebook and wrote down her name, Bea Hilger.

Once again, more questions than answers. Why was that protest group watching the building full of plastic bottles in the middle of the night? If there wasn't a work crew there, what were all the bottles doing there? And how did they get there? The fire-resistant samples were fake? It never crossed my mind to pick one of those boards up and bang it on the edge of the desk. I wondered if I could get into that place from the river.

I reached in the plastic tray for a tortilla chip. There were only two left. I ate them both and slid out of the booth. As I made my way to the door, one of the guys behind the service counter called, "Thank you, come back and see us soon." Then he and the two other guys laughed.

I didn't bother to say anything. I climbed into my car and turned the rearview mirror to get a better look at my face. Yeah, the green paint made me look pretty ridiculous.

Twenty-five

Once home, I let Morton out into the backyard and then spent the better part of a half-hour in the bathroom scrubbing the green spray paint off my face. I managed to remove most of it, except for a patch in my ear. I let Morton back in, and we watched a series episode on TV and then headed up to bed. Between dreaming about RIP and Cornell's case, I slept fitfully and ended up wide awake before 6:00 the following morning.

I turned off the alarm, shaved, showered, and was downstairs on the computer for over an hour when Morton finally wandered into the kitchen. I gave him his perfunctory scratch behind the ears and let him outside then got back on the computer. I sent an email to Aaron LaZelle asking him to give me a call when he had some time. My phone rang five minutes later.

"Aaron, thanks for calling. I didn't think you'd be in this early."

"Long night, what can I do for you?"

"I wanted to check any information you might have on an individual named Trenton Javis. He's seventeen or eighteen. I'm working an investigation, and his name turned up as a person of interest," I said, not wanting to mention Cornell's case.

"Out of my jurisdiction. You need to contact Arlene Fischer. She'll be able to pull whatever we may have. I'll send her an email saying she might hear from you."

"You got a direct number for her?"

"Yeah, hang on." He was back on the line a half minute later. "Okay, you got a color crayon and a clean spot on the wall?"

"Fire away." I wrote down the number he gave me. We talked for twenty seconds about getting together for dinner sometime in the near future, and he disconnected.

Morton and I were down in the office just after 8:00. Louie had left the coffee on overnight. Fortunately, there was still enough in there, so it didn't burn onto the bottom of the pot. I turned off the burner, dumped the remnants down the sink, and once everything cooled, made a fresh pot. I was on my second mug when I heard the stairs creaking, signaling Louie's momentary arrival.

He stepped into the office, his usual red-faced self. Gave his little wave and settled in at his picnic table desk. I set his fresh coffee mug down in front of him. He nodded and pulled the mug closer.

It took another five minutes before he finally asked, "Were you able to meet up with that guy last night?"

I gave him the short version of Terry Nelson passed out in the otherwise empty office. I didn't mention meeting Beatrice Hilger.

"This RIP organization is sounding like it's on thinner and thinner ice," Louie said.

I nodded and said, "I'm just waiting for 9:00 to roll around, and I'll call Heidi at her office. To be honest, I'm more than a little surprised she's even involved. She usually is on top of this sort of thing and would never invest in something like this. I don't get what the attraction is."

"We all make mistakes," Louie said. "Just as an example, your green clown makeup is still in your ear."

"Very funny. That's not clown makeup. For your information, it happens to be spray paint."

"Oh, well, there you go. Green spray paint in your ear makes a lot more sense."

I didn't want to tell him about Bea Hilger, so I made up a story about spray-painting some chairs for my backyard.

"Gee, I can't wait to be invited over," Louie said, meaning anything but. We chatted for a few more minutes, and then I got on the phone and dialed Heidi's office number. I ended up leaving a message. I phoned Arlene Fischer, the woman Aaron told me to call.

She answered on the third ring, "Detective Fischer."

"Oh hi, detective. My name is Dev Haskell. Aaron LaZelle is a friend of mine. He suggested I call you to see about looking over a file of a young man by the name of Trenton Javis."

"Can you give me the spelling on that name, please?"

I spelled out the name for her.

"Yeah, I got an email from Lieutenant LaZelle. He suggested I be extremely careful."

"What?"

She ignored my response. "I'll have someone pull whatever we have. The name isn't ringing a bell offhand, which is probably a good thing."

"Would it be all right if I stopped down later this morning?"

"That shouldn't be a problem right now. Of course, that can always change. Why don't we say 11:00? Anything comes up, I'll let you know. Can you give me your cell number?"

I gave her my number and disconnected. I Googled Bea Hilger and had a number of sites pop up. I clicked on Facebook and had women from Argentina, Germany, Austria, and a few in the US. Fortunately, most of the sites had pictures of the individuals, and sure enough, there was a picture of the woman who spray-painted me last night.

I sent her a message on Facebook saying I'd like to talk with her and asking her to contact me. I scrolled through her Facebook site, pretty ordinary stuff. I found it interesting that there was nothing that suggested the RIP protests, but then if she was concerned about me and my connection, maybe that made sense, which brought up a couple other questions. Were the protesters concerned about their safety? Were they afraid RIP might react in a negative or even a violent way?

I left the office an hour later and drove down to the police station. I parked in the lot across the street. I didn't recognize anyone at the front desk when I asked to meet Detective Fischer. I took a seat and waited less than ten minutes before a guy in jeans and a t-shirt opened the security door and called, "Dev Haskell?"

"Right here," I answered and hurried over. His badge and nine-millimeter pistol were attached to his belt.

"You're Dev Haskell? Virgil Amsden, nice to meet you." He held out his hand, and we shook. "Detective Fischer was called out, but I've got the file you wanted. I've heard about you," he said.

"Hopefully, on a positive note," I said.

"Yeah, pretty much. A couple of funny stories. Weren't you arrested as a high school kid? You and some girl were involved in the backseat of a car."

"Just for the record, we weren't arrested. Although jail might have been the safer place. You know how parents can get."

"Yeah, I do. Fischer has you set up in an interview room. We're a little short of space at the moment, but you'll have some privacy in there. We won't lock the door. You're pals with LaZelle over in homicide, aren't you?"

"Yeah, I've known him since we were kids, went to school together. We played hockey on a half-dozen different teams. We're good friends," I said.

He shot me a quick look but didn't comment. We turned a corner, and there were a half-dozen interview rooms on the far wall. The doors were open on all but the first one. He led me into the third room. "You need anything, just pop your head out and give a yell. My desk is right around the corner. That's the kid's file on the table. Not much to read, it shouldn't take you more than a few minutes. You want a coffee?"

I was familiar with the department's coffee. "No, thanks, I'm fine."

"All right, let me know when you're finished," he said and walked out of the room.

It was nothing if not boring, with gray walls and a gray tile floor. I pulled one of the metal chairs up to the table and sat down. The file was awfully thin. Amsden was right. There couldn't be much in it to read. The file was labeled Javis, Trenton. Apparently, he didn't have a middle name. I opened the file, and the first thing I saw was the black and white photo of a kid who looked about fifteen. The photo was two years old, which would make him seventeen today, and that seemed to correspond with what Cornell and his mother had told me.

Javis's first offense had been an attempt to steal a car. Apparently, the owner of the vehicle had caught him and called the police. His second offense, the one related to the black and white photo, had been an assault. Based on his photo displaying a swollen left eye and a fat lip, the assault had not gone well for Javis. That was it as far as criminal behavior. Nothing you'd want your kid involved in, but nothing that involved time served. Hopefully, he'd gotten his act together. I went through the file again, all five pages, and still came up empty-handed. I placed the photo on the table, pulled out my cellphone, and took a picture.

I carried the file to the door, stepped out of the room, and called, "Virgil." A moment later, he stepped around the corner.

"Finished already?"

"Yeah, you weren't kidding when you said it would only take a few minutes."

"Hopefully, that's good news. We've got a ton of kids with page after page of charges. The sad news is they're just going to keep circling the drain and, at some point, probably go down it."

"You aware of this kid at all? Ever dealt with him?"

He shook his head. "No, I glanced at the file. Like so many of them, he should try a new line of work. Crime definitely doesn't pay for him. We see it all the time. Once in a while, there's someone who straightens himself out. Unfortunately, they're the exception to the rule."

"The rest end up in more serious trouble?"

"Yeah, pretty much. In today's world, more often than not, they either try to join or are forced into joining a gang. Either way, that's a classic dead-end street. They get nailed doing something stupid, or get involved in drugs, or get killed. Too often, it's all of the above. I don't know this kid. His offenses are relatively minor, and unfortunately, he's the poster child for being on the road to hell. He'll be lucky if he makes it to twenty-five, and there's nothing we can do about it," Amsden said.

"I wish you were wrong, Virgil."

"Yeah, me too. Come on, I'll walk you out to the lobby."

We said goodbye at the security door. I thanked him again for his time and for letting me look at the file. I told him to pass on my thanks to Detective Fischer and walked out to my car. I decided to swing by Cornell's apartment building just to see if Javis might be there.

At this time of day, there were a couple of parking places on the street. I grabbed the first one I saw and walked inside. On a whim, I punched in Christine's number, 216, on the security phone. She never answered, but then it was the middle of a workday, and she was probably at work.

I double-checked my notebook. Javis's apartment number was 209. I punched in the three numbers. A female voice answered after the third ring. "Yeah?"

"Hi, I'm calling for Trenton, please."

"Who's calling?"

"I owe him some money and wanted to get him paid."

Long pause, "You still ain't told me your name."

"I don't have to tell you my name. You tell Javis if he wants to get paid, he can come see me. I'll wait ten minutes, and then I'm leaving," I said and hung up. I walked out to my car, climbed in, and waited.

Nothing happened. After close to fifteen minutes, I started my car and pulled away from the curb. I slowed at the end of the block to turn and happened to glance in the rearview mirror. A fancy-looking red SUV was pulling into the spot I'd just left. Four young guys climbed out. They looked around and then crossed the street and entered the building.

Was Javis one of the four? Or had they arrived to provide protection? I couldn't see any point in hanging around to find out, so I left.

Twenty-six

Louie wasn't in the office when I returned. Morton hopped off his pillow, stood by the door, and then cast a longing look at his leash hanging on the nail. "Yeah, probably a good idea, Morton. Lord knows Louie didn't take you for a walk."

At the sound of the word 'walk,' Morton's tail began waving back and forth at a feverish pace. I attached the leash to his collar, and we headed out. We visited his two favorite fire hydrants, and then we headed down Becky's street. I didn't see Becky on the porch, but Princess suddenly seemed to appear out of nowhere. She barked, then jumped off the front porch and ran toward her new best friend, Morton.

At the sound of her bark, he turned in her direction and then strained at his leash. Princess ran up to about three feet from Morton and stopped. She began to jump from side to side, and it dawned on me that she couldn't get past the electric fence. I reached down, unclipped Morton's leash, and he leaped toward Princess. She stared at him for a moment, no doubt wondering how he made it through the electric fence. She barked twice and suddenly took off, running toward the back of the house, with Morton following in close pursuit.

I walked up onto the front porch and rang the doorbell. Becky answered a minute later. "Oh, Dev, how nice to see you. Please, come in," she said and held the door open.

"Sorry to drop by unannounced. Morton just took off after Princess. They're somewhere in the backyard," I said, just as Princess suddenly ran across the front lawn with Morton about two feet behind her. They sped past and headed into the backyard again.

"Oh, that's perfect. Let them run their little hearts out. She needs the exercise, and from the look of things, he'll be following her, and she can't leave the yard. You up for some coffee?"

"Yeah, I could do that. I feel like I haven't seen you in weeks," I said, and then, just like Morton, I followed her, only we walked into the kitchen instead of running through the house.

"Yeah, I was beginning to wonder if it was something I said," but she smiled when she said that, so I relaxed.

"No, things just all of a sudden got crazy. I've been working the last couple of nights, and by the time I was finished, I just wanted to go home and crawl into bed."

"You could have done that here," she said as she pulled a coffee mug from the cabinet.

"You getting settled in?" I asked, hoping to move the conversation in a different direction.

"Slowly but surely. You know how it goes. You pack everything up, and then as you're unpacking at the new place, you're wondering why you bothered to bring all this stuff. I've donated clothes, books, put two chairs out on the boulevard with a 'free' sign on them. They lasted about ten minutes and were gone, and the couple that took them showed up last night with a plate of cupcakes and some flowers from their garden."

With that, she opened a cupboard and pulled out a white plate with three cupcakes. "See, not a bad deal considering I never liked the two chairs to begin with and was glad to see them being carried away." She filled a coffee mug and pushed it across the counter toward me, then did the same with the plate of cupcakes.

"Oh, thanks, Becky, but I'll just stick with the coffee."

"You won't get an argument from me," Becky said. She pulled the plate back toward her and then began to pull the paper off the sides of a cupcake. She took a bite, leaving white frosting along her upper lip. She smiled, swallowed, and slowly licked her upper lip. "You working some big case?"

"Actually, I'm just checking things out on a couple of situations. But the more I learn, the more questions seem to pop up. Have you started back to work yet?"

"Fortunately, I'm off until next Monday. But I've got a lot to do to get ready. I'm getting my internet access updated to 5G. As a matter of fact, I thought you might be the installer. They gave me a three-hour window on when they were going to be here." She glanced at the digital clock on the microwave. "I've still got two hours to go."

"Hopefully, that will go smoothly."

"Yeah, well, it's a necessary evil. I still haven't made it over to that place you mentioned, The Spot."

"No rush, if you want, give me a call when you're ready to go over, and I'll pick you up or meet you there. I'll introduce you to the bartender, and then in a private moment, you can tell him you don't want anything to do with me."

"Oh, Dev, I'd never say something like that."

"Oh, no, that's okay. It will just put you in good with everyone at the bar."

"If that's the case, then why do you still go there?"

"I'm kidding, Becky."

"Oh, sorry."

"Hey, I'd better gather up Morton and get back to work. Great to see you. I meant what I said. Give me a call if you don't feel like walking in there alone. It's a nice place, nice people."

"Thanks, I'll keep it in mind."

I finished my coffee and slid off the kitchen stool. As we walked out to the front porch, we passed a bunch of flowers in a vase on a coffee table. "Are those the flowers from the folks who took your free chairs?"

"Yes, aren't they lovely?"

"They are. What a nice thing to do," I said as we stepped out onto the front porch. I was about to call Morton, but there he was with Princess. They were lying on the grass in the shade of a maple tree. "Well, it looks like everyone got their exercise. Come on, Morton. We've got things to do."

He just looked at me and didn't move. I walked over, clipped his leash to his collar, and we headed out of the yard. "Thanks, Becky. Enjoy the rest of the day, and thanks for the coffee."

"Don't be a stranger, Dev," she called. I gave her a wave as we turned the corner and headed to the office.

The vase of flowers got me thinking about the long-stemmed roses that Javis had brought Cornell's mother. As we headed up the street to the office, Louie's Ford Fiesta was nowhere to be seen, so I put Morton in the backseat, and we drove over to University Ave.

Twenty-seven

Cornell's apartment building was just three blocks off University Ave. I figured Javis probably didn't own a car, so if he had a job, it was probably nearby. The roses had to have come from a retail outlet—either a flower shop or maybe a grocery store with a flower section. I was pretty sure he hadn't paid for the things. There was a Cub Foods store almost a mile from the apartment building. I parked in the lot and went inside. There was a flower section toward the rear of the store. The section held approximately a dozen different kinds of flowers, mums, tulips, daisies, and a few I wasn't familiar with. A woman was in the process of placing fresh bundles of cut flowers wrapped in cellophane into the buckets of water.

"Excuse me, would you happen to carry any cut roses?" I asked.

"Oh, no. I'm sorry, but the price we'd have to charge is too dear. They don't sell, and we end up tossing them. You might try Walker's Flowers. They're just a few blocks away. Do you know where they're located?"

"I do. Thanks for the tip. I'll give them a try. You wouldn't happen to have a young man working here named Trenton Javis, would you?"

She shook her head and said, "No, at least not as far as I know."

"Thanks for your help," I said. I got back in the car and drove up the street. Walker's Flowers was on the corner in a single-story, white-stucco building. They'd been in that location for at least fifty years, and I'd probably driven past a million times. I was able to pull to the curb and park in front of the shop. I glanced into the backseat. Apparently, Morton was taking a power nap after chasing Princess.

I climbed out of the car and headed toward the door. A sign on the front read 'Open 8 a.m.-7 p.m., Monday - Saturday.' I went to pull the door open, but it was locked. A buzzer suddenly sounded, I pulled on the door again, and it opened.

"Hi, how can I help you?" a woman called from behind the counter. I wasn't more than two feet inside the shop.

"I wondered if you have any long-stemmed roses."

"We do. Any particular color you're looking for? We have quite a selection over here in our cooler," she said, stepping out from behind the counter. She wore jeans and a light blue t-shirt emblazoned with 'Walker's Flowers' in white letters. She had shoulder-length dark hair, and as she walked over to a wall of coolers, I guessed her age at maybe forty-five. Her name tag read

Marilyn. Buckets of different types of flowers were sitting on tiered shelves in four coolers. There were a half-dozen buckets with different colored long-stemmed roses.

"What's the charge for a dozen roses?"

"The roses are thirty-five dollars for a dozen. That includes the sales tax."

I nodded and asked, "Do you have a young man working here by the name of Trenton Javis?"

With a questioning look on her face, shook her head, and asked, "No. What is this about?"

"Actually, I'm not here to purchase any flowers, but I wonder if you might have had an incident a week or so ago. A young guy stealing a dozen long-stemmed roses."

"Why do you ask?" she said, suddenly sounding guarded.

"I'm a detective. I'm investigating another situation, and long-stemmed roses may be involved."

"Oh, thank God. I thought the police had given up. We called and filed a report. The officer gave us a card with his name, and he wrote the case number on the card, but we haven't heard anything since. It's why we had the lock installed on the door. The young man waved a gun and threatened to shoot me."

I noticed there were security cameras hanging from the ceiling in two opposite corners of the shop. "Did you get the incident on film?" I asked and nodded toward one of the cameras.

"Yes, we sent a copy to you. Didn't you see it?"

I ignored her question and said, "If I showed you a picture of the suspect, do you think you might be able to identify him?"

"Believe me. I'll never forget him pointing that gun at me. And just a young kid."

I pulled out my cell phone and clicked on the black and white photo from the police file I'd looked at two hours earlier.

"Does this individual look familiar?" I asked as I handed my phone to her.

"Oh. My. God. Thank goodness you got him. When did you arrest him? Oh, Jesus. I can finally get a decent night's sleep."

I went on to explain that I wasn't with the police department, but I would be contacting them. She gave me the email address they sent a copy of the security tape to and then called to her husband in the back room.

Vince Walker stepped from the back. He stood an even six feet with dark brown hair and brown eyes. Marilyn had me show him my image of Javis. We went back to his office, and he ran the security tape for me. There was no question it was the same person as the police photo. Trenton Javis. I gave Walker my email address, and he sent a copy of the gunpoint robbery to me. I thanked them, promised to keep them posted on whatever happened and left.

I was just a few minutes from Martin Meyer's office, and so I headed down there to give him an update. Morton was stretched out and now snoring in the backseat as I pulled in front of the Meyer Legal Office. I climbed out of the car, looked up and down the street for a Prius or a white Barracuda with flames, and headed for the office door. There was a buzz, and the door un-locked as I approached.

"Hi, Edith, thanks for letting me in," I said as I stepped into the office. She pressed the buzzer, locking the door once it closed, and said, "Good to see you, Dev. How are things going?"

"I think very well. I'll find out for sure once I speak with Martin. You're doing okay? Any more crazy clients coming in?"

"No, fortunately, not" she said and smiled. "Let me just check with Martin. He's been working on a brief, which usually means 'Do not disturb,' but I know he'd want to talk with you." She picked up the phone and a moment later said, "Martin, Dev Haskell is here to see you. Okay. He said to go on in. Good luck," she said.

As I stepped into Martin's office, he looked away from his computer screen, pushed the keyboard off to the side, then rolled his wheelchair back and forth so he was facing me. "Perfect timing. I can use a break. How are things going, Dev?"

"I think better than expected. I may have caught a break in Cornell's case."

"Oh God, we can only hope. I'm working on a brief now and grasping at straws. What do you have?"

I repeated my earlier suspicions about the long-stemmed roses Javis took Cornell's mother and then told

Martin about Walker's Flowers and Javis stealing a dozen long-stemmed roses at gunpoint.

"And they identified him from the police photo you had?"

"Yes, and in case there was any doubt, they showed me the security tape they have of the incident, and it's definitely the same person as the police photo, Trenton Javis. I believe he's seventeen. He apparently lives with his mother and two younger siblings in the same building, just three or four doors from Cornell and his mother's unit. I just wanted to let you know. My next stop is going to be the police department and my friend Aaron LaZelle."

Meyer leaned back in his wheelchair and seemed to think about that for a moment. "I think you should hold off on that, Dev."

"Hold off on it? Are you kidding? They'll have to let Cornell go."

He shook his head. "No, they won't. They'll offer to look into it. They'll want to study the images. Maybe they'll identify the gun as a different caliber or something. Anyway, they'll come up with wanting to interview Trenton Javis personally before they release Cornell. They won't find him. His fingerprints aren't on the weapon. It was wiped down. We'll be back where we started."

"But he stole the dozen roses and took them to Cornell's mother, Christine. Walker's Flowers has the tape of him waving the gun at Marilyn and walking out with the roses."

"Yeah, and the cops have Cornell locked up, and as far as they're concerned, they've got the guy who shot Penny Larson. All he has to do is say he borrowed the gun from Cornell, and we're back to where we started. What we need to do is find this kid, talk him into testifying, and then we'll get Cornell released."

"Are you sure? I mean, it seems that—"

"I'm really sorry, Dev. But unfortunately, I'm very sure. I know you've worked with these guys a lot. You trust them, and they trust you, but please believe me. We don't have enough yet. We need to get Javis. We need him to tell the cops the truth. Then we'll be able to get Cornell released. If we try to get him released without Javis testifying, they'll simply build an even stronger case than they have now. Find this Javis person. He's the key."

Twenty-eight

I didn't like it, but on a certain level, I had to agree with Meyer. I could go down to the station and plead my case with Aaron, but in the end, the arresting officer was Detective Sergeant Norris Manning. The same guy who attempts to attach my name to every crime committed in Saint Paul. The same guy who has locked me up a number of times only to have to release me. The only way Manning was going to release Cornell was if he could pin Penny Larson's murder on me. Much as I didn't want to admit it, Martin Meyer was absolutely right. I had to find Trenton Javis.

I phoned Cornell's mother, Christine, and ended up leaving a message to call me. Since Morton was still asleep, I drove over to the apartment building, hurried inside, and punched in the code to Javis's unit, 2-0-9. No response. I tried it two more times and got the same result. I went back to my car, climbed behind the wheel, and waited, then waited some more. There was no sign of Javis. I left after ninety minutes and headed back to the office.

I climbed out of the car, took Morton for a quick walk, and then headed up to the office. Louie had apparently been napping, and our arrival woke him.

"Oh, man, what time is it?" he asked and hit the return on his keyboard to check the time. He looked pleased with what he saw. "Mmm, you up for going over to The Spot for one?"

"I got a couple of things I want to take care of. Go ahead, and I should be able to catch up with you in a half-hour."

"Everything okay?"

"Yeah, just have to make a couple of phone calls and line some things up for tomorrow."

"Okay, I'll see you two over there," Louie said. He shut down his computer, tossed a newspaper into his briefcase, and headed out the door. I called Christine Thomas again as I watched Louie waddle over to The Spot. I got dumped into voicemail and hung up rather than leave another message.

I turned on my computer and logged onto my Facebook site. There it was, a message from Bea Hilger. I clicked on the message. ***'Happy to chat send me your phone number. B'***

I sent her my phone number along with the message, ***'Call me anytime.'*** I checked out a couple of other things and headed over to The Spot. As per always, Morton nearly pulled my arm out of the socket charging along the bar to get to Louie and some pork rinds. Louie had a handful ready for him as Morton rounded the corner. He inhaled the pork rinds and licked Louie's hand clean in just a second or two.

"You having your usual, Dev?" Mike, the bartender, asked.

"You know, Mike, I think I better take a pass. Maybe just a glass of sparkling water for a change. Louie, you ready for another?" I asked.

"I don't see why not," he said and drained the glass in front of him.

Mike grabbed the empty and headed down the bar. I placed a ten-dollar bill on the bar.

"You working tonight?" Louie asked.

"Yeah, just checking out a couple of things. But if something clicks, it could end up being hours, so I better take a pass on the beer."

"Sorry to hear that," Louie said just as Mike set down his fresh drink. He placed a glass of sparkling water in front of me, grabbed the ten-dollar bill, and headed for the cash register.

"You were going to be looking into that plastic recycling company for Heidi. Did you ever find out anything?" Louie asked and took a sip.

"Yeah, I did—none of it good, by the way. The finished product samples they're using are apparently fake. From what I could determine, there doesn't seem to be any legitimate plan to get things up and running. Other than a fancy office in the Wells Fargo building, I can't see how they're spending their money. The thing I don't get is Heidi is always on top of these investment opportunities. I mean, she's really smart. That's why she's been so successful, but on this one, it's like she has her mind on something else and isn't paying attention or something. I don't know. I think—"

My cellphone ringing cut me off, Cornell's mom. "Hi Christine, thanks for returning my call," I said and stepped outside just as the jukebox was kicking off with 'Zombie' by the Cranberries. "…With their tanks, and their bombs, and their bombs, and their guns…"

"Where are you, Dev? I hope I'm not interrupting anything," Christine said.

"No, not at all, Christine. Just walking to my car, and someone drove past with the radio blasting. Thanks for returning my call."

"Sorry it took so long, busy day and then a meeting at the end of the day that was only supposed to last ten minutes but went on for almost an hour. I tell you… But it sounded like you had a question. How can I help?"

I crossed my fingers and said, "I wondered if you might happen to have a phone number for Javis."

"A phone number? Oh, gee, sorry, but I don't. In fact, I'm wondering if he ever even called. I can't remember ever speaking with him on the phone, and I don't recall Cornell ever mentioning a phone call. Is everything all right?"

"Oh, yeah. I just had a couple of questions for him, is all. Have you seen him since he delivered the cut roses?"

"No, now that you mention it, I haven't. I've been so preoccupied with Cornell's situation I just haven't considered much else."

"Understandable, Christine. I'll try to reach him some other way. In fact, don't even mention to him that I'm trying to get in touch."

"You sure? I could go down the hall and knock on the door if you—"

"No, no, thanks for the offer, but you don't have to do that."

"Well, things are so crazy around here now. With this gang nonsense going on, no one is letting their children out."

"Gang nonsense?"

"Oh, it happens periodically. The local gang is always looking for new members and up to absolutely no good. Why they all aren't arrested and thrown in jail, I'll never understand. Oh, listen to me. I'm sorry. Umm, anyway, I don't have his number."

"Not to worry, Christine. I'll get ahold of him. Don't mention it if you see him."

"All right. Good talking to you. Let me know if there is any way I can help."

"I'll be sure to do that. Thanks for returning my call," I said and disconnected. The suggestion of a gang problem hadn't occurred to me. I wondered if Javis was in a gang or attempting to join a gang. I headed back into The Spot.

"Everything okay?" Louie asked. The Cranberries were just finishing. I noticed the empty bag of pork rinds on the bar next to his drink, which meant sometime during my two-minute phone call, he'd fed Morton the rest of the bag.

"Yeah, everything is fine. That was Cornell's mom returning my earlier call. I was hoping she had someone's phone number, but she doesn't. Hey, I'd love to stay for a couple, but I'm about to head over to Heidi's and go over a couple of things with her. You in tomorrow morning?"

Louie nodded and said, "Unless something changes, I should be in all day. If you finish up at Heidi's, stop back down."

"Yeah, I'll try, but don't wait for me."

"Good luck," Louie called as I led Morton out the door.

Twenty-nine

I let Morton in the back seat. I settled in behind the wheel and phoned Heidi. I got dumped into voicemail after two rings. "Hi, Heidi. Hey, I've done some checking into your client RIP, Inc., and we should talk. I've got some time to stop over tonight if you're in the mood," I said, suggesting a number of possibilities. "Give me a call."

I thought about it for a moment and figured she was maybe just in the bathroom or driving or something. I debated calling her again and decided against it. I drove home, let Morton out the kitchen door, and went upstairs. I tossed my t-shirt in the overflowing laundry basket and put on a reasonably clean shirt from my closet. I let Morton back in, filled his water dish, gave him a biscuit, and got back in my car. I drove up the block to the Solo-Vino, grabbed two bottles of wine, and headed over to Heidi's house.

I decided with the news I had to tell her about RIP, Inc., two bottles of wine would help ease the pain and maybe direct her in another direction. I was thinking about a number of possibilities as I pulled to the curb in front of her house. The house was dark, with the exception of the dining room lights that I could see through the living room windows. It looked like candles might be lit on the dining room table.

I thought about that for a moment and wondered if showing up unannounced maybe wasn't the best idea. It wasn't until I opened the car door that I noticed the car parked in front of me. A white Prius, License number 376 PCE. One of the RIP, Inc. guys. Here? Tonight? Ruining my plans?

I considered going up to the door and knocking and just as quickly dismissed that idea. I pulled away from the curb, drove around the corner, and parked. I climbed out, walked down the alley, and entered Heidi's backyard. The shutters on the dining room windows were closed, but I could peek through the crack where the shutters were joined.

The lights in the room seemed to be dimmed. The candles were lit. A guy was seated with his back to me. His dark hair appeared to be dyed. Even with his back to me, I recognized him as one of the two arrogant pricks who'd stepped off the elevator in the Wells Fargo Building the other day. Russell Greeney, one of the principles of RIP, Inc. What the hell was Heidi thinking?

She sat just to his left, looking gorgeous and wearing a cleavage-revealing silky white blouse and smiling. At the moment, she appeared to be feeding a forkful of a dessert with whipped cream to that creep Greeney. I felt my blood pressure rising, and it took all of my concentration not to pound on the window.

"Hey, what the hell are you doing?" a voice shouted.

I looked over the fence at Heidi's next-door neighbor. He was standing on his back porch, holding a cigar in his hand. A cloud of blue smoke surrounded his head.

"Hey, douche bag, did you hear me? I said, what in the hell are you doing? You some kind of pervert?"

"Just looking at the window. The owner asked me to check the flashing around the window, and I—"

"Bullshit. It's a brick house, you dumb shit. You stay right there. I'm calling 911," he said. He jammed the cigar into the corner of his mouth and pulled out his cellphone. That seemed to be my cue to leave quickly and I ran out of the yard.

"Hey, get back here, you peeping Tom. Yeah, I want to report some pervert looking in—"

I ran up the alley, jumped behind the wheel, started the car, and pulled away. As I passed the alley, I glanced down, and there he was, charging up toward the street, cigar in his mouth, red-faced, and shaking a fist. I took a right at the corner and accelerated. I glanced in the rearview mirror a couple of times but didn't see him. So much for my plans tonight.

Halfway home, I thought of a fallback option. I drove past the office, turned at the corner, and took a left two blocks later, Becky's street. I spotted Princess in the front yard. She'd just caught a ball on the bounce, and I figured Becky threw it. Only it wasn't Becky.

Some guy in shorts and a t-shirt. A bumper sticker for the Midway Gym, wherever that was, was on the SUV parked in front of Becky's house. He picked up the ball Princess dropped and was getting ready to throw it again. Fortunately, Becky wasn't in the front yard or out on the porch. I took a left at the corner and headed home.

I put the wine bottles in the refrigerator, pulled out a beer, and settled in front of the TV. Morton and I headed upstairs just after 11:00.

We drove down to the office early the following morning. On the way down, I debated driving past Heidi's and Becky's to see if the cars were still there. I decided the way my luck had been running, I'd just be piling more misery on top of my previous evening. We were the first ones in the office, so I made the coffee. I checked my emails, and there was the email from Walker's Flowers with camera footage of Javis stealing a dozen roses at gunpoint. Louie arrived maybe forty-five minutes later.

"Oh, you guys are in? I didn't expect to see you until close to noon. Heidi throw you out this morning?"

"No, she wasn't home last night, and we both seemed to be dragging, so we just went home. Things go okay at The Spot?"

"Yeah, I didn't stay too long. Had one more, and it was time for me to go home. What's your day look like?"

"I'm going to try to locate this Trenton Javis kid. The more I learn, the more he seems to be a key player in the case." We chatted for a bit. I reviewed the

Walker's Flowers tape a half-dozen times. The more I watched it, the more Javis appeared as a frightened child. You never want anyone pointing a gun at you, and it's even more dangerous when the individual is frightened or nervous. I was ready to watch the tape again when my cell phone rang. The call came through as unknown, but I answered it anyway. I crossed my fingers and hoped it wasn't Heidi's neighbor.

"Haskell Investigations."

"Dev Haskell, please," a woman said. She sounded familiar, but I couldn't place her.

"You got him,"

"Hi, Dev, wow, you sounded so professional when you answered the phone. It's me, Bea. Just calling to see if you ever got all that green spray paint off your face," she said and laughed.

"Hi, Bea. Great to hear from you. Yes, to answer your question. I was able to get the paint off my face. It took a couple of days. Every time I thought I got it all, someone would point to an area I couldn't see. The last bit was in my ear."

She laughed at that. "So, did you still want to get together?"

"Yes, of course. I want to pick your brain regarding RIP," I said and immediately flashed back to the image of Heidi feeding the whipped cream dessert to that jerk with the dyed hair, Russell Greeney.

"I could meet you for coffee this morning if you have time."

"Absolutely, I'll make time," I said, knowing I really didn't have anything scheduled. "You pick a spot, and I'll meet you there."

"There's a little place over on Cleveland Ave called Tillie's. You know where it is?"

I did. It was only two blocks from where Penny Larson had been shot. "Yeah, I do know, as a matter of fact. Corner of Cleveland and Marshall Avenue, right?"

"That's it. See you there in an hour. Is it okay if I bring a friend?"

"Not a problem. I'll see you in an hour," I said, and we disconnected.

"Good news?" Louie asked.

"Maybe. One of the RIP protesters. I hope to pick her brain."

"So what happened with Heidi?"

"Oh, it never happened. She was out at a meeting and wasn't going to make it home until late," I lied. "Actually, that turned out to be okay. Anything I can learn from this woman this morning will only add to what I already know."

I hung around the office for another thirty minutes and then drove over to Tillie's.

Thirty

The official name is Tillie's Farmhouse. It's located on Cleveland Avenue, around the corner from Marshall Avenue. If you stood on the corner, you could just make out the blue house where Penny Larson lived. The restaurant is in a one-story brick building with a black awning across the entire front of the building emblazoned with the name Tillie's Farmhouse. Among other things, they're known for great food with a Scandinavian touch.

I was thinking we'd just have coffee, but once I stepped inside, I figured Bea would scam me for a late breakfast. I was ten minutes early, and Bea was ten minutes late, so on average, we were both on time. The friend she brought with her turned out to be Diane Haggerty, the housemate of Penny Larson I'd spoken with on the front porch.

As Bea stepped into Tillie's, she glanced around, and I gave her a wave. The two women headed over to my table and pulled out their chairs.

"Hi, Bea, thanks for setting this up. Diane, small world, good to see you again."

They both smiled and gave me a nod.

"Okay, before we get started, I'm buying. No arguments. You come here often, Diane? It's close to your place."

"Oh, we live together. I mean in the same house," Bea said.

"Really? I had no idea. So you lived with Penny, too?"

"Yeah, actually, she was the person who got me involved with protesting RIP."

"And you mentioned you're not involved with the protesting, Diane."

She shook her head, "No, between classes and working, I don't have the time. I don't disagree with a lot of it, but I don't have the time."

"Penny and I made the time," Bea said and shot a quick look at Diane. "But I—"

"Good morning, nice to see you again. Can I get you a coffee or tea?" the server asked.

"Coffee, black," Diane said.

"Same," Bea said.

The server smiled and left.

"So RIP, you told me that the samples I saw were fake."

"Yeah, they didn't manufacture them. It's not their product," Bea said.

"And not the business they're really in," Diane added.

"Well, then, what business are they in?" I asked.

The two women looked at one another. "You tell him," Bea said.

"Tell me what?"

"They've got this group of people who invested a lot of money, thinking they were going to save the world from plastic waste. But that's not the business they're really in," Diane said.

"So tell me, what do they do?"

"Drugs."

"Drugs? What does that have to do with recycling plastic?" I asked.

"The recycling plastic is just a cover. All those plastic bottles they have in that warehouse building, that's just a cover. The real business is the building. It's located on the river, and they have cocaine shipments delivered by boat in the middle of the night."

"Are you sure? No offense, but this is sounding more than a little far-fetched. Why would they seek out legitimate investors to fund a drug operation?"

"Because they're money hungry. I think their original idea, way back when, was legitimate. But they were spending more than they were taking in. The more investors they got on board, the more in debt they became. Somehow, somewhere, they got linked up with these drug dealers and some street gang, and all of a sudden, their focus turned to making money selling drugs. You've seen their operation. They're into a lot of people for a lot of money. "

"But drugs? If you know this, why haven't you contacted the police?"

"We have," Bea said. "We lacked any credible proof and protesting against RIP more or less convinced the people in charge that we were making the whole thing up."

"So are you suggesting that it was these drug people who killed Penny Larson?"

"We think that's a possibility. Holding that Cornell Thomas person responsible seems more and more unlikely."

The server suddenly appeared with their coffees. "Are you thinking of ordering any breakfast?"

"Maybe the breakfast burrito for me," Bea said.

"Yeah, same for me and a side of monkey bread," Diane added.

It dawned on me they both ordered without looking at a menu.

"Sir?" the server asked.

"Just coffee for me, thank you."

I watched for a moment as she walked away then returned to the subject at hand. "So you reported this to the police, and they didn't react?"

"Not exactly," Bea said. "They basically said they investigated the situation and came to a conclusion. In other words, our suspicions couldn't be verified. They told us they would continue to monitor the situation."

"Meaning they aren't going to be doing anything," Diane said.

"I gotta be honest. I'm having a very hard time getting my head around this thing. I know one of the investors. In fact, that's why I'm even involved. Otherwise, I wouldn't have the slightest idea. My friend wouldn't just go to the cops if she suspected any of this. She'd race over there or call the police and tell them about it. She's not a lightweight. She's very successful and would never do anything illegal. She's as law-abiding as they come," I said and then pictured Heidi last night, feeding that whipped cream dessert to that idiot Russell Greeney and wondered. "Cocaine? Really?"

They both nodded.

"Does the name Trenton Javis ring a bell with either of you?" They seemed to think for a long moment, and then both shook their head, no.

"And you're convinced about this drug thing?"

They nodded, and Bea said, "We've caught them having meetings in the middle of the night with people arriving on a boat to that building. They came in at two or three in the morning. What else could it be?"

"You have any pictures of this, maybe a recording?"

They shook their heads.

"No, we don't," Bea said. "But it's in the middle of the night, they're speaking Spanish, and they're armed. We've seen them with rifles getting out of the boat. Carrying bags of something."

"When you say we, who exactly do you mean? Did either one of you see or hear this?"

They shook their heads, and Bea said, "Penny was the one who put it all together. She was out there in the middle of the night and saw these people pull up in the boat. She saw the guns, heard them speaking Spanish. Two guys were carrying big leather bags."

The server arrived with the breakfast burritos and the plate with monkey bread. The monkey bread looked like it came out of a Bundt pan and was covered with a wonderful-looking caramel. It smelled delicious."

"Help yourself," Diane said as I stared.

"You sure?" I asked.

"Huh, you're paying. Go ahead."

I pulled one of the gooey little biscuits from the pile and placed it in my mouth. It was warm, delicious, and sticky. "Mmm, very good," I said with my mouth full and reached for another piece. They both giggled.

"We were thinking, maybe you could do some investigating," Bea said.

"Yeah. It would seem that if you could confirm this drug thing, that would obviously end the investor's interest and get the police involved. Umm, except that we wouldn't be able to pay you," Diane said.

"Don't worry about that. When the cops interviewed you about Penny's murder, did you mention this to them?"

"Yes, but as soon as they found the gun at her ex-boyfriend's house, they never came back. Never called us or mentioned anything else," Bea said.

"Did you get in touch with them and say he didn't do it?"

They both shook their heads. "We just thought, since he had the gun in his possession, well, you know, he was guilty."

"Yeah, the article in the newspaper seemed to say it was a done deal, and they got the guy that killed her."

I remembered talking to a reporter once who told me it's more important to be out there first and wrong than it is to be second and right.

"What do you think?" Bea asked.

"I think there's suddenly a lot to go over, and my investigation just became awfully complicated."

We talked some more. The girls finished their burritos and got a take-out box for what was left of the monkey bread home. We promised to stay in touch and left Tillie's. I watched them walk to the corner and disappear.

Thirty-one

On the way back to the office from Tillie's, I debated driving past Heidi's and decided that was not the best idea. Besides, I had another dumb idea. I drove past Becky's, and the SUV with the Midway Gym bumper sticker was still there. Oh great, my morning was complete.

What better way to get the icing on the cake than to head over to the police station and meet with Aaron LaZelle. One of the officers at the front desk called up to Homicide, and ten minutes later, I was on the elevator with my escort, Officer Denise Sibley. Saying we'd worked together over the past few years was too strong a statement. We'd been involved in a few cases, and she had interviewed me twice. Both times I'd been one of a number of people who had additional information on an ongoing case. We'd gotten along okay.

We joked on the way up to the homicide section. She seemed in a really good mood. She input the security code on the keypad and said, "He'll be talking with you in interview room 2. You know the way, or do you want me to escort you?"

"Not a problem, I know where it is," I said, thinking an interview room was kind of strange.

"Good chatting with you, Dev. Enjoy," she said and grinned.

A couple of folks smiled or waved as I walked through the section toward the interview rooms. I passed Aaron's office on the way. The lights were off, and the door was closed. That made me wonder even more what the deal was. Maybe he wanted to keep things looking professional, so no one got the idea he was giving me inside information.

The interview rooms were around the corner. The door to number one was open, and the room was empty. Two detectives were standing next to the door to number two. They nodded and smiled as I approached.

The door was open, and I asked, "Is he in there?"

"Oh yeah, been waiting for you. Better hurry," one of them said.

"Okay," I said and hurried into the room. As soon as I stepped inside, the door closed behind me. I focused on the metal-topped table and the man with the bald pink head sitting on the opposite side, facing me, Detective Norris Manning.

"Oh, what the hell is this? Manning? I was supposed to meet with Lieutenant LaZelle."

"He's busy. Have a seat, Haskell."

"No way. I'm not in the mood to get reamed out by you, again. I've been through that too many times. Tell LaZelle when he wants to talk, he can—"

"Take a seat, Haskell."

"No. I haven't done anything wrong. I'm not going to talk with you." I turned and took hold of the doorknob. The door was locked. "Oh, come on, Manning. I need this like another hole in my head. Can you just let me out of here? This isn't going to go well for either one of us, and I—"

"Haskell, would you quit whining like a little baby and sit down. You've been investigating a case I'm involved in, and I'd like to get your opinion."

"Oh, all of a sudden, you want my opinion? You gotta be kidding me."

"Sit down, please. I'm asking nicely."

I took a deep breath, closed my eyes as I exhaled, and then walked toward Manning seated at the table. There were three files in front of him. I sat down and stared.

He stared back for a moment and said, "Thank you. Give this a look. You may find it interesting." He handed a file to me.

I opened it, focused on the three black and white booking photos of Cornell Thomas in the file. The first page just listed basic information, physical characteristics, address, age, that sort of thing. I lifted the page. The first thing I saw was an 'anonymous' phone call that came through at 8:48 a.m., identifying Cornell Thomas as the shooter and giving his address. "Your file on the arrest of Cornell Thomas. How did you know this is what I'm working on?"

"You're listed as being on his defense team. You've visited him at least twice that I know of. I'd like to know what you've found out."

"That's privileged information, Manning. I'm not going to tell you anything. If you want to know that badly, call his attorney, Martin Meyer. Don't lock me in a room with you."

"You've got everything we have on this case in that file lying on the table in front of you. Aren't you just the least bit curious?"

"And then you'll accuse me of somehow illegally gaining access to the file, and the prosecution will find a way to eliminate my testimony. No thanks, here you can have this back," I said and tossed the file across the table.

"Suit yourself," he said and placed the file on top of the other two. "Haskell, I've never done this before, and I'm more than a little uncomfortable dealing with you."

"That goes both ways, Manning."

"We've had our disagreements in the past."

If I bit my tongue any harder, it was going to bleed. "So, what's the problem?"

Manning looked around and then leaned forward and lowered his voice. "Keep investigating. You may be on the right track for a change."

"What?" I said as Manning stood and picked up the files.

"You're free to go," he said and walked toward the door."

"Hey, Manning, wait a minute. What do you mean? I—"

The door opened, and Manning stepped out of the room. One of the detectives stepped into the room and said, "If you want to nap, I'm going to have to put you in a cell; otherwise, get your ass out of here."

I stepped out of the interview room and started to head back the way I'd come. "Oh, here's a shortcut, Haskell. Follow me." I followed the detective in the opposite direction and ended up out in a hall. "Take a left at the end of the hall and then the first right. You should be right back at the elevators if you followed directions," he said and then closed the door behind me.

I must have followed his directions because two minutes later, I was back in front of the elevators, wondering what in the hell had just happened. I took the elevator down to the main floor. I turned in my visitor's pass at the front desk and walked out to my car. I'd parked in the gravel parking lot across the street. I sat behind the steering wheel for a couple of minutes, wondering what had just happened, and never came up with anything that sounded remotely plausible. I was sure of one thing, Manning would never try to help me. I turned on the car and headed back to the office. I drove past the office and pulled in front of Rooster's. Taffy was working the counter.

"Hi, Dev. How are you doing today?"

"To tell you the truth, I'm not sure. It's turning out to be a crazy day, and it's not even noon."

"Maybe a barbecue pork sandwich would help."

"Couldn't hurt, and you better make it two. Oh, and could you throw in two more bones, please?"

"Coming right up." She was back in just a couple of minutes. I paid and went out to my car. I opened the passenger door and tossed the bag on the front seat. As I closed the door, I caught sight of a black Prius parked across the street up in about the middle of the block. I glanced both ways. There was no traffic coming. I walked around the front of the car and then took off running up the street toward the Prius. It suddenly came to life, made a U-turn with tires screeching, sped up to the freeway exit, and disappeared. I walked back to my car, waited for a car to pass, and then I made a U-turn and headed down to the office.

Louie was typing away, and Morton was stretched out on his pillow. As I stepped inside, Morton suddenly bolted upright, hopped off the pillow, and hurried over, sniffing the air.

"How about some lunch, Louie?"

"Perfect timing," he said. "How'd your breakfast meeting go?"

"Oh, interesting. There were two women, and it turns out they both live in the house where Penny Larson was shot. Nice talking with them," I said and pulled one of the take-out boxes from the bag and set it on Louie's desk.

Morton's tail began wagging back and forth, banging against the front of my desk. "Easy boy, easy," I said and reached down with a bone. He snatched it out of my hand and hurried back to his pillow.

"Oh, he's going to be busy for the rest of the day," Louie said.

I settled in at my desk, opened the food tray, and took a bite of my barbecue sandwich. The day suddenly seemed to improve. Louie and I ate in silence for the next fifteen minutes until my phone rang. I had to wipe the barbecue sauce off my hands before I answered.

"Hi, Dev, sorry I missed your call last night. I was, umm, in a meeting until late. What's up?" Heidi said.

"Oh, some general information on RIP, Inc. None of it very good, I'm afraid."

"That may be outdated. They're expecting an investor to climb on board shortly. Someone who is going to invest at a level that will give them room for the next twelve months."

"Oh, really. Who is the investor?"

"Even if I knew, I'm not at liberty to say, and I don't know, to be honest. I don't need to know as long as they invest."

"So you learned this at your meeting last night?" I asked.

"Yes, along with some other things, but it sounds like they'll be getting back on track very soon. In fact, we should meet sometime just to see what you found out, but the pressure looks like it's going to be off, at least for the next twelve months."

"That's good news, Heidi. Say, would you have time for dinner this evening? I could give you a quick summary, and you know, maybe we could get on to other matters."

"Oh, that sounds wonderful, Dev. I wish I could." I wanted to ask if she had any of that dessert with the whipped cream left, but what was the point? "Maybe we could meet up some other time. Once my schedule opens up."

Your schedule? I know what you can do with your schedule, I thought. "Let me know when you have some time. I'd like to see you," I said.

"I'll keep it in mind," Heidi said.

We disconnected, and I tossed the cellphone on my desk.

"Everything okay, Dev? You don't look too happy."

"Yeah, everything is fine," I said and tossed the remnants of my sandwich back in the take-out box. I got up, grabbed Morton's leash, and clipped it onto his collar. He stopped gnawing on the bone and gave me a look that suggested something along the lines of 'What the hell do you think you're doing? I'm perfectly content.'

"You going for a walk?" Louie asked just as a chunk of barbecue fell out of his sandwich and tumbled down his tie.

"No, I've got to find a guy. Morton will keep me company. See you later."

"Yeah, thanks for lunch, Dev," Louie called as we headed down the stairs.

Thirty-two

We headed over to Cornell's building and parked. Javis had to show up sooner or later, and he was the answer to the dozen or so questions I had bouncing around in my thick skull. I had to park almost at the end of the block. I lowered my window and adjusted my sideview mirror to focus on the entrance to the building and then waited. Morton was content to gnaw on his bone, undisturbed. Two kids rode past on bikes. An older woman walked past, pulling a small cart with a grocery bag. At one point, a guy pulled up in a red convertible, and a woman strutted out the door of the building in a yellow outfit that appeared to be about four sizes too small. Some guy carrying what looked like a twelve-pack of beer staggered into the building. I've just described almost three hours.

A red Chevy Tahoe pulled in front of the building and waited. After a number of minutes, the door to the building opened, and out walked someone who looked an awful lot like the photo of Javis. His jeans were belted below his ass, and his hands were in his pockets, apparently holding the jeans up. He had on red boxers and a white strappy t-shirt. The t-shirt might have given you a second thought if he'd been muscular, but he wasn't.

Someone in the Tahoe called, "Let's go, Flower Child. You're keeping us waiting here."

He flashed a half-dozen different signs, I supposed gang signs of some sort, and climbed into the Tahoe. He hadn't even closed the door when they raced up the street past me and screeched around the corner. As they passed by, my car vibrated with the base from their 10,000-watt amplifier and the sub-woofers. I followed the Tahoe through downtown onto East 7th street. They took a left onto Payne Avenue and, after a few minutes, turned right onto Jenks Avenue.

The homes in the area had been built as single-family homes in the early 1900s. One by one, they'd been converted to multiple units over the past century. It was now affordable housing, but there was a reason it was affordable. I pulled to the curb as the Tahoe stopped in the middle of the block, and five guys climbed out. Javis appeared to be the youngest by at least five years. The house had a front porch, and three guys were seated on the porch. They appeared to be drinking beer. One of them looked like he was smoking a joint in between sips of beer. Just the sort of neighbors everyone hoped for.

Once they slapped hands with one another, the five walked into the house, and the three guys originally on the porch remained there. After sitting behind the wheel for the better part of an hour, I climbed out, grabbed Morton's leash, and we took a walk around the next block. Morton held the bone in his mouth the entire time. I bought two bottles of water at the gas station and walked back to the car. I let Morton into the backseat and pulled a plastic bowl from the trunk. I set the bowl on the floor next to him, filled it with water, and then climbed in behind the wheel. We went for another walk around 5:00 and one more just a little after 7:00.

I never saw anyone enter or leave the house. The same three guys continued to sit on the front porch. Occasionally one would get up and go inside. He'd return three or four minutes later. I figured they were acting as guards. By 9:00, it was getting dark. At 9:30, it was dark. At 10:00, I backed into the intersection rather than drive past the house, and we headed home.

Just to be on the safe side, I checked all my doors and windows to make sure they were locked. I tossed Morton a biscuit and ate some cold macaroni and cheese I found in the refrigerator. It wasn't half bad. I googled Jenks Avenue on the internet, no alley. So, it wasn't like those guys climbed in another car and drove off. Against my better judgment, I got back in my car, drove through downtown, and turned onto Payne Avenue. This time, once I got close to Jenks Avenue, I pulled to the curb, climbed out of my car, and walked across Jenks as I headed up Payne. The red Tahoe was still parked in the same place.

I walked over to the gas station and bought a Dr. Pepper and a candy bar. I crossed Payne Avenue and sat down on the bus bench, so I could look up Jenks Avenue and keep an eye on the Tahoe. I finished my Dr. Pepper. I got off the bench twice as different buses approached. Eventually, I finished my candy bar.

It was after midnight when three guys strolled out of the house and headed for the Tahoe. Mercifully, one of them was Javis. I hurried over to my car, pulled a U-turn on Payne, and drove like a bat out of hell toward Javis's apartment. I had to park a block away and around the corner. I hurried back to the building and waited along the side. Then I waited some more. At 2:35 in the morning, I walked back to my car and drove home.

I checked the doors and windows again then went upstairs to bed. Morton was sound asleep with the bone nestled between his front paws. I turned off my alarm clock and planned to sleep as late as I could. I think I fell asleep before my head hit the pillow.

As luck would have it, I was wide awake just a little after 6:00 the following morning. I was in the process of checking Heidi's Facebook site when Morton finally wandered downstairs. I gave him his head scratch and let him out the kitchen door. Once he finished breakfast, we headed down to the office. A full pot of coffee was on, but Louie was nowhere to be found. I figured he probably had an early morning court appearance.

I phoned Cornell's attorney. "Martin Meyer Legal Office," Edith answered.

"Hi Edith, Dev Haskell. Is Martin available?"

"Hold on while I see," she said.

"Martin Meyer," he said a moment later.

"Hi Martin, Dev Haskell, thanks for taking my call."

"My pleasure, Dev. What's up?"

I went on to tell him about my brief interlude with Detective Manning yesterday. I described my history with Manning, and why I'd been concerned he might be pulling a fast one. I finished up with, "Do you have copies of those files?"

"Supposedly. I mean, at this stage, if he intentionally left something out, we would have no way of knowing. It strikes me as strange that he would contact you and pull this meeting. You think he was trying to intimidate you?"

"You know, normally I would, but the more I think about this, I'm wondering if he wasn't being completely legitimate. You've got those files, you said?"

"Yes, we do."

"Could I swing by this morning and go over them?"

"By all means. I'm here all day. Stop in anytime."

"I'll be over in a bit," I said and disconnected. I pulled open my desk drawer. The bag from Rooster's with the second bone was in there. I pulled the bag out, wrote a note to Louie, and left Morton on his pillow, gnawing away.

I drove over to Becky's house. Unfortunately, the SUV with the Midway Gym bumper sticker was still parked in front of the house. I was ready to drive past, but Becky and the guy were both sitting on the front porch drinking coffee.

Becky waved and called, "Hi, Dev," and I felt I had no option but to pull over and meet the boyfriend. Fortunately, I could use the bone as my excuse, nice guy that I was, and then beg off to get to an appointment. I pulled in front of the SUV and parked. I grabbed the bag from Rooster's and got out of the car.

"Hi, Dev. I hope you weren't going to just drive by," Becky said as I walked up the front sidewalk. As I approached, Princess suddenly rose to her feet and hurried down the porch steps. "Oh, I think she might like what you have in that bag."

"Yeah, I stopped there yesterday and thought of her, well, and Morton too. He's back in the office gnawing away on his."

"Kevin, this is the guy I told you about. The one who's made me feel at home in the new place. Dev, this is my brother, Kevin."

Kevin flashed a friendly smile and said, "Nice to meet you. Becky was telling me all about you."

"Must have been a pretty dull conversation," I said, and they both laughed. I unwrapped the bone and handed it to Princess. She snatched it, hurried back up onto the porch, and settled into a distant corner.

"Can you stay for a coffee?" Becky asked.

"Yeah, I can, as long as it's already made. Don't put a new pot on if it's not."

"It's all made. Give me just a second, and I'll be back," she said and hurried into the house.

I climbed up onto the porch, and Kevin shifted his chair over so I could pull one between him and Becky's chair. As I sat down, he said, "Hey, before she comes back, thanks for being so nice to her. This was a tough move, and you showing her around and having a dog, and all, just made it a lot easier."

"Oh, my pleasure. She's a nice lady. It was a pleasure to meet her. Princess was giving Morton a run for his money, literally. They were chasing one another around the house until they were ready to drop."

"You do take it black, don't you, Dev?" Becky said, stepping out onto the porch. She was dressed in nice fitting cutoff shorts and a black t-shirt that read, 'Just a woman who loves Bob Seger.' As she set the coffee mug down, I caught a slight hint of a nice perfume.

"Oh, thanks, Becky. So, Kevin, let me guess. She had a half-dozen things that each weigh about a ton, and she asked you to carry them up to the attic."

They both laughed. Kevin shook his head and said, "Fortunately, that wasn't the case. Everything was pretty much put away."

"Dev moved a bunch of boxes for me before you came," Becky said to him.

"Much appreciated," Kevin said.

We chatted for a bit. Kevin lived up in northern Minnesota, the town where they'd grown up. They hadn't seen one another for over a year, and in short order, they were discussing what people from high school were doing and who was married. I sat and listened until

I was finished with my coffee and then apologized for having to run off.

"It was really nice to meet you, Dev. I'm heading out later today, so it was nice to associate a face with all the stories. Thanks for your help moving Becky's stuff," Kevin said as he shook my hand.

"Honestly, she had it all pretty much done."

"Thanks for stopping, Dev, and thank you for the bone. Princess will be your lifelong friend."

"Yeah, she and Morton, peas in a pod. Take care you two. Safe trip up north, Kevin."

"Nice to meet you," he called as I made my way to the car. The day suddenly seemed a lot better, and I was glad I decided to stop. Her brother, who knew?

Thirty-three

I didn't realize I'd been humming along with the songs on the radio until I pulled in front of the Meyer Legal Office and turned off the car. Edith buzzed the door as I approached.

"Good morning, Edith. Hope everything is going well for you today."

"Oh my, aren't you just Mister Happy this morning. Enjoyable evening?" she asked and grinned.

"No, in fact, quite the opposite, but today is a lovely day, and I get to see you and Martin."

"Oh, brother," she said and picked up the phone. "Yes, Dev Haskell is here. All right. You can go on in, Dev. He's been expecting you."

"Thanks, Edith," I said and walked into Martin's office.

Martin was seated at his desk typing away on his computer. "Grab a chair, Dev," he said without looking up. As I sat down, he stopped typing and pushed three manila file folders across the desk to me. "These are the files we received from the police. Go through these and see if anything might be missing. In the scheme of things, they're rather thin, but then Cornell has never had any interaction with the police until this incident."

I pulled the files toward me and opened the one on top. Copies of the three photos of Cornell I saw in the interview room with Manning yesterday stared back at me. The second sheet was the personal information on Cornell. Things like weight, height, and address. The third sheet was the one listing the initial phone call and the anonymous phone call the following morning. There were transcripts of the calls. The first call came through at 9:37 pm.

"911, what's your emergency?"

"Yeah, my wife and I are on Marshall Avenue. We, we found a woman on the front porch. I think she's been shot. Oh, Jesus, you need to send an ambulance right away."

"Tell me the address, please."

"Jesus, you need to hurry. There's blood all over, and she's—"

"Please tell me the address, sir."

"I already did that, umm, it's 1997 Marshall Ave. She's, no honey, don't touch her. Oh, my God. Oh, my God. Please hurry."

"Emergency Medical Team has been alerted, and they are on the way. Is there anyone there with you, sir?"

"Anyone? No, it doesn't look like it. Honey, ring the doorbell, see if someone—No, damn it, ring the doorbell. Oh God, please hurry. Please hurry."

The caller's name, Thomas Kennedy, and his phone number were listed at the bottom of the transcript.

The anonymous call the following morning came through at 8:48 am. I made a mental note that Javis was at Cornell's apartment around 8:30.

"911, what is your emergency?"

"Yeah, umm, I think some dude just shot a woman."

"Where are you calling from, sir?"

"I'm on my phone."

"Where did this shooting occur?"

"It's at a blue house at Marshall and North Moore Street. Dude just shot the girl, umm, shot her last night, I mean. Yeah, that's when it happened. Last night and then he ran off the front porch and disappeared. His name is Cornell Thomas, and he lives at Capitol Plaza South. Building address is 422. He's in unit two-one-six. Oh, and he hid the gun under his pillow."

Male caller disconnected. Number not available. No name given.

I pulled out my notebook and wrote down the name of the initial caller, Thomas Kennedy, along with his phone number and address. "Did you call this guy who first reported the shooting?" I asked Meyer.

"I spoke with him on the phone. Seemed nice enough. Not surprisingly, he and his wife are still upset with the situation. There's a copy of the police interview in the file. They live a block away on Iglehart. They did not know Penny Larson or any other residents in the Marshall Avenue house."

I shook my head. "Just reading this, that second call seems to scream 'set-up.' The call comes through the next morning. The caller won't identify himself. Reading the transcript, it suggests someone is coaching the caller. Were you able to listen to the audio?"

Martin shook his head. "Not yet. I want to eventually, but the transcript was enough to go on initially."

I paged through the rest of the file and then worked my way through the other two. Everything seemed in order except for the call identifying Cornell as the shooter, and a good portion of the case hung on that phone call. Well, that and the fact that the ballistics test confirmed the Glock 17 with the serial numbers filed off and recovered from beneath Cornell's pillow was indeed the murder weapon.

Once I finished going through the files, I asked Martin, "What's your impression of this Thomas Kennedy?"

"Impression? From the way he conducted himself during our conversation, my sense is he's a successful, responsible individual who wishes he wasn't involved in this and would give anything to have been able to save the Larson girl's life. My sense is she was probably dead before he and his wife found her."

"I'd like to talk with him."

"You took down his phone number, didn't you?"

"I did."

"Give him a call. He's aware he'll most likely be called before we go to trial. Have you heard anything else from the detective?"

"Manning? No, I haven't, and I don't expect to. I'm beginning to think he may sense the arrest of Cornell might not hold up in court, but he doesn't know where to turn."

"Did you mention this Javis person to him?"

I shook my head. "No, I didn't. Only because I'm still not sure. I'll be in touch with Manning later today. But first, I want to talk to Kennedy and his wife."

I promised Meyer I would stay in touch. I waved goodbye to Edith on my way out. She was on the phone and buzzed the door, so I could leave. I drove back to the office and phoned Thomas Kennedy. I was dumped into voicemail and left a short message explaining the reason for my call. He returned the call a half-hour later.

"Haskell Investigations," was how I answered when Kennedy's name appeared on my phone.

"Yes, Mr. Haskell. This is Thomas Kennedy. You're a private investigator?"

"I am. I'm working with Martin Meyer. I believe you've already spoken to him."

"Meyer? Oh, yes, the attorney. He's representing the man arrested for the murder of the Larson girl."

"Yes, he is. I'm wondering if I could take a couple of minutes of your time and meet with you and your wife. I like to hear what you saw that evening. By the way, thank you for calling 911. A lot of people would have simply run the other way in that sort of difficult situation."

"I don't think we'll ever forget it, unfortunately."

"Would it be possible to talk with the two of you? I'd be happy to meet wherever you would feel most comfortable."

"Hang on just a minute. Let me check," he said. I could hear a brief conversation but couldn't make out what, exactly, was being said. Kennedy was back on the phone a moment later. "If you wouldn't mind meeting at our home, say 5:00 this evening."

"Sure, I can do that. What's your address?" I asked, even though I already had it. He gave me the address, and we said goodbye.

Thirty-four

I took Morton for a quick walk and headed over to Cornell's building. I had to park at the far end of the block. Once in the small lobby, I punched in 2-1-6, Cornell's apartment, on the off-chance his mother, Christine, might answer. She didn't.

I was about to phone Javis's unit when I happened to glance out the door. The red Tahoe was just pulling up to the curb on the wrong side of the street. I automatically touched the pistol tucked in my belt and breathed a little easier. I crossed my fingers and prayed Javis was being dropped off. Instead, the driver climbed out of the car. Just like Javis, his jeans hung below his rear. He gave the finger to whoever was inside the car and then proceeded to pull his jeans down even further and began to pee. When he was finished, he pulled his jeans up to just below his rear. He climbed back in behind the wheel, and the car just sat there, waiting.

A couple of minutes later, I heard a noise from the other side of the door. The door opened, and there was Javis. He got a strange look on his face and was about to side-step me.

"Oh, Javis, long time no see. How are things?" I asked, backing him up half a step.

"I know you?"

"Don't you remember? We met a long time ago," I lied. "Hey, what do you say we catch up? It's been a while."

He shook his head and said, "I ain't got time right now. A car with my pals is out there waiting for me." He attempted to step around me.

I placed a hand on his chest and said, "You should probably make time."

He tried to slap my hand away. I pushed him back into the hallway, staying right on top of him until I heard the door close behind me. "We need to talk, Javis. Your friend Cornell Thomas is locked up and being held for murder."

"I don't know anything about that. The police came and took him away. They found the gun in his bedroom. He had it hid under his pillow."

"Come on, Javis. You know that's not the way it went down."

"Yes, it is. It was even on the news. The gun was in his bedroom. It even had all the serial numbers filed off."

"You know, Javis, you just proved my point. No one knows about the serial numbers being filed off. Let me make a wild guess. Would this just happen to be the same gun you used stealing roses at Walker's Flowers? That takes a lot of balls, waving a gun at an unarmed woman in a flower shop. You're quite the man."

"Ahh," he screamed and swung at me. I blocked it and punched him in the nose. He staggered back and raised both hands to his nose. Blood oozed out over his fingers. "God, you didn't have to do that. You didn't have to hit me."

"You're going to get a lot worse if you try something like that again. I want you to come down to the police station with me and—Ahh," I groaned when he kicked me between the legs. I slowly slid along the wall down to the floor, gasping.

Javis took off out the door.

I took a couple of deep breaths, slowly rose to my feet, and stepped into the entrance lobby. Javis was waving his arms and running toward the red Tahoe. Someone inside the car opened the rear door. He jumped in, and the Tahoe sped up the street, skidded around the corner, and disappeared from sight. I leaned against the mailboxes built into the wall, closed my eyes, and took a number of deep breaths. I waited a couple of minutes before I looked up and down the street. Once I was convinced the Tahoe had gone, I made my way to my car at the far end of the block. I was still in pain as I drove back to the office.

I gingerly managed to climb the stairs and stepped into the office. Louie had a file spread out on his picnic table desk. He took one look at me and asked, "Are you okay?"

"I will be. Just getting my breath back is all."

"You better sit down, Dev. You're not looking so well."

"That little dip-shit, Javis kicked me right where it hurts."

"Javis, you finally found him?'

"For maybe half a minute. I gave him a bloody nose, and then when he looked like he was ready to start crying, I relaxed my guard, and that's when he kicked me. I ever find that little bastard, I intend to pay him back, big time. Any doubt I had about Javis being involved has been erased."

"Can I get you something?"

"Like what?" I groaned.

"I don't know, an ice pack or something."

"No, thanks, Louie, but I'll be okay. Just give me a couple of hours. Oh, God…"

I sat at my desk for the next twenty minutes and slowly recovered. All I wanted now was a rematch with Javis. I pulled out my cellphone and checked my contact list for 'Pain in the ass' and called.

After four rings, a voice answered, "Detective Manning."

"Yeah, Manning, Dev Haskell. I've been thinking. We should talk."

"Haskell? Thinking? Where did you learn that?"

"Do you want the information I have or not?"

"Dealing with unpleasant situations is part of my job description, Haskell. Why don't you come down here and we can—"

"No way. I want to meet in a public place. Somewhere I'll feel safe."

"Sorry, but it's policy, I can't meet with you in a sleazy bar."

"Manning, you want to set this case right, or do you want—"

"All right, all right. God. Against my better judgment, you tell me where and I'll be there."

"You know where Irvine Park is?"

"Do I know where—Yes, I know where Irvine Park is. A half-block from the Ramsey Mansion."

"I'll be there in thirty minutes."

"I can hardly wait to see you," Manning said.

As I disconnected, Louie looked at me and shook his head. "It's bad enough that Javis person tried to eliminate your chance of having children. Now, you're meeting with Detective Manning?"

"It's time. I wanted to have more to go on, but I've got enough to get things started. I just hope he listens."

"And if he doesn't?"

"Then I get to deal with this punk, Javis, on my own," I said and smiled.

Thirty-five

Irvine Park is a New England-style public square that was platted in 1849, pretty much the beginning of history for our city. The park is surrounded by some of the oldest homes. The area began a renovation in the 1970s to include a gorgeous fountain in the center of the park along with a gazebo and benches. It's the city's most popular park for a wedding.

My drive from the office wasn't quite ten minutes. I was feeling pretty much back to normal after being kicked by Javis and I took up a seat on one of the dozen benches surrounding the fountain. It wasn't five minutes later when a black Caprice parked on the opposite side of the park from me. The tires were black, no white wall. There was a spotlight attached to the car halfway up the front windshield. So much for being unmarked. I watched Manning step out of the car and heard the horn beep when he clicked the fob locking the doors. He glanced around, apparently checking for someone hiding in the bushes before crossing the street.

I watched as he approached, still glancing from side to side. His white shirt made his pink head appear just that much brighter. He gave another look around the park, just in case someone was hiding, and then sat down at the opposite end of the bench from me.

"So, Haskell. You wanted to meet, and here I am. What is it you want?"

"I want to talk about Cornell Thomas. We both know the kid is innocent."

"Where did you get that information?"

"Come on, Manning. I know you don't think he's guilty. I think I have an idea on who may have been involved."

"And just what proof do you have?" Manning asked, sounding anything but friendly.

"How about a video of him using the same gun in a robbery thirty minutes before your so-called anonymous phone call was made."

"What do you mean a video?"

"Just that, from a security camera. The video was sent to the department. No one bothered to follow up."

"You've seen it?"

"Not only have I seen it. I've got it on my phone. You want to watch it?"

Manning slid over next to me and said, "Play it for me."

I clicked on the link from Walker's Flowers, and the video began playing. Javis was holding the Glock 17 at a ninety-degree angle, shouting at Marilyn Walker.

"Tell me again when this was taken," Manning said.

"The morning after the shooting. It's from Walker's Flowers over on University Avenue. The kid holding the gun is named Trenton Javis. Those long-stemmed roses he stole, guess who got them?"

Manning shook his head, suggesting he didn't have any idea.

"Cornell's mother, Christine Thomas. And when Javis took the flowers over at 8:30 in the morning, Christine was in her bedroom getting dressed for work. Cornell ran down to the first floor to get the mail, so Javis was more or less on his own for two or three minutes. I'm pretty sure he hid the weapon, the Glock 17 he's holding in that security video. I think he's the one who hid it under the pillow. Oh, and just to make it a little crazier. Javis is in a gang. By the looks of things, I would guess he'd been recently made. Want to know what his nickname is?"

"What?" Manning asked, looking up at me.

"Flower Child."

"And you think he murdered the Larson girl as part of a gang initiation?"

"No, at least I'm not sure about that. I do think he made the anonymous call the next morning after hiding the gun under Cornell Thomas's pillow. He may know who killed her, but I can't see him doing it. One other thing. I reviewed the files you sent Martin Meyer, the defense attorney."

Manning nodded.

"That anonymous call, the caller says Cornell shot her and then ran off the porch. The medical examiner's report stated the shot distance was twenty-five to thirty feet. Oh, and Javis mentioned to me earlier today that the serial numbers on the Glock had been filed off. To my knowledge, that fact was never reported."

"No, we held that information back. It was never released," Manning said.

"That's pretty much all I know. I'll send you a copy of this video as soon as I get back to the office along with the department address it was originally sent to."

"You know where this Javis kid is?"

"Javis? He's with his buddies in a red Chevy Tahoe. They spent most of yesterday over on Jenks Avenue, just off of Payne."

"A gray house with a couple of thug wannabes sitting on the front porch?"

I nodded. "There were three of them out on the porch all day yesterday. Javis and four others climbed out of the Tahoe and spent the entire day in the house."

"We're familiar with the place. There's rumors of a new cocaine source. Those animals in the house are rumored to be the local distribution center."

"A new source? Where? How?"

"We don't know that yet." I shook my head. "What, Haskell, you know something?"

"Maybe bits and pieces. It all of a sudden makes sense, sort of, maybe. But it's a long story, and it would put the murder of Penny Larson at the center of everything."

"Tell me," Manning said.

"I got a call from a friend who has invested in a plastic recycling company, Recycled Industrial Plastics, Inc. RIP for short. They've got an office up on the thirty-fourth floor of the Wells Fargo building, a production office in Inver Grove that a guy actually lives in, and then a sort of warehouse full of empty plastic bottles."

"Is there a point to any of this?"

"Well, I just met with two women yesterday. As a matter of fact, they live in the house where Penny Larson was murdered." I went on to tell Manning about my breakfast meeting with Diane and Bea and their suspicions about RIP.

"And they're protesting against this company?"

"Yeah, because they think the plastic recycling is bogus and the real intention is to take over the drug trade in the city."

Manning pulled out his phone and said, "You mind if I make some calls? There are a couple other people who should hear this."

"Tell you what. You've got my phone number. If you want to set something up, that's fine with me. In the meantime, let me go back to my office and forward this tape from the flower shop to you and that address it was originally sent to."

He seemed to think about that for a moment and then said, "Yeah, okay. I'm going to try to put something

together in the next hour or two, so keep yourself available."

I nodded and began to walk back to my car.

"Oh, and Haskell. Nice job," Manning said.

"High praise coming from you. Thanks."

Thirty-six

I hurried back to the office. Louie was gone, and Morton was napping on his pillow. He opened one eye as I entered the office. As soon as he saw it was me, he took a deep breath and went back to sleep. I fired up my computer and sent a copy of the security video to Manning along with the police department email address where Walker's Flowers sent a copy of the video. I also included the apartment address for Javis, and I mentioned the red Tahoe, adding that, unfortunately, I didn't have a license plate number.

Thirty minutes later, Manning sent me a text message thanking me for the email. He mentioned a meeting tomorrow morning at 9:00 that he would like me to attend. I replied I would be there.

I phoned Martin Meyer and gave him an update. He seemed pleased with the information and told me to stay in touch. I debated calling Heidi but decided against it since I wasn't sure what, exactly, her relationship was with Russell Greeney, and I couldn't risk having her tell him anything.

I took Morton for a long walk around four and then took him home. I headed over to chat with the Kennedys. I arrived at their home on Iglehart ten minutes early. I debated removing the pistol from my belt and decided I would just untuck my shirt and cover it.

Thomas Kennedy answered the door. I pegged him at being in his mid-fifties. He had neatly trimmed white hair and wore bifocal glasses. He was wearing dark blue trousers and a starched white shirt. The suit coat and tie had been discarded.

"Mr. Kennedy? Hi, my name is Dev Haskell," I said as I stepped inside.

"Yes, we've been expecting you," he said as he closed the door behind me and held out his hand. "Come on back to the den. Amy and I are having a glass of wine. Can I interest you?"

"That would be great."

We walked past a nicely decorated living room, through a dining room, and into the kitchen. An open bottle of red wine sat on the counter. Kennedy pulled a wine glass from a cabinet, filled it, and handed it to me. I followed him into the den.

His wife Amy was seated on the couch. She had blonde hair and was wearing black slacks and a top with horizontal black and white stripes. She took a sip from her wine glass and set it on the coffee table. A wedge of what looked like brie cheese and round crackers sat on a wooden cutting board on the coffee table.

"Amy Kennedy," she said and held out her hand.

"Pleased to meet you. Dev Haskell. I want to thank you both for agreeing to talk with me. I'm sure you would like nothing better than to have this entire situation behind you."

"Please take a seat. How can we help?" Kennedy said.

"Well," I said as I sat down in a brown leather recliner. "As always, there are all sorts of questions that arise. I've read the police reports. I've spoken with the police, the defense attorney, and with Cornell Thomas, the young man accused of the shooting."

"And you think he's innocent?" Kennedy asked and took a sip of wine.

"I'm just trying to make sure the right individual, or individuals, are held accountable. Could you tell me what you saw that evening?"

The Kennedys looked at one another. Amy gave a slight nod to her husband. He began by saying, "In all honesty, there really isn't much to tell. We were on our evening walk. We've been doing it for the past couple of years."

"I had a cancer incident four years ago," Amy said. "Endometrial cancer. Fortunately, it was in the early stage, and we were able to get into the Mayo clinic. That got our attention, and we've been busy exercising for our health ever since."

"We adjusted our diets, exercise on a regular basis. Amy runs every other day. We walk three miles every other evening, and we pass the house on Marshall at the end of our walk. As we walked past that night, Amy glanced at the house and said, 'Tom, does that look right to you?' I glanced over, and I could see a leg lying on the porch floor. A black shoe was next to it. I stared for a bit but couldn't detect any movement."

"Tom called, 'hello' a couple of times, and then he told me to wait on the sidewalk. I'm embarrassed to admit it, but my first thought was someone had too much to drink."

"I kept calling as I approached, thinking this didn't seem right. Of course, I never got a response. I remember it as if it happened five minutes ago. There are four steps up to the porch. I was on the second step when I saw the woman, a young girl actually, and I told Amy to stay where she was."

"Well, I wasn't about to do that," Amy said. "So I hurried up to Tom. Oh my, the blood, it was all over the porch floor.

"There was a folding lawn chair lying on its side, and my first thought was she's fallen out of the chair and hit her head on the railing. But at the same time, I knew that wasn't the case. I called 911. Amy rang the doorbell to see if anyone was home. I think the police arrived in four or five minutes."

"It was four minutes," Amy said and nodded.

"It felt like four hours. I checked her wrist for a pulse. There wasn't one. She was obviously dead, and at that point," his voice started to break. He cleared his throat and took a deep breath. "At that point, I just wanted to get Amy away. We stepped off the porch, and the police finally arrived.”

“Did you see anyone around? A car speeding away? Something? Anything?”

They both shook their head. “No, up until that moment, it was a normal quiet evening. We never heard a gunshot if that’s your next question,” Amy said.

“It probably took me twice as long to tell you this as the actual event. The whole thing couldn’t have been more than a minute. My understanding is she had been dead for at least a half-hour, and no one driving past would have been able to spot her. We just happened to walk past, and Amy glanced over at the right moment to see the foot.”

“Are you aware of any activity going on at that house?”

“Activity? You mean like wild parties and that sort of thing? No. I don’t know how long it’s been a rental. But we’re not aware of anything,” Amy said.

“We know a couple who live two doors down. They’ve never mentioned anything,” Tom said. “It’s a busy street. A number of busses are up and down the street. I guess one passes by maybe every twenty minutes or so. Lots of traffic heading into or coming from Minneapolis. A single gunshot wouldn’t necessarily be noticeable. I guess all the girls work in the service industry when they’re not in school.”

“We went to the girl’s funeral. It was up in Saint Cloud. We wanted to say something to her family, but in the end, we, we just couldn't," Amy said as a tear rolled down her cheek.

"Very sad," Tom said as he reached over and took hold of Amy's hand.

We were quiet for a long moment. I was drawing a blank as far as any other questions to ask. "We're all very fortunate to live the lives we have, and this awful incident…" I couldn't come up with anything else and shook my head. "Thank you for caring enough to see if she was all right and then for making the call to the police."

"We can't believe this happened in our neighborhood," Amy said.

I set my nearly full wine glass on the coffee table and said, "Thank you for your time. I'm sorry to resurrect this incident again. I know you just want to get it behind you."

"Will that ever really happen?" Tom asked.

Thirty-seven

I drove back to the office. Louie wasn't in, and Morton was at home. I made some brief notes, turned off the coffee pot, and got it ready for the morning, so all I'd have to do would be turn it on. I debated going home and decided I'd check in with Louie over at The Spot.

He was seated on his usual stool at the end of the bar. As I walked in, Mike leaned over the bar, looked for Morton, and asked, "How did you find your way over here without Morton?"

"He wanted to see if I could make it on my own."

"Get you a beer?"

"Yeah, better give Louie another drink, too."

"Coming up," he said.

"What'd you do with Morton?" Louie asked as I pulled out the stool next to him and sat down.

"He's taking it easy at home. How'd your day go?"

"Same thing, different day. How about you?"

I told him about meeting with Detective Manning and that I'd spoken with the Kennedys, although I didn't go into any detail. "I'm getting together with Manning

and some other folks down at the police station tomorrow morning. I'll see what they have to say. I'm hoping
we can get Cornell Thomas released sooner rather than
later. Manning seemed to imply their air-tight case suddenly isn't quite so air-tight."

"Any idea who's responsible?"

"Maybe a general idea, but nothing specific. Hopefully, after the meeting tomorrow, we'll have a little better direction."

Mike set my beer on the bar and a fresh glass in front
of Louie. I pulled all the cash from my wallet, a five-
dollar bill and four ones, and handed it to him.

"Thanks," Louie said and took a sip. We chatted for
maybe twenty minutes, when my phone rang.

"Hi, Becky," I said, then nodded at Louie and
stepped out the side door.

"Hi, Dev, hope I'm not interrupting anything."

"No, not at all. Everything okay?"

"Oh yeah, in fact, the reason I'm calling is I went
past this fun-looking little restaurant the other day called
the Dog House. It's got a patio, and you can bring your
dog in there and order dinner. Are you familiar with the
place?"

"I am. It's been a while since I've been there, but
their specialty is hot dogs. They've got about a dozen
versions of the things. I've taken Morton there. If you
bring your dog, they give them a dog biscuit."

"Oh, that really sounds fun. Would you be interested
in going there?"

"Yeah, I'd love to. You thinking of bringing Princess?"

"I was if that would be okay."

"Sure, when were you thinking?"

"Tonight, if you can make it. If not, maybe tomorrow or the next night."

"Yeah, I think we can do tonight. I'm just finishing up an appointment and—"

"Oh, I didn't mean to interrupt."

"Not a problem. I've got to grab Morton at home. You want to meet there in an hour, or we can pick you guys up?"

"Those two in a car together? Mmm, bad idea, I think. Let's meet there in an hour. First one there gets a table out on the patio."

"I'll see you there," I said, disconnected, and hurried back into The Spot.

"Everything okay?" Louie asked as he watched me drain what was left of my beer.

"Yeah, Becky's having a problem moving some stuff. Things are just too heavy. I told her I'd give her a hand." I set my empty glass on the bar. "I'll catch you tomorrow. You going to be in?"

"Yeah, I should be," Louie said.

"I've got the coffee all set to go. All you have to do is turn it on."

"I'd better write that down," Louie said as I headed out the door.

I hurried to my car and then thought, as nice as it was for the Dog House to give a biscuit to the dogs, that would only keep them occupied for a couple of seconds. I climbed behind the wheel and headed up to Rooster's.

Taffy was working. There were six people in line ahead of me, two couples and two guys. The couples must have been first-timers because they pondered over the menu posted on a 4 x 5 sheet of plywood attached to the wall above the counter. Eventually, they made a decision and stepped off to the side. The two guys were regulars and knew what they wanted.

I stepped up to the counter. "Hi, Dev," Taffy said. "Your usual?"

"Actually, no, I just wanted to get two bones if I could."

She smiled and said, "Coming right up." She stepped into the kitchen and was back thirty seconds later. She handed me the paper bag and said, "No charge."

"You sure?"

"Positive. Say hi to Morton for me."

I pulled out my wallet to give her a tip, opened it, and realized I'd spent the last of my cash at The Spot. "Oh, sorry."

"Don't worry about it, Dev."

"I'll catch you next time. Thanks, Taffy," I said and hurried out the door.

As I left, one of the people waiting said, "Do you believe that guy?"

I drove home to get changed and pick up Morton. I slipped on a reasonably clean Hawaiian print shirt with beer bottles lined up around the bottom of the shirt and a less wrinkled pair of jeans. I debated again about the gun but ended up sticking it in my waistband and letting the Hawaiian print shirt hang out. I gave myself a quick shave just to neaten up. I wiped the shave cream off the shirt collar, and we headed out to the car.

Morton hopped into the back seat. He immediately stuck his head into the front and sniffed the bag from Roosters. He knew exactly what was in it, and his tail was going a mile a minute by the time I climbed in on the driver's side.

"No, Morton, sit. Sit, Morton," I said then grabbed the bag and placed it on the floor of the passenger seat.

Morton gave a little whine, but he settled down and we drove to the Dog House. The place is in a two-story brick building. 'DOG HOUSE' in red neon letters with an image of a dog at either end runs back and forth across the front of the building. The front door is surrounded by white wood trim resembling the entrance to a doghouse. I grabbed the bag from Roosters and immediately got Morton's undivided attention. As I let Morton out of the backseat, I caught a black Prius driving past out of the corner of my eye. By the time I focused on the license plate, it was too far down the street to read. We headed toward a side gate that led onto the patio. As we entered the patio, I looked around for Becky and Princess but didn't see them.

"Hi, need some help?" a guy in a white apron asked.

"Yeah, looking for friends, but I think we're the first ones here. Can I get a table?"

"How many will there be?"

"Myself, a woman, and two dogs."

"That's perfect. We've got one table left. This one right here," he said, pointing to a table just inside the gate. If you want to grab it, I'll be back with menus and dog biscuits."

"Thank you," I said. I settled into a chair. Morton took up a position next to me and stared at the bag from Rooster's. The table was round with a glass top and an umbrella in the center. I counted a total of fifteen tables on the patio. Maybe half of them had a dog nearby. The waiter was back a moment later with two dog biscuits and menus.

"Here you go," he said, placing the menus on the table then setting a dog biscuit on each menu. "Get you something from the bar?"

"Yeah," I said, glancing at the menu. "I think we'll start with the salsa and chips, and better give me a pitcher of your IPA and two glasses.

"Coming right up."

Morton was up on all fours with his tail wagging. I tossed him one of the biscuits. He caught it in mid-air and devoured it in three quick bites.

Just as the waiter delivered the salsa, chips, and beer, Becky and Princess stepped out onto the patio from inside the restaurant. I gave a wave to catch their attention, and they headed in our direction. Morton was on his feet again with his tail wagging the moment he saw Princess.

"Perfect timing. The beer just arrived," I said.

I got a peck on the cheek from Becky. As she settled into her chair, she said, "We'll see how it goes with these two."

"I brought a secret weapon," I said and nodded at the bag.

"Don't tell me, a bone?"

I shook my head. "No, two bones. One for each, otherwise there would be trouble. Why don't you give Princess that biscuit? Once she's finished with it, I'll give them the bones, and hopefully, we'll have the evening more or less to ourselves. Can I pour you a beer?"

"Yes, please," she said and moved her beer mug toward the pitcher.

I filled both our mugs. We toasted one another and sat down. Both Morton and Princess were focused on the bag from Roosters.

"Will you look at these two. All right already, here," I said, dumping the bones onto the patio. They each snapped up a bone and then moved a couple of feet apart just to make sure they wouldn't have to share. We chatted for a good half-hour. We ordered dinner, and our hotdogs arrived ten minutes later. It was turning out to be the perfect evening. We were laughing and telling each other stories. Morton and Princess were focused on their bones. Becky ordered a second pitcher of beer. The evening held great promise. Life was good.

Thirty-eight

T he first indication I had that things might not be going my way was when the gate opened, and three guys with jeans pulled down beneath their rear ends stepped onto the patio.

One of them, the largest of the group, pointed at me. "You," he said and wiggled his index finger at me, suggesting I follow him.

"I don't think so," I said.

Becky got a worried look on her face and said, "Dev?"

"It's okay. I'll handle this. Guys, I think you better leave. There are security cameras taking your picture right now."

The other two idiots quickly looked around for the cameras.

I began to stand as the big guy raised his strappy white t-shirt, exposing a pistol stuck into his blue and white striped boxer shorts.

"Take it easy, man," I said a second before he hit me, knocking me backward. I fell into my chair and tumbled onto the patio. Becky suddenly grabbed our empty beer pitcher and slammed it into the side of the guy's head. One of the other idiots began to pull a pistol from his boxers. Becky grabbed him by the wrist with her left hand, stretched his arm out, and slammed the palm of her right hand into his elbow. There was an audible crack just before his pistol fired. Fortunately, it was pointed toward the sky. She tore the pistol from his hand as the third guy, standing there wide-eyed, began to run toward the gate. Unfortunately, his second step kicked Morton's bone. Morton attacked, biting his way up the guy's leg. He tried to pull Morton off, and that was when Princess clamped onto his arm and wasn't about to let go.

"You okay?" I asked Becky. I picked the two pistols up from the patio and handed her one. "Shoot them if they move."

"I might just shoot them anyway."

At this point, everyone on the patio was fleeing inside the restaurant. Morton and Princess were growling at the guy they'd chewed up. His leg and arm were bleeding. The guy Becky slammed with the empty beer pitcher was still unconscious. The fool with the damaged elbow was leaning against the fence with his eyes closed, whimpering.

I heard a crashing sound coming from the street and looked out the gate. The red Tahoe had just backed into the car parked behind it and now raced forward, smashing into the car parked in front of it. Surprise, surprise, Javis was behind the wheel. I pulled my pistol from my belt and opened the gate.

Javis saw me coming and slammed into the car behind him a second time. I aimed my pistol at his rear tire and fired. A hiss and a quickly flattening tire responded. I took four steps and fired into the front tire. The Tahoe began leaning to the right. I waved my pistol. Javis shook his head and raised his hands. I yanked the passenger door open.

"Don't shoot. Don't shoot. I thought we was just gettin' dinner," Javis pleaded.

"Turn off the car and slide onto the passenger seat."

"Don't shoot. Honest. I told them not to do this. I told them—"

"Turn off the car, now. Or I promise I will shoot your worthless ass."

"Okay. Okay, man. There, it's off. See, I did just what you wanted."

I motioned with my index finger just like the thug had done to me a minute ago.

"Okay, okay, stay cool, dude. I'm doing just what you want. Coming your way," he said as he hoisted himself over the console and onto the passenger seat.

"Let's join your friends," I said. I grabbed him by the t-shirt and pulled him out onto the ground. "You carrying?" I shouted as I patted him down using my left hand. My right hand held my pistol up against the back of his neck.

"No, no, I ain't got a gun. Honest. I'm telling you the truth."

"You try anything, you're dead," I said and pulled him to his feet just as I heard a siren heading in our direction.

Becky kept the gun pointed at the three thugs. The guy she'd hit with the beer pitcher was more or less conscious and sitting against the wrought iron fence. The left side of his face was in the process of swelling and changing from red to purple. The idiot the dogs attacked was still bleeding, but Morton and Princess had returned to their bones. He tried to move once, but Princess wasn't having any of it and growled. The guy with what was probably a dislocated elbow was holding his arm and still whimpering.

Javis sat down next to the guy with the purple face.

A cop car pulled up in front. I could hear the siren from a second car coming from the opposite direction. "Maybe put the gun down, and I'll keep an aim on these idiots," I said and slowly lowered Becky's arm toward the glass-topped table. "Where'd you learn those moves? You're really good."

"I've got a black belt in Karate. I have to be honest, Dev, this is not my idea of a fun night."

"That makes two of us," I said just as two cops stepped onto the patio with their guns drawn. "Drop your weapon, now," one of them yelled at me. I set the weapon on the table and raised my hands. "Down on your knees," he said, and I knelt down.

"That guy was trying to kill us. You need to arrest that dude," Javis said.

"We'll get to you in a moment. The smart move would probably be to shut up until then," the cop said as he handcuffed my hands behind my back, then helped me to my feet and sat me in a chair.

Two cops came in through the gate. One of them was a woman. One of the cops said, "Francie," and nodded at Becky.

"Ma'am," she said to Becky. "I'm going to ask you to assume the position. Just going to check you for a weapon. Do you have any sharp objects on your person, a syringe, knife, or—"

"I've got my car keys in my front pocket and my cell phone." The woman patted Becky down and then had her sit in a chair next to me.

We'd been seated for maybe five minutes when Detective Manning came in through the gate. He took one look at me and the four guys leaning against the fence and shook his head.

"Hey, Manning. You think you could get them to take these cuffs off me so I can finish my dinner?"

He closed his eyes for a brief moment as if he couldn't believe it and said something to one of the uniformed cops. The cop came over and undid the handcuffs.

Manning stepped over and said, "What'd you get yourself into this time, Haskell?"

"We were just eating hotdogs when these fools came in, pulled guns, and tried to take us away."

He looked at Becky. "Ma'am?"

"Yes, that's pretty much it. Well, except for the at-tempted assaults, at gunpoint, I might add. One of them, that cry baby holding his arm, shot at us. Fortunately, he's a lousy shot."

"She hit me. She, she broke my arm, and it really hurts."

Becky shook her head. "I didn't break your arm. I should have, but I didn't."

"This have anything to do with Cornell Thomas?" Manning asked.

"Yeah, it does. The guy I told you about, Trenton Javis, that's him there," I said and pointed at Javis.

"Hey, I don't even know you, Dude. You tried to attack me in my building. I had to defend myself."

"He's the one on the videotape from the flower shop," I said.

"Yeah, I recognize him. What about these other three?" Manning asked.

"All from the same gang. I have a feeling, if you suggest some options, they may be willing to cooperate."

Becky and I were interviewed. I ate my hotdog as I talked with the officers. Becky didn't seem all that happy. I suppose I couldn't really blame her. Who likes to have their dinner interrupted by someone waving a gun around?

Manning let Becky and Princess go home. He wanted me down at the station. Becky offered to take Morton home and told me I could pick him up in the morning. I followed Manning to the police station in my car. He pulled into the secure parking lot that had a twenty-four-hour guard, and I was able to follow him into the lot. Once up in his office, he sat me down at his desk and started asking questions.

"So what's up with these guys? You've got three guys with felonies, one of whom has an outstanding warrant for failure to make a court appearance, and they're interrupting your hotdog dinner? By the way, you must be a hell of a date, Haskell. Did you make the Desjardins woman pay?"

"Don't sell her short, Manning. If it weren't for her, you'd be trying to interview me in the city morgue."

"So, what did they want?"

"They didn't say, specifically. But I'm sure it's because I fingered Javis for planting that gun under Cornell Thomas's pillow. Like I told you this afternoon, this is bigger than just the Penny Larson murder. I'm not trying to make light of that situation. These guys are looking to do distribution for the two idiots running RIP, Inc. I think you've got a pretty good chance of getting that information and more from these fools."

Thirty-nine

It was sometime after one in the morning when Javis was brought into the interrogation room. Manning and a female detective named Sandy Lindell from the gang unit were seated at the steel table. Two officers escorted Javis to his chair then attached his handcuffs to a fourteen-inch chain that was bolted to the steel table.

I was in the viewing room with another officer from the gang unit. He hadn't bothered to introduce himself, and at that hour of the morning, I didn't really care.

Javis appeared to be nervous. Suddenly the 'romance' of being an important guy in a gang had gone out the window, and now he was sitting in front of Manning and Lindell all by himself.

Manning was his usual caustic self, and I was thankful it wasn't me seated across from him. Once Javis was seated and the cops who escorted him in had left, Manning waited for what seemed an eternity before he said anything. In actuality, it was only ninety seconds.

"So, Mr. Javis. We have you on charges of assault. Assault with a deadly weapon. Reckless endangerment.

A number of driving offenses. Driving without a license. Attempted murder. Filing a false—"

"No, wait. Hold on a minute. I wasn't in there when they did all that. I thought they were just stopping to get hot dogs. Everyone was hungry and—"

"Not what we heard from your pals. Boogie Monroe told us you followed Haskell to the Dog House. You intended to kidnap Mr. Haskell. You drove the car, a red Tahoe, didn't you?"

"Yeah, I was driving, but I didn't go in there. I thought they was just getting dinner."

Manning nodded and said, "I know what you mean. Say, you mind if I call you Trenton?"

Javis shook his head, "No, that's okay. That's my name."

"Good. You can call me detective or sir." Javis nodded. "So, like I was saying, we know you were driving, even though you don't have a license. In fact, you're going to be held for reckless endangerment. Smashing into two vehicles, twice. Right there, we're looking at jail time, and we haven't even gotten to the serious charges. You see, Trenton, you knew they were going there to get Mr. Haskell, didn't you?"

"Well, see I—"

"Let me give you a hint, Trenton. They told us all about you. Oh, yeah, in fact, forgive me, but do you want to be called Trenton, or would you prefer to be called Flower Child? You know on account of the roses and all."

Javis looked like he was about to say something, but nothing came out of his mouth.

"Trenton, we know about the roses. It's funny. It wouldn't be that big a deal except that you took them at gunpoint. We call that armed robbery. Of course, we'll probably bump that charge up to attempted murder. After all, you did threaten the woman at Walker's Flowers with a gun. What do you think, Detective Lindell?"

"What I think is, right there, you're looking at ten years behind bars, Javis. What we'll probably do is charge you with that first. You'll go to court, and it'll be a slam dunk for us. We got it on film. You waving the gun around and running out the door with a dozen roses. We know you took the roses to Christine Thomas. When you did that, since she was in her bedroom and her son Cornell had gone down to get the mail, you planted that pistol under his pillow. That makes you an accessory to murder. We're talking more like thirty years with that."

"But I didn't shoot her. Boogie did. I never got out of the car. I didn't know they were going to shoot her. He gave me the gun and told me I had to get rid of it and, and I didn't know what to do and then all of a sudden, it just kind of popped into my head."

"See, the problem there is, that's what you say, but Boogie told us he didn't do that. Your word against his, and well, we just gave you the list of some of the crimes you've committed. I'm not sorry to be the one to tell you, but you better get used to a jail cell."

"But Boogie is the one who shot her, not me," he said and started to cry.

"That's what you say. But Boogie said that you shot her, and he didn't."

"No, Boogie, shot her. Honest, I'm telling you's the truth."

"That's what you say, Trenton," Manning said and shook his head. "But, then there's the problem of your phone call the next morning telling us Cornell Thomas shot her and that the gun was under his pillow."

"I didn't make that phone call."

"You sure? Because we've got a recording of the phone call, and it sure sounds like you. We'll be making a voice comparison later, but my guess is you made that call. Once we prove you lied to us, well, anything you say is basically gonna get tossed out. You might want to take a second or two and think about this. You're looking at doing thirty years. You'll be almost fifty by the time you get out."

Javis shook his head. "They made me make that phone call. Told me what I had to say."

"And you were there when she was shot. You made the phone call. You are an accessory to the murder of Penny Larson, and you are going to be tried as an adult," Manning said, his voice almost to the point of but not quite shouting.

Javis had tears running down both cheeks. "She was going to go to you guys. Tell you about the drug deal. The gang is planning to make all kinds of money, and we, I mean they, they just had to get rid of the bitch before she talked. Boogie got paid a couple grand, and he bought his girlfriend a gold chain. A fancy gold chain with diamonds.”

“Who is his girlfriend?” Manning asked.

“Her name is Melanie. She lives with her sister in the Skyline Tower on St. Anthony Avenue.”

“She have a last name?” Manning asked.

“I don’t know, honest,” Javis said, shaking his head.

“So you drove Boogie and his pals to get Dev Haskell. Why?”

“Because they told me I had to drive. I didn’t want to do it, but they said I had to. They made me do it.”

“Yeah, I get that, but why? Why Haskell? What did he do?”

“He’s been following these two guys. I don’t know their names, but they’re rich guys. They’re buying the cocaine, and they were going to let us distribute it.”

“And you don’t know their names?”

He shook his head. “I heard they got a place somewhere on the river.”

“Would you happen to know where this place is?”

“No, I don’t. But I bet I could find out if you let me go,” Javis said and sniffled.

Manning nodded at Lindell. She stood, walked to the door, and pressed a button. A moment later, the door opened, and two officers stepped in.

“I get to go home?” Javis asked.

Manning shook his head. "I don't think so. You're going to be charged with armed robbery at Walker's Flowers for right now, and we'll just have to see if you're willing to work with us before we decide what to do with all the other charges." Manning nodded at the two uniformed officers. "Lock him up. We'll touch base tomorrow."

"But wait, I thought you were gonna let me go home. I can't stay here," Javis said and began to cry as they led him out of the room.

Manning turned, glanced at the tinted windows in the viewing room, and gave a thumbs up. I wanted to talk to him and after a moment went out of the viewing room, but I never found him.

I ended up going home. After our patio experience at the Dog House, I triple-checked all my windows and the front and back door to make sure they were locked. It was after 2:00 in the morning before I crawled into bed. I set my alarm and immediately fell asleep.

Forty

The alarm woke me the following morning. I debated trying to catch another hour, all the while knowing that wouldn't work. I crawled out of bed, looked around for Morton, and then remembered Becky had taken him to her house. I hit the shower, had a dish of yogurt with honey for breakfast, and went to the office. Louie wasn't in yet. I turned on the coffee and fired up my computer.

I checked the news stations and YouTube but never found any mention of our incident last night at the Dog House. Louie arrived a half-hour later. I poured him a mug of coffee while he caught his breath after climbing the stairs.

After a couple of sips, he said, "Where's Morton?"

"He spent the night at Becky's," I said and went on to tell him about last night's incident.

"These guys pulled a gun on you?"

"Yeah, if it wasn't for Becky clocking the guy with the empty beer pitcher, I don't know what would have happened. Certainly, nothing good."

"And they're all arrested?"

"Yeah, at least for the time being. I'm meeting with Detective Manning at 9:00. I'm guessing they'll be going after this gang, and hopefully, Greeney and Lanzo, the RIP guys who bankrolled this drug deal, will get locked up."

"Have you mentioned any of this to Heidi?"

I shook my head. "I don't think she would intentionally alert them, but I didn't want to take the chance. I could see her calling Greeney and asking him if what I'd told her was true. It's just better if she doesn't know, at least for the time being."

"Sounds like a real mess," Louie said.

"Yeah, I'm afraid so."

I was down at the police station ten minutes early for our 9:00 meeting. "How can I help you?" the sergeant at the front desk asked me.

"Hi, my name is Dev Haskell. I'm here to attend a meeting with Detective Norris Manning in Homicide."

The guy gave me a funny look for a second and then picked up the phone. He held the phone to his ear for a bit and then said, "No answer. You sure you have the right time and day? I'm pretty sure he's out at the moment. In fact, I know he is."

"Out? Did something come up and—tell you what. Give Aaron LaZelle a ring. I can talk to him."

He shook his head. "LaZelle is out. He's with Manning, actually."

"Are they running an operation? I was supposed to be involved and—"

"All I can tell you is they're out at the moment."

"What about Sandy Lindell? She's with the gang—"

"She's out too."

"What the… They're all out. Where are they?"

"I'm afraid I'm not at liberty to give you that information."

"But I'm—okay, never mind. Could I leave a business card for LaZelle and Manning?" I asked.

"That you can do."

I pulled out my wallet, handed him two business cards, and went back to my car. I drove over to Becky's to get Morton. I parked in front of her house. It was a nice morning, sunny, with a pleasant temperature. The drapes were pulled on the front window. No one was on the porch. I climbed the steps and rang the doorbell. I heard a bark inside and some footsteps. Someone was at the door. A moment later, I heard the security chain on the door being removed, the door lock snapped, and Becky opened the door.

"Oh, hi Dev. Here to get Morton?"

"Yeah, thanks so much for bringing him home last night. I didn't get out of the police station until close to 2:00 this morning."

"Oh, God. Well, if it's any consolation, I think I slept off and on in fifteen-minute increments."

"Oh, I'm sorry to hear that." Morton suddenly poked his head around Becky. "Hey, Morton, good morning." I bent down to scratch him behind the ears and asked, "How did he do?"

"Not a problem. They were involved with their bones."

"Thanks again for taking him. I feel like I owe you dinner. Would you two like to come over this evening? I was thinking of maybe doing some steaks on the grill. We could just relax. My backyard is fenced, so we could all just take it easy and—"

"Oh, thanks, but I think we'll just keep a low profile here, if you don't mind."

"No, whatever you want to do. Umm, thanks again for your help last night. If you hadn't been there, I don't—"

"Yeah, I'm just glad everything worked out. I should probably get back to work here. Umm, you take care, Dev," she said and opened the door a little wider so Morton could step out onto the porch. As soon as he was out of the house, she closed the door. I heard the lock snap and the security chain being put back in place.

So much for a friendly conversation, I thought, and we headed to the car.

"That was fast. Back already?" Louie said when we stepped into the office.

"Yeah, Manning and everyone were gone, so there wasn't a meeting. I went over to grab Morton, thinking I could scam some coffee from Becky, but she clearly didn't want to talk. As soon as he stepped out onto the porch, she said goodbye and locked the door."

"Maybe give her some time to take it easy and process the events of last night, Dev. It has to be pretty traumatic for her. She certainly didn't expect something like that to happen."

"Yeah, I guess." Morton had settled onto his pillow and looked like a mid-morning nap was in his immediate future. I sat down at my desk and phoned Walker's Flowers. My call was answered on the third ring. "Walker's Flowers," a woman said, and I immediately pictured Marilyn Walker in the light blue t-shirt.

"Hi, is this Marilyn?"

"Yes," she said, drawing out her response.

"Marilyn, Dev Haskell, I'd like to order some flowers."

"Oh, hi Dev, how nice to hear from you. What are you thinking of, roses?"

"Actually, no, some sort of nice bouquet for around forty or fifty bucks. Do you make deliveries?"

"We do. Now it wouldn't be delivered until this afternoon if that's okay."

"Yeah, that would work out just fine. You choose what kind of flowers." I gave her Becky's address and then my credit card number.

"Now, I'll enclose a card with the delivery. Would you like to leave a personal message?"

"A personal message, I think just put 'thank you for saving the day' and then an exclamation point."

"All right, Dev. Now that will go out this afternoon. Anything else I can help you with?"

"No, I think that will do it for right now. Nice to talk with you, Marilyn. Oh, the guy that stole those roses a couple of weeks ago has been arrested. I sent that security video to a detective regarding another matter. He's in jail as we speak."

"Oh, that's wonderful news. Thank you. You've made my day. I tell you what, no charge on these flowers."

"That's very nice of you, Marilyn, but don't do that. Charge me."

"Really? I mean, I think we owe you and—"

"No, charge me, and thank Vince for sending the security video to me."

"Thank you, Dev. I'll make sure this woman gets some wonderful flowers."

"Thank you, Marilyn," I said and disconnected.

"You better knock that stuff off, or someone's going to make the mistake of thinking you're a nice guy," Louie said. "What kind of flowers did your order?"

"I just told her to choose some."

"Did you suggest a color, red, yellow, blue, white, or maybe something pink?" Louie's comment got me thinking for a long moment. "Hey, did you hear what I just said?"

"What? Oh, yeah, sorry when you said those colors, it got me thinking. I was gonna check on something, and I don't think I ever did." I pulled a file from the small stack on my desk, notes on Cornell's case. There was a sheet from a yellow legal pad in the file. The note read,

'College Club. Check photo of bride with groomsmen in different color tuxedos.'

"Hey, you going to be here for a bit?" I asked.

"I'm here all morning," Louie said.

"I have to run and check on something. Shouldn't take more than an hour."

"Go on. I'll just be typing away," Louie said.

I hurried out the door, cursing myself for forgetting. I drove up to Lexington Avenue, took a right, and drove a mile to Summit Avenue. The Governor's mansion and the College Club were a block and a half down Summit. I pulled into the circular drive in front of the College Club, parked, and hurried inside.

A woman carrying what looked like two crystal vases was just coming down the elegant staircase. "Hi, can I help you?" she asked as she set the vases on an antique buffet.

"Yeah, I hope so. There was a wedding here a couple of weeks ago. The groomsmen all wore different colored tuxedos. I wanted to talk to the photographer at that wedding."

She smiled and laughed. "Oh yeah, hard to forget. It was really cute, the tuxes and the matching shoes."

"Would you happen to have the name of the photographer?"

"Not off the top of my head, but I'm sure I'd have it in the file. Follow me," she said and reached for the vases.

"How about I carry the vases?"

"Oh, would you mind? They're heavy."

"I'd be happy to do it," I said and picked up the vases. She was right. They were heavy. I followed her down the hall and into a large room. We walked down two steps and onto the wooden floor.

"If you would just place the vases on the bar, that would be great. I'll be back in just a moment," she said and hurried out of the room.

I set the vases on the bar. I looked at the room and the small stage at one end. It suddenly dawned on me that this was the ballroom. Four or five round tables were folded up and leaning against a far wall. Six or seven stacks of chairs stood next to the tables. A set of double doors led outside onto a porch that overlooked the back of the Governor's mansion. I walked over to see if I could maybe catch a glimpse of the Governor himself, but the only thing I saw was a pair of squirrels chasing one another around an oak tree.

"Here we go," the woman called as she entered the room. I found an extra business card, Gregory Preston," she said and handed me the business card. "He's very good."

"Oh, this is great. Thank you so much."

"Anything else I can help you with?"

"No, this will do it. I'll give him a call."

She walked me to the front door, maybe just to be sure I really left.

Forty-one

The Preston Pictures studio was over in the Merriam Park neighborhood, not all that far from where I was. Rather than call, I drove over and parked in front of the two-story brick building. Preston Pictures was one of four businesses in the building. They were located up on the second floor. I knocked on the wooden door, opened it, and stepped into an office. All four walls in the place were covered with framed photos, lots and lots of weddings, a few babies, and a couple of outdoor events.

"Hello," a voice called, and a moment later, a guy stepped out of a back room. "Hi, what can I do for you?"

"Greg Preston?" I asked.

"Guilty as charged," he said.

"Hi. My name is Dev Haskell. I'm interested in a photo you took back on May fifteenth. It was a wedding at the College Club. All the groomsmen were in different colored tuxes."

He smiled and said, "Oh yeah, they got a lot of the attention that would usually go to the bride. Fortunately, she had her head screwed on right, and since the tuxes were her idea, she didn't care."

"Would you happen to have any of those images?"

"I've got a number of them, all digital, mind you. What's this about?"

I went onto explain Cornell's situation, and he smiled.

"I'm pretty sure I've still got the original shots. I Photoshopped them to remove background clutter. God bless Photoshop. Step into my studio, and I'll bring them up on the screen."

I followed him into the back room. A lighting booth was off to one side. More framed photos covered the walls. Three large desktop computers were positioned on a counter. He sat on a stool and turned on the computer. A moment later, he brought up a file and clicked on it.

"Catherine Gibbons and Chuck Van Sistine, if I remember," he said and scrolled through a series of items. He eventually stopped and clicked on a box, another file immediately appeared, and he scrolled down a long list.

"Whoops, I think this is what you're looking for." He brought up an image of a lovely bride in a long wedding dress holding a bouquet of flowers. She was flanked by three men on either side, each one wore a different colored tux with matching shoes. I stared at the image for a long moment and said, "That's incredible. I mean, it really is."

"Yeah, I gave them a very nice discount in order to get their permission to use this in advertisements. I'm having the image framed as we speak, so it should be on the wall out there by early next week."

I studied the background. Cornell wasn't in it, nor was anyone else for that matter. "I'm actually looking for a guy who would be running in the background."

"Oh, yeah, that's right. This is the Photoshopped version. Let me bring up the originals." He clicked on something, and a half-dozen smaller images appeared. He clicked on three of them, and there was Cornell with a smiling face as he glanced at the backs of the wedding party. There was no question it was him.

"Oh, thank God. You've got him. That's him. That's Cornell. Can I get a copy? I'll pay you."

He chuckled at that. "It's cost-prohibitive. Tell you what, I'll print off two copies of each. I'd like to use your name and advertise the fact that, along with weddings, I can also do a jail release."

I handed him a business card and offered to sign a contract if he wanted. He printed off two copies of each photo. I thanked him profusely and headed back to the office.

Forty-two

I arrived back at the office thrilled with six 8 x 10 images of Cornell running past the College Club. The date and time of day, 20:51, which meant 8:51 p.m., was in the lower righthand corner in fluorescent green numbers. Louie was just loading his laptop into a computer bag as I stepped into the office.

"You heading out?" I asked.

"Yeah, with any luck, I'll be back before 3:00. You get what you were looking for?"

"Yeah, better than I could hope. I might be able to spring Cornell this afternoon."

"Oh, fantastic. Hey, gotta run. Catch you later," Louie said and hurried down the stairs. I heard him groan as he made his way down to the first floor. Then watched him waddle across the street to his Ford Fiesta. A black, sooty cloud erupted from his tailpipe when he started the car. He waited for a bus to pass and then drove up the street.

I placed calls to Aaron Lazelle and Manning and ended up leaving messages in both instances. I tried calling Heidi and left a message. I decided a personal visit to Heidi might be the better idea. I grabbed the folder with the photos of Cornell running past the wedding, put Morton in the back seat, and we drove over to Heidi's house on the off-chance she was home. Surprisingly, she was, or at least her car was parked in front. I rang her doorbell and knocked on the front and back doors but never got an answer. I took a round-about way through her neighborhood, thinking maybe she'd gone for a walk, but I never saw her, and so we left.

From Heidi's, we drove over to the Meyer Legal Office on University Ave. Edith buzzed the door open as I approached. "Hello, Dev. How are you this morning?" Edith asked as I stepped into the office.

"Just fine, thanks for asking. Can I see Martin for a minute?"

"You can. He's on a phone call at the moment. He should be off in just a bit. How's everything on your end?"

"Good," I said. "I'm hoping some things are going to break loose on Cornell's case, maybe even as soon as today, and I wanted to give Martin a heads-up."

"You're expecting good news?"

"Yeah, hopefully. I'm keeping my fingers crossed."

"Oh, he just got off the line. I'll let him know you're here," she said, picking up the phone.

Martin suddenly appeared in the doorway. "Edith, I want to speak with—Oh Dev, perfect timing, come on into the office," he said and backed up his wheelchair.

I gave Edith a little wave and followed Martin into his office. "Take a seat," he said as he wheeled around his desk and faced me. "I'm just off the phone with the city attorney's office. It sounds like there may be some changes about to happen in the Cornell Thomas case."

"Changes? Did it sound like they were going to release him?"

"Yes, hopefully, as soon as this afternoon. They're going to be dropping all the charges against him."

"Here's a little added insurance in the event there's a problem," I said and set the folder on his desk with the pictures of Cornell running.

He opened the folder and stared at the first photo, then paged to the other two. "What's this?" he said.

"That's Cornell running in the background the night of Penny Larson's murder. Given the time they were taken, they support Cornell's alibi that he was out running. That scene was photographed next to the Governor's mansion at 8:51, and he still has a good two miles to go before he's finished and then walks home. That makes it virtually impossible for him to be at her home when she was shot. The photos were taken by a professional photographer. The time and place are documented. You just have to get those images down to the police."

"Is this what's going on? The city attorney's office was pretty vague other than to tell me charges will be dropped."

"Actually, no," I said. "As far as I know, they're unaware of these photos. I do know there were some arrests made last night as part of a broader investigation, and the Larson murder is related to that investigation." I went on to tell him about the incident at the Dog House, the arrest of Trenton Javis, his three pals, and the linking of Franklin Lanzo, Russell Greeney, and the RIP building along the river where the drugs were supposed to be delivered.

"And you were there last night when they interviewed these characters?"

"I was there for just one, Trenton Javis. That was sometime after midnight. I'm guessing they got information from the other three individuals last night, and they were back at it first thing this morning. I've got calls into Detective Manning and Lieutenant LaZelle but haven't heard back."

"Think you should call them again?"

I shook my head. "No, right about now, I'd guess they've got their hands full. They've got to get warrants on Lanzo and Greeney and then find them. They'll undoubtedly get more information on this gang and bring some of them in. It's going to be a busy day for all involved."

"And the police have not seen these photos."

"No, I thought you might find it enjoyable to bring them to the department's attention."

"Oh, this will be fun. I'll alert them to this new evidence in just a moment. If I place the call, would you like to deliver them down to the station?"

"I can do that if you'd like. I think it would be wise to have them placed in the hands of either Manning or LaZelle, just to be safe. They'll no doubt serve as the icing on the cake for Cornell's release."

We talked for a half-hour. Meyer placed another call to Aaron LaZelle, but since he was still out, he didn't call Manning. I left the photos with him. Morton and I headed back to Heidi's.

We pulled in front of her house and parked behind her car. From what I could tell, the car hadn't been moved since the last time we were there. I walked up to the front door and rang the doorbell. I waited for an answer, rang it again, and then knocked on the door. She never answered.

I tried the side door, got the same results, and peeked in the kitchen window. There was no sign of activity inside. No dishes were piled on the kitchen counter. I went back to the front door. The mailbox was empty. I wasn't aware of her traveling anywhere, not that I'd ever know. If she was out of town, her car would either be in the garage or out at the airport. Other than our crazy night the week before we hadn't had any interaction for quite some time. Maybe she was meeting with someone and they drove. I didn't know what to think, and so I headed back to the office.

I parked across the street and took Morton for a quick walk. I purposely avoided walking past Becky's and figured, after last night, maybe she just needed a break from me. By the time we got back to the office, Louie's Ford Fiesta was parked behind my car.

We headed upstairs. Morton began picking up speed the closer we got to the door. Once we stepped inside, I understood why. Louie was in the process of eating a barbecue sandwich from Rooster's. A Styrofoam takeout tray was waiting on my desk, and there, resting on the middle of Morton's pillow, was a fresh bone. Morton literally leaped from the office door to his pillow and started in on the bone.

"Oh, Louie, thanks for thinking of us. Nothing like a late lunch. This is great. I'm guessing things went fairly well in court."

"Better than we could have hoped. I figured, what better way to celebrate than lunch."

"Mmm-mmm," I said through a mouth full of barbecue pork.

"How'd thing's go for you?"

"Good, Martin Meyer got a call, and charges on Cornell Thomas are going to be dropped. He should be released this afternoon. I still haven't heard from Aaron LaZelle or Manning. I stopped at Heidi's a couple of times, but either she's not around, or she knows it's me and isn't answering. I stopped at Becky's, picked up Morton, and invited her over for dinner."

"What are you going to serve?" Louie asked and took another large bite of his sandwich.

"I'm going to serve whatever I want. She declined the invitation and then closed the door and locked it."

"Oh, so she's catching on, just kidding. Maybe give her a couple of days. A physical assault, guns, everyone running off the patio and into the restaurant. I know that's an everyday occurrence for you, Dev. But that's heavy-duty stuff for normal folks. She just needs some time to process all of it."

"Yeah, I suppose. Not that I have any other choice."

We chatted for a bit. Louie left a barbecue stain on his shirt, which was becoming par for the course. I finished my sandwich and was nibbling on a French fry when my phone rang. Aaron LaZelle finally returning my call.

"Hi Aaron, thanks for getting back to me."

"Sorry it took so long. It's been a crazy day. I must have just missed you this morning."

"You mean my phone call?"

"No, Manning's little early morning chat with Trenton Javis. They put him in a cell for maybe thirty minutes, and he suddenly got religion and wanted to talk. That led the other three to tell their versions. By 5:00 this morning, we had two teams out there making arrests. That led us to the two you mentioned, Frank Lanzo and Russell Greeney. We got Lanzo coming out of his office heading for the airport. Somehow we missed Greeney. We know he had a flight scheduled to Miami, but he never showed up. You told me you met with Terry Nelson?"

"Yeah, he's the production manager or something with RIP, Inc. He offices in this building, actually I think he lives there. He—"

"Yeah, he was picked up. They've actually placed him in detox. He'll be there for at least seventy-two hours."

"Did you get a call from Martin Meyer, the attorney representing Cornell Thomas?"

"I did. He's my next call."

I filled Aaron in on the wedding photos with Cornell jogging past in the background.

"They're in the process of doing up the paperwork. He should be released in the next hour or so."

"Do you know if he's made a call to his mother?"

"I have no idea."

"Just asking, I could be down there and give him a lift home."

"No problem on this end if you want. He should be released from the Adult Detention Center in the next hour. Give your name at the front desk, and they'll bring him out to you."

"Would you mind making a call for me, just to alert them? The smoother this release goes, the less chance for a harassment lawsuit."

Aaron seemed to think about that for a moment and then said, "Yeah, I can do that. Just make sure you show up."

"I'll head over there shortly," I said.

"Sounds like things are shaping up," Louie said once I disconnected.

"Seem to be. I'm going to head over and give Cornell a lift home when they release him. It shouldn't take long. If you decide to head over to The Spot or go home, just leave Morton here. He's working on his latest project."

Morton ignored both of us and remained focused on his bone.

Forty-three

I drove over to the Adult Detention Center and found a parking spot on the street. I walked into the lobby and headed for the front desk. One of the officers had just hung up the phone as I approached and said, "How can I help you?"

"Hi, my name is Dev Haskell, and I'm here to give Cornell Thomas a ride. Charges have been dropped against him, and he's being released."

The desk sergeant behind him leaned over and said, "We got a call on that about a half-hour ago. Haskell, I remember you. Didn't you end up in an elevator with some Russian nutcase a few years back?"

"More like ten years ago, but yeah, unfortunately, that was me."

The sergeant laughed. "Made my day, great entertainment."

I smiled and headed for an orange plastic chair.

"He should be out here in about ten minutes or so," the sergeant said. He turned to his compatriots. "You guys should have been there. This Russian fella grabs Haskell by the collar..." He was laughing just enough that I couldn't understand what else he told them. Suddenly, everyone erupted in laughter. The sergeant pointed at me and laughed even harder.

I waited nearly fifteen minutes, and suddenly a door opened, and Cornell Thomas stepped into the lobby. He gave a quick glance around and headed for the door.

"Cornell Thomas?" the desk sergeant called just as I stood. The color seemed to drain from Cornell's face. "A gentleman here to give you a ride," the sergeant said and nodded in my direction.

"Hey, Cornell," I called.

A wave of relief seemed to wash over him, and he grinned when he saw me.

"Just thought you could use a lift home. Let's get you out of here," I said as we shook hands. Cornell let go of my hand and gave me a long, hard hug.

"You stay safe, Haskell," the desk sergeant called as we headed for the door.

As we stepped outside, Cornell slowed, closed his eyes, and turned toward the sun.

"Oh, Dev, thanks for being here. I'm so glad to be out of that place. One more day and think I would have lost my mind."

"I'm just glad you're out of there. What did they tell you?"

"Only that the charges against me had been dropped, and I was going to be released. I wasn't about to argue."

"Did you call your mom?"

He shook his head. "No, I didn't have access to a phone. They started the release process almost immediately, and I didn't want to hold them up. I just needed to get out of there."

"Well, then let's get you home," I said and pointed to my car. We climbed in, and a moment later, I pulled into traffic. Being the end of the day, rush hour had begun. We hit every stoplight along the way. That just gave me time to give Cornell an update, starting with Trenton Javis.

"You got to be kidding me. Javis was with these gang members at the Dog House?"

"Yeah, he drove. I don't know this for a fact, but it sounds like placing the gun under your pillow was his initiation into joining the gang. I'll be interested to see what he's charged with. I'm pretty sure he's going to be doing some time."

"I never would have guessed him for a gang-banger. He just seemed…I don't know, lost or something." I pulled to a stop in front of his building. "You want to come in? My mom would love to see you."

"Oh, thanks, but I got another stop to make. Give my best to your mom, and congratulations on getting out."

"I couldn't have done it without you, Dev. You got things moving, thank God."

"Stay in touch," I said. We shook hands, and I watched until Cornell stepped into the building. As he opened the door, he turned, gave a wave, and disappeared inside.

I drove back to the office. I parked in front of Louie's car, just in case he left before me. That way, all that soot and ash or whatever it was when he started the engine wouldn't end up on my car. Morton was the only one in the office, and he appeared to be content working on his bone. He gave me a quick look as I entered and then went back to the business at hand, gnawing.

I grabbed his leash and said, "Morton, let's go for a walk."

He looked at me as if to say, 'What? Really? Can't you see I'm busy?'

"Morton, walk, let's go." He clamped onto his bone, gave me another look, and rose off his pillow. I clipped the leash onto his collar, and we headed down the stairs. We did a twenty-minute walk. I made a point of avoiding Becky's house. Morton carried his bone the entire time.

I opened the door to the back seat of my car, and he settled in, happy to give his undivided attention to the bone. I drove up the street and headed toward Heidi's house. With the various arrests made, not the least of which was Frank Lanzo, I figured she should know.

Her car was still parked in front, which was very unlike her. I pulled in behind her car and climbed out. I'm not sure Morton was even aware I'd left the car. I walked up to her front door and rang the doorbell. I heard it chiming inside. I noticed the shades were pulled on the living room windows. I couldn't remember a time when she'd done that.

I rang the doorbell again and still didn't get an answer. I debated knocking and decided against it. I climbed in my car and drove down the street. I took a right at the corner, turned down the alley, pulled in front of her garage, and parked.

I checked just to be sure I had my pistol stuck in my belt and climbed out. I opened the rear door for Morton. I got another look from him, but after staring for a moment, he clamped onto his bone and hopped out of the car.

I tried to lift Heidi's garage door, but it was locked, which only made sense. I opened the gate to the backyard. We stepped in, and I quietly closed the gate. The garage was built with the same red brick as the house. There was a locked door at the far corner and a window on the side of the garage with a flower box below the window. The flower box had six red geraniums planted in it.

I peeked in the garage, and all my questions were answered. There it was, a white Prius. Russell Greeney's car. I had a tough time believing Heidi would park on the street so that Russell could park in her garage. We hurried out of the backyard and into the alley. I carefully closed the gate behind us, took out my phone, and called Aaron LaZelle.

My call dropped into his voicemail after the fourth ring. I phoned again, and this time, it dropped into voicemail after the second ring. I phoned once more, and this time he answered, "Jesus Christ, I'm busy," he said.

"Don't hang up. I think I found Russell Greeney."

"Found him? Where?"

I gave him a quick rundown.

"So you didn't actually see him?"

"No, but her car has been out on the street for the better part of the day, which she never does, and his Prius is parked in the garage. Shades are drawn in the house, and she's never done that, at least not in her living room."

Aaron seemed to think about that for a moment and then said, "Okay, stay put. We're on our way."

"I'm in the alley. I've got my car parked, blocking the garage door. But he could jump in her car out on the street. It's a red Mercedes."

"You stay where you are. Do not try to enter that house. I'm going to have them block the street off at either end of the block. Stay where you are, Dev. Promise?"

"Yeah, I heard you the first time. Just get here."

"On our way," he said. Based on the heavy breathing, it sounded like he was already running.

Around ten minutes later, I heard some noise coming from the front yard. Something sounded like a door slamming, and a guy yelled, "Go, go, go." I figured it was the cops. A squad car turned into the alley down at the far end and was slowly making its way up the block.

Just as I was thinking it was about time, the garage door suddenly rose, and there was Greeney with Heidi. It looked like she was gagged with a t-shirt tied behind the back of her head. Her hands were cuffed in front of her with a set of pink handcuffs with fluffy pink feathers. I recognized them from an occasional—

"Oh, what the hell," Greeney shouted when he saw my car and then focused on me. "Hey, wait a minute, you're that bastard Hassle. They were supposed to take care of you. What in the hell are you—"

Heidi took off toward me. Greeney took three steps, grabbed her by the hair, and pulled her back. I pulled out my pistol as she gave him an elbow in the ribs. He let go of her hair and went to kick her, missed, and hit Morton, or rather Morton's bone.

Morton growled, barked, and clamped onto the calf of Greeney's leg. He screamed, pointed his gun at Morton, and I fired.

Two cops ran into the garage just as Aaron Lazelle opened the gate and stepped into the alley. "Don't shoot. Don't shoot. He's one of us," he shouted.

The squad car sped up the alley and screeched to a stop. Two officers hopped out.

I had an arm around Heidi and held her against my shoulder. Morton gave another bark and growl at Greeney, daring him to make a move. Then he picked up his bone, gave Greeney the evil eye, and settled in next to my car.

"How 'bout I take that, Dev," Aaron said and cautiously took the gun from my hand.

I untied the t-shirt around Heidi's head. "Oh, thank God, Dev. Yuck! He tied his sweaty t-shirt over my mouth. Ick. Ick. Ick." I pulled her close and held her head against my shoulder.

They eventually loaded Greeney onto a gurney and wheeled him out to the ambulance parked in front. Unfortunately, I'd only grazed his shoulder. Morton had ripped a hole in his leg, and the EMT had wrapped it in gauze. Heidi was in the backyard talking to an EMT.

A black BMW came down the alley. It slowed as it approached, then stopped and lowered the passenger window. "Oh, good, that guy is the window peeking pervert I called you about the other day," Heidi's neighbor said and pointed at me.

"Yeah, thanks for your call. We finally got him," Aaron said.

"Good work." He gave a salute and pulled into his driveway.

"You sure seem to get around," Aaron said.

"I was looking in the dining room and saw Greeney here the other night."

Aaron seemed to think for a moment then said, "When we arrived to arrest Lanzo this morning, he was on his phone. I wonder if he was talking to Greeney. He probably thought this would be a safe place to lay low."

"Maybe," I said.

"Yeah, well, thanks, Morton. Talk about bad to the bone…"

Epilogue

Morton and I spent the night at Heidi's, but it was nothing like the usual wild time. I slept on the living room couch. Morton slept under the coffee table with his bone. Heidi remained in her bedroom with the door locked. I offered to stay the following night. I invited her to sleep in the guest room at my place. She decided she'd be better just staying home and slowly, but surely, hopefully, getting back to normal.

I waited a few more days before Morton and I went to visit Becky. I had a bone from Rooster's for Princess, and I was going to ask Becky out for dinner. That didn't work out the way I planned. When we came around the corner, there was a moving van backed into the front yard. At first, I thought they were maybe delivering something large like a piano, but then it dawned on me that the crew was hauling furniture out of the house, not into it. We walked around the truck, and there, in the front yard, was a brand new 'For Sale' sign.

"Is the owner here?" I asked one of the crew. I think he was the same guy I spoke with when they were hauling furniture into the house.

"No, she left town a couple of days ago. Kind of strange. She'd only been here for a few weeks. It's like she was fleeing from something or someone," he said and gave me a look.

We headed back to the office. I dropped the bone for Princess on Morton's pillow. Now he had two bones, and he looked like he was in heaven. He took turns chewing on one and then the other.

No Heidi, no Becky. I spent the rest of the day trying to figure things out and feeling sorry for myself. I never really came up with anything other than life is crazy. Louie was tied up at the courthouse and we were about to head home when my phone rang.

"Heidi, hello. How are you?"

"I'm fine, Dev. Thanks for asking. More importantly, how are you?"

"Oh, doing okay. Just working away."

"Yeah, sure you are. I'm wondering if you'd have time for dinner. Sorry I'm calling so late. If you can't—"

"Oh, no, no, I can make it."

"Oh, good. Plan on bringing Morton, too. I owe both of you. I think I finally figured out what I need."

"Are you sure? I mean, he'll be fine at home."

"Bring him. Plan on spending the night and tomorrow morning. I need to thank you, big time."

"Oh, yeah, that sounds, umm—What can I bring?"

"Not a thing. I've already got everything here. You show up whenever you feel like it. The door is open. I'll be waiting on the couch."

"See you in seven minutes," I said and grabbed Morton's leash.

Yeah, life really is crazy. "Come on, Morton. We gotta go…"

The End

Thank you for taking the time to read **Bad to the Bone.** If you have a moment please consider leaving a review on Amazon. I'm an independent author and it really helps.

Don't miss this sample of **Silencio!** The next book in the Dev Haskell series.

Sneak Peek

Silencio!

Second Edition

MIKE FARICY

Prologue

As I held the door Melissa Donnelly said, "Oh, thanks." We were leaving Starbucks after our first meeting. We'd corresponded back and forth a few times on a dating site. She seemed about as bored as I was on the internet, and after three texting sessions, we decided to meet for coffee. I thought the in-person meeting had gone pretty well. She was an attractive blonde, liked to smile, and had a delightful laugh.

"Thanks again for making the time, Melissa. It was great to meet you. You're even nicer than you seemed online if that's possible."

"You are a really good liar, Dev Haskell. Believe me. The pleasure has been all mine. It was wonderful to meet you. No pressure, but I'll leave it in your court if you want to get together again."

"You free Friday night? I'm wondering if we could maybe meet up just for a beer or a glass of wine. There's a place just across the street from my office called The Spot. I pop in there once in a while," I said, thinking there was no point in mentioning I was in there just about every day.

"The Spot? That sounds so cute, but I don't know where it is. Across the street from your office?"

"Yeah, on Randolph Avenue. You can't miss it. It's on the corner of Randolph and Victoria. Just a small little neighborhood local."

"I'd love it. You name a time, and I'll meet you there."

"Why don't we meet up around six. We can have a glass of wine and maybe grab dinner somewhere. How about you pick the dinner place?"

"I'll put my thinking cap on," she said and gave me a peck on the cheek. She squeezed my hand for a moment then crossed the street to her car. She waved, blew a kiss, climbed in, and drove down the street.

That was great, I thought, as I climbed into my car and headed home. I'd dropped off Morton, my golden retriever, at home before meeting up with Melissa. I figured right about now he was probably due for a walk. I pulled in front of my place ten minutes later. I planned to grab Morton. We could take our walk down at the office and then head over to The Spot just for one.

I hurried up to the front porch, placed my key in the lock, but the front door wasn't locked. You gotta be kidding me. I always lock the front door. Was I that focused on meeting Melissa in person that I forgot to lock the door? Get a grip, man.

At first, I thought the noise was from my radio, but it seemed to be coming from the front room. Then there was the pizza box on the floor, and Morton was stretched out, dining on pizza crusts.

"Morton, where in the hell did that—"

"It's about damn time. Get your dumb ass in here," an unfortunately familiar voice called.

Fat Freddy Zimmerman was stretched out on my couch, oozing over the edge. Another pizza box rested on his lap. He stuffed the last half of the final piece into his mouth. "You better pat down douchebag," he said to the muscle-bound thug watching the cartoon on my TV.

"What the hell are you guys doing in my hou—"

"You heard what he said. Shut the hell up and assume the position," the thug said. He spun me around, pressed the side of my head against the wall, shoved a foot between my legs, and kicked them apart.

"Nice to meet you, sir. I can tell you right now I'm not carrying," I said as he reached between my legs none too gently, causing me to jump.

"Relax, Haskell, that's probably more action than you've had in months," Fat Freddy said and laughed.

"He's clean, boss," the one-watt thug said and stepped back.

I remained pressed against the wall. "Is it okay to move? I'm not going to scare you if I turn around, am I?"

"I hope that wasn't meant as an insult, Haskell. Austin might take that the wrong way, and then there's no telling what could happen."

"Oh, no, not an insult. I just didn't want to get on the wrong side of Austin."

"Much better, Haskell. Turn around so I can see your smiling face."

I turned around, careful not to rub Austin the wrong way. He was a good six inches taller and maybe a hundred pounds heavier than me, none of which was fat. Even his muscles had muscles. He glared down at me. I stepped to the side so I could see past him and focused on Fat Freddy, who was in the process of licking his fingertips. There was half a crust in the pizza box, and as he set it on the floor, Morton hurried in. He let Fat Freddy scratch him behind the ear and then snatched up the crust.

"Dog after my own heart. God only knows why he's still with you," Freddy said.

"Why are you guys here? How did you get in?"

"Your dog Morgan let us in. Not that it's important," Freddy said and laughed. Idiot Austin let out a fake laugh and then stopped a half-second after Freddy stopped. "Mr. Gustafson would like a word with you, now, Haskell. Let's go, Austin."

"First of all, my dog's name isn't Morgan. It's Morton, and just what does Tubby Gus- err, umm, Mr. Gustafson want with me?"

"I guess you should probably shut the hell up and come with us to find out. Look, Haskell, you're starting to be difficult again. Need I remind you that never, ever goes your way. Hey, I've got an idea. Maybe just get your dumb ass in the car, and then once you see Mr. Gustafson, if you still want to be stupid, you could ask him what he wants. Or, maybe just once, you could keep your trap shut, and he'll tell you what the hell he wants. Now, for your own good, please, don't say another word. Austin, if Haskell says anything, you have my permission."

"Permission to do—ooff," was all I could get out before Austin hit me in the stomach, lifting me off my feet. The room was suddenly spinning. I saw stars as I leaned against the wall and attempted to get back to whatever 'normal' had been just a moment before.

"See you later, boy," Fat Freddy said as he patted Morton on the head. "Bring Hassle out to the car, Austin. Be careful. I don't want him throwing up in the back seat."

One

Slowly but surely, I began to recover. I knew where Tubby Gustafson lived, I knew the route they probably took, but lying face down on the floor of the back seat in Freddy's Cadillac Escalade, it was impossible to determine where exactly we were. By the time we pulled through the wrought iron gates and onto the circular drive in front of Tubby Gustafson's mansion, I was pretty much back to normal, except for the dull pain where my stomach used to be.

Austin was driving, and he pulled to a stop at the front door. He hurried out of the car and opened the passenger door for Fat Freddy. As soon as Freddy's door closed, my door opened. Someone grabbed me by the ankles and yanked me out of the door, stopping at the very last second before I dropped at least two feet head-first onto the pavement. Instead, I landed on my knees, tearing both knees on my trousers. Idiot Austin grabbed the back of my collar, popping two buttons on my shirt as he yanked me on to my feet.

"Better pat him down again, just to be on the safe side," Fat Freddy said and headed into Tubby's mansion.

"When in the hell could I grab a gun?" I called after him. Brainless Austin gave me a look. "Okay, okay, sorry, just asking."

Fortunately, one of the thugs stationed by the front door stepped between Austin and me and began to pat me down. I raised my hands over my head and leaned against the car. He gently patted me down, then stepped back and shouted, "Clean."

"Let's go," said some other guy, who'd been leaning against the front of the house, and held the front door open. I hurried toward the door. At that point, I would have done almost anything to get away from psychopathic Austin. The door closed behind me, and I stepped into the entryway. Another thug was seated just inside, attempting to read a comic book. He gave me a look suggesting I was interrupting an important part and tossed the comic book onto the end table next to his chair.

"I know, I know," I said and assumed the position again, leaning forward with my legs spread and my hands above my head resting against the wall.

"Okay, good to go," he said a half-minute later. I stepped into the large entry with the staircase running up the side of the wall and the gilt-framed painting of Tubby Gustafson holding a bunch of rolled documents pretending to be someone who had done something noble in his life.

Fat Freddy tossed what looked like a chocolate into his mouth and headed down the hall. We passed the dining room and Tubby Gustafson's library, then stopped at the heavy oak door to Tubby's office. Fat Freddy gave me a quick look, knocked on the oak door, and pushed it open. "Greetings, sir. Sorry it took so long. We ran into a bit of difficulty along the way."

Tubby Gustafson stood at the opposite end of the room, on the far side of his desk. Usually, when I had been summoned, I found him stretched out on a massage table with his fat oozing over the side and his privates covered by a white towel. Two scantily clad women would be massaging his hairy, dimpled shoulders.

Today, he stood wearing a pair of red plaid boxer shorts and black knee-high stockings held up by black leather sock garters. He wore a strappy t-shirt that had to be a triple extra-large size. He leaned forward with his head down, holding a golf putter. With his large stomach protruding, it had to be damn near impossible to see the golf ball. He studied something a few feet away, then seemed to concentrate and putted. A moment later, he groaned, "Damn it," and tossed the putter onto a brown leather recliner.

He turned, stared at the torn knees on my trousers, and shook his head. "What have I done to deserve this?" he said as he pulled back the leather desk chair and sat down. "Well, now what is it you want, Haskell?"

"Actually, Tub, err, umm sir, I was under the impression you wanted to see me."

"I believe the politician, sir," Fat Freddy said from behind me.

"The pol…oh, yes, yes, with everything we've had going on, I almost forgot. Thank you, Frederick. Haskell, I want you to look into something for me, actually someone," Tubby said. He opened a drawer along the side of his desk, pulled out a manila file folder, and set it on the desk. "Hmm, another failed attempt to look trendy?" Tubby asked and nodded at my torn trouser knees. "Get over here and sit down."

I hurried over to one of the client chairs in front of his desk and sat down.

"I'm interested in a gentleman by the name of Casper Trickle. I need you to take a look at him and see what you can find. He's involved in—"

"Pardon me for interrupting, sir, but as I think you know, politics, financial dealings, taxes, and the like are really not my strong suit."

"Please, stop right there, Haskell. Have I asked you to think? Do I appear to be the kind of individual who would want you to examine financial records? Do you even have a strong suit? Good lord, you probably still have a piggy bank in your bedroom."

"Only for quarters, sir. I find—"

"Silencio," Tubby shouted. "God save me. I'll want a full report on the individual mentioned in this file. You may read the file while you sit there. I do not want to hear from you until you are finished, and then I only want to hear you say that you have read the information and will proceed with an investigation. Do I make myself clear?"

I nodded and pulled the file across the desk to me. Tubby returned to his putting.

Casper Trickle appeared to be involved in acquiring companies that ended up in bankruptcy. His name sounded familiar, maybe, but I couldn't recall why, exactly.

"Would you mind if I made a few notes, Sir?" I asked just as Tubby putted.

He was quiet for a long moment and then said, "Damn it, Haskell! You made me miss. No, I don't care if you make notes. I never expected you to be able to remember what you read."

I wrote down Trickle's name and his address along with what appeared to be a business and private phone number. I paged through the file until I came to what looked like a tax form. I quickly went through the remainder of the documents. With the exception of a half-dozen grainy images, it was all financial information. I closed the file and sat quietly, watching and counting as Tubby missed one putt after another. I was up to eleven when he swore and tossed the putter back on the leather recliner.

"Finished, Haskell?" he said.

"Yes, sir, I've his name and home address, along with his office address, business phone number, and—"

"I don't give a damn about his professional life. I know the man is successful. That's why he's thinking of running for governor. I want you to investigate his personal life. Find out his background, what his weak spots might be. This investigation is to remain private. Do not, I repeat, do not mention this to anyone. I'll want this information no later than a week from today. Do I make myself clear?"

"Yes, sir, very clear. I'll see what I can find out."

"See that you do. Frederick, get him out of my sight," Tubby said as he picked up his putter and focused his attention on his next missed putt.

Fat Freddy nodded toward the door, and I followed. Once out in the hall, I said, "I wasn't aware Mr. Gustafson played golf."

"He's just begun to take it up. Let's go," Freddy said and headed for the front door. As we stepped outside, Austin and the two individuals leaning against the front of the mansion stood and pretended to be focused on whatever they were supposed to be doing.

"Austin, get Haskell out of here and take his worthless ass back to that seedy part of town he lives in."

"Glad to, sir," Austin said and glared at me. He hurried toward the black Escalade and held the rear door for me.

"Why, thank you, Austin," I said as I climbed in.

He slammed the door behind me and hurried around to the driver's side. He started the car, slowly drove out through the gate of Tubby's mansion, and sped down the street. He hadn't driven more than three blocks when he pulled to the curb, turned toward me, and said, "Get out."

"What are you talking about? You know where I live. My house is four or five miles from here. I don't want to—"

"I don't care what you want, Hassle. Get your dumb ass out of the car. I've got shit to do."

"No doubt," I said as I opened the door and began to step out. I wasn't halfway out the door when Austin floored the vehicle. Fortunately, I landed on the grassy boulevard on all fours and gave him the finger as he sped down the street. Maybe it was a good thing I wasn't in the car with him. I stood, brushed the torn knees on my pants, and started walking.

It took me two hours, and I was starving by the time I made it home. Morton was asleep on the couch in the front room. As I stepped inside, he raised his head and wagged his tail. He'd torn up both pizza boxes and scattered the bits and pieces around the room. I went out to the kitchen, finished up pasta left overs from the refrigerator and then decided a nap might be in order. Morton woke me a few hours later. I grabbed his leash from the counter, and we walked around the block.

We passed a woman along the way that I'd seen before. She was walking a little furry white dog. She usually gave us a nod and a smile. Tonight she stared at the torn knees on my trousers and hurried across to the opposite side of the street.

Once we were home, I checked the locks on all the windows, wedged chairs beneath the front and back door, and stretched out on the couch in front of the TV.

I woke up a little after one. Morton had already headed upstairs. I climbed the stairs, pulled off my torn trousers, left them on the floor, and climbed into bed.

TWO

I was up before my alarm went off. I got the coffee going in the kitchen then hurried back upstairs to shower and shave. Morton was still asleep when I headed back down to the kitchen. I was on my second cup, going through email messages, when he wandered in. I gave him the proverbial head scratch and let him outside.

I took Morton out to my car and stopped. A half-dozen eggs had been thrown on the car sometime during the night. I put Morton in the back seat, turned on the garden hose, and removed most of the egg from my car. *'Damn kids,'* I thought.

We were in the office before Louie arrived. I turned off yesterday's coffee, dumped the remnants down the sink, and made a fresh pot. I was watching out the window when Louie pulled up and parked across the street behind my car. I filled his mug with coffee and set it on his picnic table desk. I listened to the stairs creak as he slowly made his way up to the office.

"Fresh coffee waiting for you on your desk," I said. Louie gave me a thumbs-up and settled into his chair. At the moment, I was looking into the apartment across the street through my binoculars. A woman in a black thong was standing at her kitchen counter applying makeup. Not a bad way to start the day, watching, that is.

"How'd your coffee meet-up go yesterday? Did that woman even bother to show?" Louie asked once he caught his breath.

I turned around in my office chair, put the binoculars in my desk drawer, and said, "To be honest, it went a lot better than I expected. Really a nice gal. We're going to meet up tomorrow night for dinner and see where things go. I'm not gonna put any pressure on her."

"I was wondering if everything worked out. Thought you might make it into The Spot last night and give me a full report."

"First off, nothing to report. We chatted for maybe forty-five minutes, and it went fine. I drove home to grab Morton and planned to head down to The Spot, only to find a couple of visitors in my place."

"Visitors?"

"Yeah, dumbass Fat Freddy Zimmerman and some thug named Austin, who punched me in the stomach."

"They were actually inside your house?"

"Yeah, and get this, they'd ordered pizzas and were giving Morton all the crusts."

"I'm sure he loved that," Louie said and slurped some coffee.

"God only knows what he left in the backyard this morning. Anyway, they drove me to Tubby Gustafson's place. He wants me to check some guy out. Then this Austin jerk was supposed to drive me home, but instead, he kicked me out of the car about three blocks from Tubby's, and I ended up walking home. I was so beat I fell asleep on the couch in front of the TV."

"Sounds like it maybe wasn't the best evening."

"The Tubby part sucked, but Melissa, that's the woman I met online. She was really nice."

"Who does Gustafson want you to check out?"

"Oh, vintage Tubby, he had me read a file while he practiced putting golf balls. I don't think he ever made a putt while I was there. You ever hear of a guy named Casper Trickle? Apparently, he's thinking of running for governor, at least, that's what Tubby said. Not sure how he makes his money. If he's interested in politics, he probably has some scam in mind. You ever heard of him?"

Louie seemed to think for a moment. "Now that you ask, something seems to ring a bell. I can't remember what, but probably nothing good. If I recall, and I may be wrong, I believe Casper Trickle was permanently disbarred two or three years ago. He ran some shady 'loan modification' business. You know, for a price, he would get your mortgage company to lower the interest rate. He collected illegal advance attorney fees and, I think in a couple of cases, improperly borrowed money from client trust funds and failed to repay. He's your basic legal sleazeball, but then if he's going into politics, he'd probably fit right in."

"Can you think of anyone who may have dealt with him?"

Louie shook his head. "Off the top of my head, nothing's ringing a bell. But just a word of warning. If anyone is linked up with Casper Trickle, they can't be good. I'm sure if you google him, things will come up. Does Tubby have funds somehow tied up with him?"

"Not that I'm aware of. He was pretty specific. He wants personal info on Trickle. He gave me a week to find out everything about the guy."

"Funny he wouldn't check him out on his own," Louie said.

"He's probably too busy, now that he's taken up golf. God knows he needs all the practice he can get. You in the office today?"

"Yeah, I think so. I may get a call from a new client. The guy was arrested for DWI yesterday afternoon and ended up in the drunk tank overnight. It depends on if he gets out today or they hold him for a second night."

Louie fired up his computer and began typing. I grabbed my binoculars and checked the apartment across the street again. Unfortunately, the woman in the thong was nowhere to be seen.

I fired up my computer and googled Casper Trickle. Not much came up other than he had been involved in the implosion of a hedge fund called Archegos Capital Management. He somehow seemed to escape without much damage. He was listed as a retired attorney, which was par for the course.

The three online images of him suggested a well-heeled sleaze bag. Light brown hair, slightly gray at the temples. He looked to be about fifty and apparently liked expensive clothes. He struck me as a guy who appeared to be very wealthy, and in case you actually wondered, he would somehow allude to that fact within the first minute of conversation. He lived in town on Summit Avenue. A pricey street populated by large mansions built at least a hundred years ago.

I checked the county tax site, got his address, and decided to check the place out.

"I gotta run a quick errand. You going to be around for maybe an hour?"

"Not a problem. Take your time," Louie said.

Morton gave me a glance as I headed out the door. He was more involved with the pork bone he was chewing on than wanting to get off his pillow and tag along with me. I made it through all five stoplights, so it was no more than a five-minute drive over to Summit Avenue. I took a right and headed down past the Governor's mansion. Today the protestors were waving signs about voting 'no' on proposition eleven. I had no idea what proposition eleven was. I drove two more blocks, pulled to the curb, and climbed out of my car. If what Tubby said was correct and the guy was thinking about running for Governor, I found it interesting he lived just two blocks from the Governor's mansion.

Trickle's mansion took up two corner lots. I slowed my pace as I walked past. The house was a three-story red-stone structure with a slate roof and there was a six-foot-high wrought-iron fence around the property. Three large oak trees were in the front yard. Four security cameras were mounted along the front of the house. I turned the corner and walked along the side of the house. I counted two more security cameras, one on either corner of the house.

I held my cellphone in my left hand and gave one and two-word answers to a fake phone call as I pressed the camera button and took pictures of the place.

The three-stall brick garage behind the mansion had a rental unit on the second story. There was a brick patio off to the side of the garage, and two muscle-bound guys were on the patio in gym shorts and strappy red t-shirts bench pressing some serious weights. One of the guys, blonde with a crewcut, stood as he spotted while the other was on the bench doing some serious lifting. The guy spotting gave me more than a casual glance as I walked past. I gave a simple nod, clicked my cellphone camera a few times, and kept going.

The back of the garage ran along the edge of the alley. The wrought-iron fence butted against the back corner of the garage. At least two more security cameras were mounted on the garage. Rather than walk up the alley, I went around the entire block and climbed back in my car.

I drove past Trickle's place, and now three cars were parked in front of the house. A red convertible, a black SUV, and at the moment, a white van labeled Duncan

Flowers. I slowed as I drove past the open gate, but I didn't see anyone outside. Rather than make a second pass and possibly attract attention, I headed back to the office.

Three

When I entered the office, both Louie and Morton were sound asleep. Morton slowly opened one eye, saw it was me, and drifted back asleep. Louie snorted when I closed the door and returned to breathing heavily. I drummed my fingers on my desk, wondering who I could call regarding Casper Trickle, when a light suddenly blinked on in my one-watt brain. Heidi Bauer. My on-again, off-again friend with benefits that I hadn't seen in several months.

I still had her number on speed-dial. I brought her name up, tapped the screen, and crossed my fingers, hoping she'd answer when my name appeared on her cellphone.

She answered after the third ring. "So, you heard. I guess the news is all over town," was how she answered. I'd been here uncountable times and knew exactly where this was going.

"Hi, Heidi. Just checking in to see if you're okay," I lied, having no idea who she broke up with this time. "I was more than a little surprised. Just for the record, I think the guy is an absolute idiot. The worst decision of his life. You doing okay?"

"What are you talking about?"

Shit. "I thought you broke up with what's his name."

"Cletus Devon? No, Dev, that was over two months ago. I was talking about my car getting totaled."

"Well, yeah, that was the other thing I was going to mention," I said, having never heard about it. "But you're okay after the car being totaled?"

"I'm fine, I guess. It's just a major pain in…well, you know. Of course, I'm suddenly getting jacked around by my insurance company. I'm driving a mid-range rental and wearing sunglasses, so no one will recognize me in the thing. I put Cletus's clothes in a box out in the garage six weeks ago, and he still hasn't picked them up. I tell you, right now, life is a pain in…So why did you call? I didn't think I'd ever hear from you again."

"You know that's not going to happen. I was thinking, if you're not too busy, I'd bring dinner over tonight, and we could catch up. No pressure, and if you don't want to, I get it, and I won't bug you anymore. Just thinking you could maybe use a night off, relax. I'd be happy to give you a back rub if you still like them."

"Yeah, right, like I would give those up. You know, Dev, this might be just the thing I need. I suppose you'll want something in return."

"No pressure, but there is something else I was thinking about."

"I knew it, typical."

"Sorry to disappoint, but I'm not talking about bed-room antics. I'm curious if you've ever heard of a guy named Casper Trickle. He's apparently thinking—"

"Casper Trickle? Oh yeah, who hasn't heard of him? I suppose I could fill you in, at least a little. Fortunately, other than investing in his stock, I've never had to deal with him. Let me do some checking and get up to date. What time were you thinking?"

"Maybe dinner time. I can bring dinner and a bottle of wine. Your only task will be to relax and take it easy."

"I'm sold. See you tonight, and thanks, Dev. It's nice to hear your voice again."

"Same here, nice to hear you. I'll see you tonight," I said, and Heidi disconnected.

"Was that Heidi I heard you talking to?" Louie asked, blinking his eyes open. He rolled his shoulders a couple of times, and I could hear them pop and snap all the way over at my desk.

"Yeah, I called to see what she knew about Casper Trickle and somehow got talked into bringing dinner."

"Oh, I think the evening will probably work out to your liking. It usually does when she's involved."

"One can only hope," I said. I took Morton for a long walk toward the end of the afternoon. We stopped in at The Spot for a minute just to touch base with Louie. He fed Morton two handfuls of pork rinds, and we headed out the door. I dropped Morton off at home, changed clothes, and grabbed two bottles of wine from Chuck at Solo Vino. I drove to Carmelo's and picked up two sun-dried tomato pesto dinners. Ten minutes later, I pulled in front of Heidi's. It was exactly 6:00.

She opened the front door before I even climbed the three steps to ring the doorbell. "Well, don't you look like you're on a mission."

"Dinner and wine, and I want to hear all about the car. First question, are you okay?" I asked as I handed her the bag with the two wine bottles. I followed her into the kitchen and set the Styrofoam dinner trays on the counter.

"Yes, I'm fine. I wasn't even in the car at the time. It's just frustrating."

"You weren't in the car? Who was driving?"

"Driving? No one was driving, Dev. This was that phone pole that went down when they were working on the lines."

"That was your car?" I'd seen it on the news, a red BMW 850 convertible, not exactly cheap. Somehow, the telephone pole had fallen on the car and crushed it. The local news station led with the story four or five nights ago. The vehicle looked like it was about six inches high, with the phone pole resting right down the center of the car.

"Yes, unfortunately, that was my car. A total loss, now we're arguing about what the value is, or rather, was. The good news is, I wasn't in the car at the time. The bad news is, I've been dealing with my insurance company ever since."

"Anything I can do to help?"

She looked at me for a moment, then shook her head and said, "Never mind, bad idea. So, what have you been up to for the past few months?"

We ate in the kitchen and chatted through dinner and a bottle of wine. Once the second bottle was opened, we moved into the den, and Heidi brought me up to date on Casper Trickle. The bottom line was he sounded like a well-connected guy who did all the right things until you really looked at the particulars. He was tied into the past and present mayors, the city council, a bunch of legislators, and a couple of judges. He donated to both political parties and all the sure winners in various campaigns. He would most likely be labeled as an independent.

"I've met him a few times, nothing personal, but deep down, I think he'd always make sure he came first in any deal. Kind of slimy was my impression," Heidi said. "I'll email you a list of people who are less than pleased with him, some former investors, a neighbor, and a couple of attorneys who dealt with him in court."

"Thanks, much appreciated. I'll take a look at that tomorrow morning," I said, hoping she caught on to my 'tomorrow morning' suggestion. If she did, she didn't react. "More wine?" I asked, thinking maybe another glass might loosen her up a little more.

"Oh, I'd love one, but I'd better not. I've got an early morning meeting with two potential investors, and I want to be at my best."

I was hoping that meant we might adjourn and head upstairs to bed. After a painfully quiet moment, I said,

"Well, I should probably take off and head home. Thanks for the info on Trickle."

She climbed off the couch, gave a revealing stretch, and said, "Oh, I think I'll sleep like a baby after that wine."

"Hey, I never gave you that back rub. I could—"

"That's okay, maybe some other time. Thanks for coming over with dinner and the wine. It's nice to see you again," she said and held out her hand.

I couldn't believe it, a handshake? From Heidi? You gotta be kidding me! She had really changed. I took hold of her hand and gently pulled her toward me for a kiss, hoping that might get her into the mood. She smiled as she drew close and then, at the last minute, turned her head, so I kissed her on the cheek.

"Good luck in your meeting tomorrow," I said as she gently pulled away and headed toward the front door. I followed reluctantly, wondering what I'd done wrong. She turned at the front door, looked at me, and suddenly laughed. "Oh, look at you. So disappointed. I love it. Come on, you big baby." She took me by the hand and led me upstairs.

It was still dark when she kissed me. My first thought was, *Really, again?* Then she said, "I've got to get down to the office early and prepare for this meeting. The coffee's on downstairs. Let yourself out and lock the door. Thanks for a wonderful evening and the back rub. I really enjoyed myself."

When I woke again, it was daylight. The digital clock on her dresser read just a few minutes after seven. My distant memory of the evening slowly came into focus, ending with her kiss and telling me to let myself out. I dressed, filled a travel mug with coffee, and drove home. Morton was just coming down the stairs as I stepped in the front door. I let him out into the backyard and went upstairs to shower. I pulled on a pair of jeans and a faded blue t-shirt with yellow letters that said St. Paul Police over the left breast. Once we finished breakfast, we headed down to the office. I couldn't remember if Louie was coming in or if he was in court this morning, so I made a full pot of coffee. He showed up about twenty minutes later.

"So, how'd your evening go?" he asked after a couple of sips.

"Nice night. I took dinner over to Heidi, and we caught up. She filled me in with some general information on financial deals with Casper Trickle, none of it very good."

"And?"

"And then I went home and came down here. She's going to send me a list of folks who aren't too thrilled with Casper Trickle, so hopefully, I can talk to some of them and have enough information to make Tubby Gustafson happy."

"And that was your night? You didn't, ahhh, you know…"

"Louie, it was more of a business meeting. I was interviewing her."

"Yeah, okay, but in the past, when you two got together, there was almost always fireworks."

"Sorry to disappoint, but we were both strictly business this time." He gave me a look that suggested he might not be buying my explanation, but there was nothing he could do.

Four

It was close to 10:00 before I began calling the names on the list Heidi sent me. I ended up leaving a message on the first four calls. I was prepared to do the same on the fifth call when a guy named Colin Demming answered after the third ring. "Demming."

It took me a moment to realize he was live.

"Hello? Anyone there?"

"Hello, Colin. My name is Dev Haskell. I got your name from a friend. I'm checking on someone I was thinking of doing some business with. He seems to have a somewhat mixed set of reviews and recommendations, and I wondered if I could get some input from you."

"Hmm, happy to help if I can. Who are we talking about?"

"A gentleman by the name of Casper Trickle."

"One piece of advice. Don't walk. Run in the opposite direction just as fast as you can. Get the hell away from him and never look back. Block any communications from him. In the end, he'll only do one thing, and that's Cost. You. Money. He'll be more than happy to take every last dime. He has ruined more than one life."

"That doesn't sound too promising," I said and chuckled.

"There is nothing funny about Mr. Trickle. All of us are surprised he's not behind bars. Virtually everyone I know who came in contact with him lost a substantial amount of money. A number of us are involved in a lawsuit that's bound to go on for eternity."

"The little information I have is that he was disbarred. Is that correct?"

"That's correct. As charming as he seems, the man is rotten to the absolute core. He'll be more than happy to lie to your face. Any financial figures he provides will, at best, be inaccurate, inflated, or outright falsehoods."

"What about more personal information? He seems to have a lovely home on Summit Avenue. Is he married? Does he have children? Is he involved in a church?"

"He's involved in all of the above, or at least he was at one time. He's been divorced for a number of years, at least eight, maybe ten. There were two children in the marriage. They must be college age by now, maybe even graduated. He's active in a church when it suits his needs. The saving grace for the man is the fact that he is politically connected to the powers that be. If you're running for office, he would be one of the first contacts you would make in fundraising, regardless of your party. He likes to back winners, and that seems to pay off."

I thought about the two guys lifting weights on the back patio of Trickle's home. "Are you aware of anything along the lines of, mmm, physical intimidation?"

"If you're referring to the two muscle-bound Neanderthals that have paid a visit to at least a couple of individuals, yes, I'm aware. But only on a second-hand basis. Fortunately, I've not had that experience. The three individuals I'm aware of who share that dreadful experience are not about to mention it to anyone. Suffice it to say, they were frightened to the point where one moved out of state, another hired round-the-clock protection. The third died of a heart attack about six weeks after his run-in with those two creeps. All three eventually dropped their legal proceedings."

"Would you be able to give me their names?"

"I'm sorry, but I won't. They've been through more than enough and not a reflection on you, but they won't talk to you or anyone else regarding this. They simply want to get away from Casper Trickle as fast and as far as possible."

"How does he keep doing what he's doing?"

"Trickle? Deep down, he's crooked as the day is long, and he's connected. I'm sorry, tell me your name again."

"Haskell, Dev Haskell."

"Forgive me, Mr. Haskell. I'll plead old age. I'm fifty-eight."

"Hardly old," I said.

"There are days," Demming said. "Mr. Haskell, as I said, the man is connected. I've seen it too many times and not just with Trickle. Things seem to be going well and then suddenly fall apart, whether it's the stock you purchased, the person he put you in touch with, or the great idea you ran past him for advice. You wake up one morning to find yourself suddenly screwed. Trickle's surrounded by a legal shield you're unable to penetrate. They don't take your phone calls. You end up having to close your office or let go of ninety percent of your staff. The gentleman you thought you knew, the guy you trusted and relied upon, he's off to Mexico, or Europe, or Southeast Asia, and you're left holding the bag. That's if you're lucky and haven't had a heart attack from stress."

"And then he starts all over again?" I asked.

"Like clockwork. If you watch and keep tabs, you suddenly realize that's his damn game. The information is out there. The problem is people always think they know better, and before they know it, they've been played. He's brought in a competitor, bid a higher price on the property, found someone to do the job for less. Whatever it is, you end up doing all the work, and Trickle seems to benefit."

"Incredible," I said.

"More like sinful and no doubt illegal, but I get your point. One of these days, someone's going to figure out how to deal with him, and I don't mean spending twenty years filing lawsuits. It will be swift and to the point."

"Do you know of anyone currently involved with him?"

"I'm not involved any longer, other than to be part of one of many lawsuits, which seems to be going nowhere, I hasten to add."

"Are you aware of a gentleman named Gustafson who is involved with him?"

"No, sorry, but that name isn't ringing a bell. Do you know someone involved with him?"

"No, I just heard a rumor about him looking into politics and wondered, is all. Would you mind if I contact you down the road with a question? Unfortunately, everything you've told me seems to match up with the little bit of history I'm aware of."

"Not a problem. Feel free to call at any time. But please, take my advice. If you're involved in some way with Trickle, get out. Sell at a loss if you have to but get out."

"Well, thank you for the information. I think we'll look somewhere else and keep our distance from Mr. Trickle."

"Believe me, that's the best thing you can do."

"Thanks again for the time, Mr. Demming. Nice chatting, wishing you all the very best," I said, but he had already disconnected.

To be continued . . .

Not to worry, things are bound to get worse. Better grab your copy of **<u>Silencio!</u>** And find out just how bad. Enjoy the read.

Books by Mike Faricy

Crime Fiction Firsts

A boxset of the first four books in four crime fiction series:

Russian Roulette; Dev Haskell series
Welcome; Jack Dillon Dublin Tales series
Corridor Man; Corridor Man series
Reduced Ransom! Hot Shot series

The following titles comprise the Dev Haskell series:

Russian Roulette: Case 1
Mr. Swirlee: Case 2
Bite Me: Case 3
Bombshell: Case 4
Tutti Frutti: Case 5
Last Shot: Case 6
Ting-A-Ling: Case 7
Crickett: Case 8
Bulldog: Case 9
Double Trouble: Case 10
Yellow Ribbon: Case 11
Dog Gone: Case 12
Scam Man: Case 13
Foiled: Case 14
What Happens in Vegas… Case 15
Art Hound: Case 16
The Office: Case 17

Star Struck: Case 18
International Incident: Case 19
Guest From Hell: Case 20
Art Attack: Case 21
Mystery Man: Case 22
Bow-Wow Rescue: Case 23
Cold Case: Case 24
Cash Up Front: Case 25
Dream House: Case 26
Alley Katz: Case 27
The Big Gamble: Case 28
Bad to the Bone: Case 29
Silencio!: Case 30
Surprise, Surprise: Case 31
Hit & Run: Case 32
Suspect Santa: Case 33
P.I. Apprentice: Case 34
Rebel Without a Clue: Case 35
Puppy Love: Case 36

The following titles are Dev Haskell novellas:
Dollhouse
The Dance
Pixie
Fore!
Twinkle Toes
(*a Dev Haskell short story*)

The following are Dev Haskell Boxsets:
Dev Haskell Boxset 1-3
Dev Haskell Boxset 4-6
Dev Haskell Boxset 7-9
Dev Haskell Boxset 10-12
Dev Haskell Boxset 13-15
Dev Haskell Boxset 16-18
Dev Haskell Boxset 19-21
Dev Haskell Boxset 22-24
Dev Haskell Boxset 25-27
Dev Haskell Boxset 28-30
Dev Haskell Boxset 1-7
Dev Haskell Boxset 8-14
Dev Haskell Boxset 15-19
Dev Haskell Boxset 20-24
Dev Haskell Boxset 25-29

The following titles comprise the Jack Dillon Dublin Tales series:
Welcome
Jack Dillon Dublin Tale 1
Sweet Dreams
Jack Dillon Dublin Tale 2
Mirror Mirror
Jack Dillon Dublin Tale 3
Silver Bullet
Jack Dillon Dublin Tale 4
Fair City Blues

Jack Dillon Dublin Tale 5
Spade Work
Jack Dillon Dublin Tale 6
Madeline Missing
Jack Dillon Dublin Tale 7
Mistaken Identity
Jack Dillon Dublin Tale 8
Picture Perfect
Jack Dillon Dublin Tale 9
Dublin Moon
Jack Dillon Dublin Tale 10
Mystery Woman
Jack Dillon Dublin Tale 11
Second Chance
Jack Dillon Dublin Tale 12
Payback Brother
Jack Dillon Dublin Tale 13
The Heist
Jack Dillon Dublin Tale 14
Jewels To Kill For
Jack Dillon Dublin Tale 15
Retirement Scheme
Jack Dillon Dublin Tale 16
The Collector
Jack Dillon Dublin Tale 17

Jack Dillon Dublin Tales Boxsets:
Jack Dillon Dublin Tales 1-3
Jack Dillon Dublin Tales 4-6

Jack Dillon Dublin Tales 1-5
Jack Dillon Dublin Tales 1-7
Jack Dillon Dublin Tales 6-10

The following titles comprise the Hotshot series;
Reduced Ransom! Second Edition
Finders Keepers! Second Edition
Bankers Hours Second Edition
Chow Down Second Edition
Moonlight Dance Academy Second Edition
Irish Dukes (Fight Card Series)
written under the pseudonym Jack Tunney

The following titles comprise the Corridor Man series:
Corridor Man
Corridor Man 2: Opportunity knocks
Corridor Man 3: The Dungeon
Corridor Man 4: Dead End
Corridor Man 5: Finger
Corridor Man 6: Exit Strategy
Corridor Man 7: Trunk Music
Corridor Man 8: Birthday Boy
Corridor Man 9: Boss Man
Corridor Man 10: Bye Bye Bobby

Corridor Man novellas:
Corridor Man: Valentine
Corridor Man: Auditor

Corridor Man: Howling
Corridor Man: Spa Day

The following are Corridor Man Boxsets:
Corridor Man Boxset 1-3
Corridor Man Boxset 1-5
Corridor Man Boxset 6-9

All books are available on Amazon.com
Thank you!

Contact the author:
- Email: mikefaricyauthor@gmail.com
- Twitter: @Mikefaricybooks
- Facebook: Mike Faricy Author
- Website: http://www.mikefaricybooks.com

Published by

MJF Publishing

www.ingramcontent.com/pod-product-compliance
Lightning Source LLC
Chambersburg PA
CBHW051310300726
48976CB00002B/345

* 9 7 8 1 9 6 2 0 8 0 4 7 7 *